Good Student 3
Nicey Nice 3
Zong Zong Boogaloo 4
Bad Luck Cat 7
Music Awards Show 9
Pukelid Terrace 11
Poetry Class 13
Protest 15
Artist 18
Vagina Monologues 20
Punching Cans 22
Happy Talk 23
Preschool Graduation 26
Imaginary Friend 27
Birthday Party 28
Inverse Crosswalk 30
Bad Boy Factory 33
SHART 34
Passive-Aggressive Man 38
Burning Man 41
Anti-PI Conference 50
Seven Deadly Sins (by Jacques de la Merde) 52
Poly Sci I 54
Poly Sci II 56
Tequila Drinking Contest 57
The Program to Increase Speaking Skills 59
Golden Years 60
Doritoed 61
Johnny Yo-Yo 63
Zit 64
Academy Awards 67
Trough 69
Perfect Girl 72
Burrito 75
Bum Tales 77
Petty Revenge 81
Subway 82
Burning Hot Coals 84
Triple Offer Game 85
Hill Tribe Village 86

Deluxe Imagizer 7.0 88
Monkey Suit 89
Thai Sex Show 91
Jung 92
Dog Doo 94
Tangerine 94
Korean Church 95
Racist Baby 98
Donnie the Rock Star 99
Rice Plant 100
Mexican Train 100
Haircut 102
Bidov's War 104
Pizza Face 106
It's the Thought that Counts 107
Ho Hike 108
Philosophy Class 109
Best Way to Cheat 111
Meatball 112
Cow 113
Comic 114
Farley 116
Lucky Beaver 118
Purple Day 120
The Catalina Project 123
Coasting 125
Golden Corn 127
Big Game 128
Interview 129
Sneeze War 132
Coffee Table 134
Smitty's Pub 137
Options 142
The Man Who Hated People 143
Boss 144
Crosswalk Syndrome 145
Cool Old Queefer 146
Star 147
Wine Bar 149
Leprechaun 151

Anti-Depressant........152
Sonic Fart Chair........154
Double A........156
Drunn Kanhigh........158
A Good Licking........160

Good Student

Hey everybody! My name is Jack. I'm a twenty-seven-year-old drunk college student. Well, I guess I'm not always hammered. But that is a big part of who I am! It was part of the manual they gave me when I first got here. They told me to be drunk – and to chase girls too! So I'm always working on some scheme to ride the pony. Girls love me. In between all the chicas and beer are classes. They're annoying but most of the time I show up.

I go to the University of Arizona and I've been here about nine years now – not counting a semester or two I took off here or there. This is the greatest school on Earth. I'm paying a boatload of money for tuition, but it's worth *every* penny. And the loans are all deferred until I graduate anyhow so who cares! I can't believe how lucky I am. I even scored a part-time job at Dreamy Coffee Shop, so I get to learn all about the real world and study at the same time too!

I'm majoring in medieval poetry and my professors are all pretty cool. None of them has ever had a real job, but they have something that others lack – these people have *wisdom*. And every day I'm just sitting there soaking it all up like a sponge.

A lot of crazy things have happened to me at U of A. I have screwed up a lot but I have learned some stuff too. Life is pretty unpredictable and you only live once. YOLO! So I'm going to become a world-famous rapper one day! Either that or a comedian. When I first got here, I didn't know very much. I guess I was kind of an idiot. But now I pretty much know it all.

Nicey Nice

Early on freshman year I had a great epiphany. I discovered a way to get everyone to like me. Whenever I saw someone doing something that was questionable, I just went along with it. I never said anything! You only live once I figured so I decided to live and let live. No matter what anybody did, I was always cool with it. And this made me a good person! I was a *good guy*. I never pointed out the negative consequences of anyone's actions. I even came up with a special phrase to use in these situations. "That's cool." Altogether, this attitude has served me pretty well. It has been a great way to make friends since no one likes a guy who rains on their parade.

Well, the other day my buddy was shooting up heroin. I walked right up to him. "That's cool," I said. "You're pretty brave to try such an adventurous thing!" He smiled when he heard this. I think he was just glad to know I wasn't judging him. My buddy died a couple hours later from an overdose. I was kind of bummed out about it, but I guess he probably would have died anyway. I'm just glad he went to his grave knowing I was always cool.

It is wrong to judge. The only people I don't like are the ones who judge other people. They suck! Life doesn't always work out the way we hope. But this is America! And we are all free! No one can tell us what to do!

Zong Zong Boogaloo

Uncle Sal lived over by Sabino Canyon and he was kind enough to offer me one of his extra cars, a classic – an old Volkswagen Thing. The price was cheap so I cruised over to his place to check it out. At first glance I was shocked. This *Thing* was ugly as hell, it had no paint, and everything except the tires was as square as a box. I had never seen anything like it, but it was the most hideous car in the entire world so I decided to buy it.

The Thing was a mess. The interior was all torn up, springs stuck out here and there through the seats, and all four tires were bald. And that wasn't all – the side and back windows sported a bubbly do-it-yourself tint job, braking was an art form, and the accelerator stuck every time I pressed it down. Somehow I managed to drive around. But traffic lights were a bitch. Whenever one turned yellow, I had to slip my foot under the gas pedal and yanked it up. Then I pumped the brakes like a madman to get the car to stop. After a while I was pretty good at this.

The brakes did cause me some trouble though one day. It happened when I was at a stoplight. I had just performed the trick to stop and I was right behind another car, waiting for the light to change. I was also daydreaming. I was standing on stage holding a microphone, the curtain was about to rise, and – BAM! I heard a smacking noise. My body lurched forward and all of a sudden I was transported back to the real world. I looked at the car in front of me. It was right up on my bumper! The other driver had backed up and hit me! It was so rude! I stuck my head out the window and furled up my brow. "Hey asshole!" I yelled. "Where'd you learn how to drive?!" Then I realized that my foot was still on the brake and it was all the way to the floor. It took me a minute, but I put two and two together and figured out what had happened.

I was a really good driver so I decided to cancel my car insurance. Then the registration went along with it. Nothing bad could ever happen to me so I wasn't too worried about it. But since I didn't have any registration or insurance I figured I should try to avoid getting pulled over, and because of this I made a habit of driving in the right-hand lane. I spent a lot of time checking out the rearview mirror, and whenever a police car got too close, I took a right turn. I was smarter than the cops!

My car wasn't the greatest, but I was just glad to have some kind of ride. The automobile had been around for over a hundred years by now and it seemed like people were starting to take it for granted. In the olden days a guy just hung around the same village his entire life. He knew everyone! The TV and Internet didn't exist and people were all just bored out of their minds. They talked to each other! And they didn't have anything better to do than sit around shucking corn. But nowadays Americans were scattered all across the country like wild dandelions and we could do whatever we wanted. We were forgetting how useful the automobile had been in transporting us far away from our families to live all alone in a sea of strangers. One of these even brought me all the way to U of A!

Me and my buddies like to go out drinking all the time. We do this four or five nights a week. It's why we all came to U of A in the first place! Arizona has a rep. It's a big time party school. Along the way I have managed to pick up an education. It has been a tough price to pay for nightly partying, but I'm proud to say that I've been up to the challenge!

For a long time my car smelled like dead fish, and my buddies were always giving me crap about it. They hated the Thing. But then one day my brother Craig found a meatball underneath one of the seats. Well that meatball must have been there for months because it smelled bad! We all took turns sniffing it. Everyone was crinkling up their nose, but at least the mystery of the smell was solved. After that Craig dubbed the car "Bertha" and did something horrible with the meatball. I'll tell you about that later. Bertha was a girl that no one liked. Guys would ride her even though she was ugly and reeked – they just didn't want to be seen with her in public. That night we had a big party in honor of her. Craig took a forty-ouncer of Pabst Blue Ribbon and christened her by smashing it across the hood. Then we each drank about a dozen beers. It was a great time! But at a certain level of drunkenness, all good ideas seemed bad and all bad ideas seemed good, so I hopped into Bertha and decided to go for a spin.

I got her out onto the road and started heading for Mt. Lemon. I just felt like going somewhere cool and Mt. Lemon was the only place around to beat the heat. I drove and drove along the winding road all the way up to the top. An hour or so later I arrived. Then I got out and started walking around in the dark, enjoying some private time among the trees. The forest was a beautiful place – it was so tranquil. A cool breeze was blowing and the whole area just seemed so quiet and peaceful. I couldn't help but soak up the vibe. I was beginning to feel at one with nature, so I whipped out Barney and pissed on a tree. An owl spied me. "Who!" it cried. Then a chipmunk jumped up onto a rock and started scolding me. Who the hell did all these forest creatures think they were! They had some nerve. I was Jack Inhofe! And no one could stop me! So I picked up a rock and hucked it at the owl. Right away the two judgmental animals scattered. Next I tripped over a root and hit my head on a big rock. After that a huge flock of birds appeared in the air above me. There were hundreds of them and they were all darting around, popping in and out of the shadows and making a lot of noise. This lasted for several minutes. Finally one spotted me. "Caaawwww!!!" it cried. The thing's eyes were dead on me and pretty soon the birds were all circling around, glaring, and yelling in my direction. It was still dark but I knew what these creatures were. They were crows – *evil crows.* I was beginning to wonder what they all wanted. And right at that moment the leader flew down and landed in front of me on a branch.

It looked me straight in the eye. "Jack," it said, "We have a mission for you. You must go and you must seek out Zong Zong Boogaloo. This is your quest. Once you do this your life will be perfect." Then the crow flapped its wings and was off.

"Wait!" I cried. "What do you mean? What is Zong Zong Boogaloo? Where is this place? What am I supposed to do there???"

But it was gone. And the other crows were fast on its tail. The first hint of light was breaking across the eastern sky, so I watched them all until they disappeared into the horizon. After that everything was calm again. I figured it was time to go, so I hopped into Bertha and started driving back to Tucson. About twenty minutes later I passed the tree line. I was out of the forest but I was still on that crazy winding road, and it was a long way back home. To my right was a huge drop off into a saguaro-filled canyon. There were cactuses everywhere and I couldn't help but admire the view. My eyes kept drifting over to the canyon.

I was going around a treacherous curve, enjoying the scenery, when the brakes began to give out. The brakes! I had forgotten they were bad! I looked to my right. It was several hundred feet down. I would die for sure if I went over the edge, so I gripped the steering wheel as tightly as I could. I was doing my best to hold the turn. My knuckles were white on the wheel – but Bertha was just going too damn fast. She started grazing up against the guardrail. Sparks were flying everywhere. And there was a horrible grinding noise. For a moment I felt like I could hold on, but then Bertha broke through the rail and went over the edge. I was in the air now and an eerie silence was all around. I was about to die. As Bertha hurtled through the dawn sky, I decided to gaze around. City lights were sparkling off in the distance and the moon was full. I thought about the great drunk-driving hero of Arizona, Billy Bob "Catfish" Walker. He had invented "Bear Down" – the rally cry we used for sporting events, and then he had died in an alcohol-related car accident. I was about to join him in infamy! I would be dead but this was sure to make the news. For fifteen minutes everyone would know my name. I was so excited! I couldn't wait to hit the ground! But whenever you wanted something too bad, disappointment was sure to follow. I kept flying and flying and for some reason Bertha never crashed. She just flew and flew all the way back to Tucson and touched down with all four tires on Speedway Blvd. Somewhere along the way, though, things changed. Stuff was different now. And deep down inside something was gnawing away at me. I didn't know what this thing was or where to find it. I only knew its name. Somehow...I had to find Zong Zong Boogaloo.

Bad Luck Cat

Me and my buddies were drunk. It was the middle of the afternoon and we were all over at Bonzo's place. Bonzo lived in one of those hideous old motels that had been converted into apartments. It seemed like every other building in Tucson was one of these. We were all lazing around watching TV when a cat wandered into Bonzo's apartment. I was bored so, to entertain everyone, I picked the thing up and carried it out to the second floor walkway above the pool. Everyone followed me outside.

"Hey bastards," I said, "what do you think I should do with this cat?" Then I glanced over at Craig. We were always on the same wavelength.

"I don't know, Jack," he said. "The cat looks thirsty. Maybe you should give it some water?"

"Uh yeah..." I said as I stroked my chin thoughtfully, "I think I know what you mean."

I grabbed the cat by the neck and the back and held it out in front of my body. The thing went limp and got a glassy look in its eyes, but it also seemed to sense that something was up. This worried me since it had claws. I decided to be careful. So I gripped its fur tightly and began to slowly rotate around in a circle. Next I sped up. I spun around several times. And with each 360 I was picking up speed. It was the Olympics! I was an Olympic athlete and I was holding a discus!

"Go Jack!" Bonzo cried.

Rocco was excited too. "Yeah!" he yelled. "Chuck that bitch!"

I let the thing go. And somehow I managed to avoid the claws. The cat flew high up into the air. Legs were flailing about in every direction and claws were jabbing around all over. But there was nothing to grab onto and nowhere to reach. The cat just kept flying and flying. For a moment it even blotted out the sun. Then it reached its peak and started to come down. The thing flipped over into cat-upright-landing-position and hit smack dab in the middle of the pool. A perfect throw! It started swimming right away, doing the cat-paddle somehow before it even hit the water. The cat made it to the edge of the pool and climbed out. Then it shot me a look and scampered off.

"Hahahahahahaha!!!" we all laughed. It was great fun and we couldn't stop busting up. Bonzo was laughing so hard that beer shot out of his nose. And Craig was lying on the ground clutching his gut. For a few fleeting moments I felt proud of myself. I was a dumbass for sure but at least I had made everyone laugh. We needed something new anyway. Being drunk all the time was getting kind of old.

I had forgotten all about the cat until I ran into the thing and its owner a few days later. The cat's owner was a hippie chick in her late thirties. She was wearing leather boots and eating a hamburger as she walked. And she had a t-shirt on that said "PETA." This meant she was a member of People Eating Tasty Animals. It was a group I had never really understood. *Everyone* liked to eat animals. And we *all* knew they tasted good. It seemed too obvious a thing to be proud of.

The hippie was holding the cat and petting it protectively. She recognized me right away and when she did, she turned to the cat. "See that asshole," she said. "He's the one that threw you in the pool." I was shocked when I heard this because I had no idea a cat could understand English. The thing played coy, though. It perked up an ear and flicked its tail. For a second its mouth even cracked open, but it decided not to dignify me with a response. I couldn't say much in my defense anyway, so I just took the hit. The hippie was right. Only a crazy asshole threw a cat into a pool. I scratched my head for a minute and thought about this. There were all kinds of crazy. And I guess I was one of them – but at least I didn't talk to cats!

The hippie went into her apartment and closed the door. I kept walking along and ran into an old man who had melted into a pool chair. The guy looked about a hundred years old. "Son," he said, "ain't nobody got manners no more. Be kind to everyone. 'Cause when people quit on humans, they turn to animals – and nature. They're afraid to live and they know those things can't hurt 'em. And when the eggs start to dry up, a woman might up and marry a cat. A man who come along after that point ain't never gonna be more important than that cat. And it's a damn shame. I don't like seein' women alone. They're the hearts of families and neighborhoods and communities – and this whole damn country. They're the ones holdin' everythin' together. And America is missin' that. Women folk are sculptors. Every day they do a lot of chiselin' with all the bitchin' and moanin'. They see somethin' wrong and they wanna improve on it. They make guys and kids better! But a guy don't get the full effect of this until he's up an' hitched. Before marriage women tend to flatter. And that ain't worth much. They got a chip in 'em, wantin' to tie the knot, you see. They wanna catch them a prize. Zay zay gets activated by the rocket, son. But it don't go into full force without no ring. You'll find out about zay zay later..."

I didn't know what the hell that old man was taking about. But I was starting to feel bad about what I had done, so I walked over and knocked on the hippie's door. I waited for a minute but there was no answer. "Sorry about the cat!" I yelled. "I shouldn't have thrown it in the pool." Still there was no response. I was about to leave, but then the cat jumped up onto the windowsill. The thing held up its front paw and stuck out a middle toe. After that it smirked. I couldn't believe what I was seeing. The son of a bitch was flipping me off.

Music Awards Show

I turned on the TV. The music awards were on and the artist Yagalooga had just taken the stage. He was the most famous singer in all of America. Yagalooga couldn't sing a lick but he was the proud owner of a voice synthesizer. It had been surgically implanted into his throat and now, thanks to this marvel of modern science, he had the pipes of a god. The device gave him a really odd-looking, rectangular-shaped Adam's apple, but no one cared. Everyone loved Yagalooga. He was a star!

Yagalooga was also a purpler. He had tattooed his entire body purple and he was one of the first people to do this. Everyone in America was purpling nowadays. Scientists had discovered that humans were, by nature, most racist against the color purple, so people were all dyeing themselves this color by choice. It was a great step in the evolution of mankind. In the past only *some* people had been victims of the racist society, but *now* it was possible for *all* people to feel the sting of racism. The common man had equal opportunity – now he too could burn with righteous anger and strike back against the Man. It was inevitable that racism would one day be cured, but until that day arrived, people were all having too much fun purpling.

The first thing Yagalooga did was to set his drummer on fire. The man lit up like a Christmas tree. He dropped his drumsticks, jumped up, and ran around the stage screaming in pain. It was quite a sight and the crowd enjoyed it tremendously. People were all cheering. After a good fifteen seconds of this the drummer collapsed to the ground. Then a camera zoomed in on him. His body continued to twitch around for a few moments, and then – there was nothing. Smoke was still billowing up from the carcass, though, and people were having trouble seeing Yagalooga, so a roadie ran onto the stage and sprayed it with a fire extinguisher. Yagalooga went through a lot of drummers, but they were all well paid and got to live like rock stars. So he never had a trouble finding anyone new.

Next a goat appeared on stage. The crowd was baffled. Why was a goat here? Even Yagalooga seemed confused. "Baaa!!!" it cried. The thing was trotting around, bleating loudly, and annoying everyone. No one really knew what to think. But then, in an instant, Yagalooga put it all together for us – he dropped the fake confused look and then he dropped his pants. In a moment of mad fury he jumped up behind the goat and started raping it. People were all amazed. It was such an audacious stunt! Only Yagalooga could pull off something like this! And of course everyone knew what he meant. People all *got it*. Yagalooga was making a political statement. He was raping the goat to show that rape was bad.

"Yay!!!!" everyone cried.

Yagalooga was an artistic genius. He spoke through his art and the crowd understood him implicitly. People were all on their feet cheering wildly. Once everyone finally sat back down, a woman in her late thirties jumped up. She was wearing a t-shirt that said "PETA." Right away the woman started yelling at Yagalooga. It was tough to make out what she was saying, but she was from People Eating Tasty Animals so everyone figured she wanted to eat the goat. It all seemed so terribly inappropriate. The poor creature had just been raped for entertainment and now a lunatic wanted to eat it. Some people just didn't have any class. Security swooped in and took her away.

Once the woman was gone, Yagalooga walked up to the very front of the stage. He was a sexy man so the screams of young girls began to pierce the air. Yagalooga just stood there for a moment and let the love wash over him. Then one lone voice cried out, "I love you Yagalooga!" After that the room was quiet. People were all waiting for what he would do next. Yagalooga sucked some phlegm into his mouth and then he belted out the chorus of his hit song.

"I Yagalooga!"

"You Yagalooga!"

"We Yagalooga!"

"Hhhocck peeuuuhh!"

The chorus always ended with him hocking a loogie. Yagalooga seemed to have a never-ending supply of phlegm and this was one of the many great skills he possessed. At the end of the chorus, Yagalooga lifted his arms up slowly until he was standing in a Christ-like pose. Then he paused and let loose with a series of rhythmic tribal screams that had been recorded in advance.

For the grand finale, Yagalooga grabbed a samurai sword and cut off his own head. Then he gripped it by the hair and performed a flip – all while hitting an amazing falsetto. After that, he placed the thing back onto his neck and walked off stage, holding it gingerly with both hands to keep it from falling off. A doctor would fuse everything back together for him later on.

A sexy girl in a tight dress interviewed him off stage and she was very impressed by his performance. "Oh Yagalooga!" she cried, "You've done it again! How is it that you're able to outdo yourself time and time again?" Yagalooga responded with a dazzling display of verbal skill – he unleashed a barrage of sixty-nine curse words in a row. People were all stunned. It was a new record! A sign above the stage started flashing "New record! 69!" And the crowd went nuts all over again.

"Yay!!!" everyone cried.

Yagalooga was truly one of a kind. And somehow he always managed to outdo himself. Everyone knew he would be artist of the year again this year. No one was better than he was at distracting people from the music.

Pukelid Terrace

Euclid Terrace was a big apartment complex just off campus at U of A. It was famous for drunken free-for-alls and had won the nickname "Pukelid Terrace." Everyone loved the place. We all stumbled across a party there one night, and my eyes nearly popped out of my head as soon as we walked through the door. Sitting right in front of me on the kitchen table was a beer bong! When I saw the thing, a shiver went down my spine. It was gorgeous – a jet black funnel with a hose attached to the small end. This was my night. Deep down I could feel it. I was about to become a rock star!

I decided to break my personal beer bong record. Peacocks had feathers and lions had a great big mane, but I had a cheap plastic contraption that made people whoop and holler. I was ready to be the Man!

"Gimme that beer bong!" I cried. "I'm doin' a triple!"

A small crowd began to form. One freshman in particular seemed really excited. "You gonna slam it, dude?!" he exclaimed. "Wow! That's awesome!"

Bonzo filled up the funnel and handed it to the freshman. Then I put the hose into my mouth. We were all set to use gravity so I gave the kid the thumbs up and he lifted the thing high into the air. And at that moment Bonzo poured in a few extra shots of vodka. The booze was already rushing through the hose so I didn't have any time to react. I just started drinking. And all of a sudden time began to move in slow motion. I was sucking the stuff down as fast as I could and I could feel my stomach expanding. It was getting bigger and bigger. My gut was about to burst. I was going to die! And this would make me famous! I was so excited. But there was no time to think and no time to stop. All I could do was keep on guzzling. The mix just kept on shooting down my throat. And then, finally – I took one last gulp. I did it! A triple beer bong vodka! It was the greatest moment of my life.

In triumph, I lifted the hose up above my head and grinned a crooked grin. And right then an unbelievable rush hit me. Was this Zong Zong Boogaloo? Everything seemed perfect. I staggered around for a minute. Then I realized that someone was talking to me. It was the freshman. He was following me around and kept telling me how great I was. Kids were all cheering my feat. "Yay!" they cried. I was the hero of the moment. But it was a quiet victory. I couldn't even speak. My stomach had nearly burst, and now – a great sickness was rising up in my gut.

I turned to the freshman. "I'm gonna puke," I told him.

"No way dude!" he cried. He could not accept this. His hero could never throw up. A hero could not show weakness.

But then I let out the greatest and most horrendous belch a human had ever heard. It started out slow and got louder the longer it went on. The thing lasted a good ten seconds. It was like the rumble of a great earthquake. Or the approach of a train. Plates began to rattle in a nearby cabinet. The overhead light went out for a second. And then it came back on. A dog started barking out in the alley.

The crowd had cheered me on but I didn't have a friend in the world now. All the girls scattered. The sound of the belch scared everyone off and there was only one thing left for me to do. This was the part of the show no one wanted to see. I didn't have much time and figured I could keep everything down for maybe another five seconds, so I started stumbling around the apartment in desperation. There had to be somewhere to puke. Where was the bathroom? Where the hell was it?! I was running out of time. And then I saw something. A sink! The thing was full. It was piled up high with a tower of dirty dishes. But it was time for action. I hurled all over the tower. The stack teetered magnificently for a moment and then came crashing down. Dishes smashed all over the countertop and broke into a thousand pieces. Stuff was everywhere. A glass rolled lazily off the counter and shattered on the floor next to my foot. All of a sudden I felt much better. I got myself together and went back to join the party.

Someone had just started blasting the new hit by Yagalooga. Kids all heard him rapping and went crazy. They were jumping over chairs and knocking down tables, pretending to be goat-rapers. One guy was dancing with his pants around his knees. "Look at me!" he cried. "I'm a sex offender!" Another kid tried to set his buddy on fire as a joke. That cracked everyone up. Yagalooga's new song, Me Good You Bad, was a huge hit. The lyrics told the story of his terrible life as a purpler. Everything was bullshit and life was unfair for him, so he hated people and refused to give them respect. But despite this, Yagalooga expected good treatment from others. Yagalooga wasn't just a rapper. He was a teacher too.

We got hungry later on and went out for fast food at Whataburger. We were all standing in line and having fun. Everyone was being as loud as humanly possible. And then all of a sudden I remembered something. The mic! Whataburger had a microphone up front, right next to the cashier. They used it to call orders back to the cooks, but to a bunch of drunks it was way too tempting. Tonight was my night. I had already done a triple beer bong vodka so I was on a roll. No one could stop me! I swaggered up to the mic and grabbed it like I owned it. Then I brought down the house with some Yagalooga.

"I got ranch dippin' sauce
And lotsa hos

When I feel like a snack
I eat pinkie toes
Oh I munch 'em all up
Yeah that's right y'all
'Cause I'm a mass-murderin'...
Canni-*baallllll!!!!!*"

When the manager heard this, his head turned into a big angry tomato. Steam started coming out of his ears and a vein popped out of his forehead. The guy was getting ready to yell. He was all set to give us a piece of his mind. But then – his head just blew up, and chunks of brain started landing all over the place. It was not a pretty sight. And right about then I realized that we were all out of line. Yagalooga was a very important person and I was glad to have him as a teacher, but somehow I had not applied his lesson correctly. We were dissing other people, but for some reason we weren't getting good treatment in return. We wound up having to leave Whataburger before we even got our food. Then we went back home and washed off all the pieces of brain. After that I just sat on the couch and scratched my head for a while.

Poetry Class

"Hello class!" cried Peggy the Poet, her gray ponytail bouncing along happily. "Today is a special day for all my special students! Today we are going to write our first poems!" As soon as we heard this our mouths curled up into great big smiles. Then we all started to cheer and fist-bump each other. The excitement was palpable. We were *finally* going to write our own poems! The class had been studying poetry for almost an entire year, and we had accumulated a great deal of wisdom over this period of time. We were ready!

"I brought three bags with me today," Peggy said. "In the first bag are nouns, the second has adjectives, and the last one is full of verbs. A good poem has all three of these things. I need you guys to come up here one at a time and take one piece of paper out of each bag. You will have three words total! And you will use these three words to construct your very first poem. This is how I write my own poems at home!"

Peggy the Poet had written thousands of poems. She was always telling us that she "bled poetry." It was all she ever thought about. Poetry was her life. And some of her poems had actually been published – one even made The New Yorker. She was just a really smart lady. Everyone liked Peggy the Poet.

I picked my three words. Then I sat down and began to compose my work of art. About thirty minutes later Peggy decided to call on people to present their poems.

"Jack!" she cried. "Would you like to share your poem with us?"

"Sure," I said. "Why not?" I walked up to the front of the class and grabbed a marker.

"Jack," she said, "please share your three words with us first."

"Oh right," I said. "My three words are rooster, blue, and meet." After that I wrote my poem on the board.

Cock crying out
Oh so blue
Sad and lonely, hoping to go inside
Wanting to meet pussycat

- Jack Inhofe

"Uh..." Peggy said. "Can anybody tell me what's wrong with this poem?"

A guy in the back raised his hand really high. "I know, teacher," he cried. "He signed it 'Jack Inhofe'! He ain't got no middle name! Poets all got three names!"

"Right!" Peggy cried. "Other than that Jack's poem is pretty good. I love how he used *cock* – an archaic form of the word rooster. It makes me feel like I'm in a dingy old Chinese Restaurant with a placemat that says 'year of the cock' on it instead of 'year of the rooster.' What do you think class? Does this work for you? Do you all like cock?"

It was U of A. So most of the girls started nodding. A few guys too. Not everyone was happy, though. A kid by the window with pretty hair and fashionable shoes seemed pissed off.

"No fair!" he complained. "How come I didn't get cock?!"

"Now calm down, Jojo," Peggy said in a soft voice. "Life isn't a movie. We can't all have cock." But Peggy's encouragement was of no use. Jojo's feelings were hurt so he got up and stormed out of the classroom. Peggy seemed a little flustered. "Okay!" she said, straightening her ponytail. "Now where were we?"

A girl up front perked up. "We were critiquing Jack's poem," she said.

"Oh yes," Peggy said. "Can anybody tell me what else is wrong with this poem?"

The kid in the back raised his hand again. "This poem make sense," he said. "Rooster wanna meet cat. Poems ain't s'posed to make sense."

"Right again!" Peggy cried. "A good poem is like a French movie. It shouldn't make any sense. The goal is to confuse people. You want them to feel dumb – like they can't understand your nonexistent lofty concepts. And then you're supposed to laugh at them."

Protest

I was hanging out down by the bridge at Dreamy Coffee Shop drinking an iced goat's milk cappuccino when a bunch of people began to march by. It was a group protesting for their rights. America was the greatest country in the world. People could protest anything and everything. And they did. The protesters were marching along and they were all chanting in unison.

"Free the gays!"

"Free the gays!"

"Free the gays!"

The group was demonstrating because gay people were being incarcerated at a higher rate than the general population. I thought about this. How true it was! There were many stories about the high rate of gay activity in prison. And it was common knowledge that gays were all born that way. Scientists had figured this out. The more I thought about all of this, the more it began to bother me. It was just such an obvious injustice! And I felt like a fool for not having figured it out earlier. The protesters were right. What was going on in America was truly unbelievable. The police had been systematically arresting and locking up gay people! The prisons were concentration camps! And this had all happened right under our noses!

Anger began to well up inside of me. It was unthinkable that something like this could happen in a free country. Immediately I stood up, ready to join the fight. But just as I did, another group of protesters appeared. This group was from a Christian church. The Christians were worried about the gays. They wanted them to be straight. All of a sudden the Christians started protesting the protest. And they had their own chant.

"Cure the gays!"

"Cure the gays!"

"Cure the gays!"

It didn't take long for the two competing protests to converge upon each other, and then the screaming really started. Faces were red with anger – there was fury on both sides. Christians were yelling at gays. And gays were yelling at Christians. Christians were telling gays they were going to hell. And gays were screaming that Christians were all bigots or secretly gay. Everyone was yelling at everyone.

Meanwhile, over in a nearby alley, a bum was lying on his back, drinking out of a bag and observing it all. It had been several minutes since he had screaming anything incoherent, so he grabbed his bottle and stood up. "Yaaaa!!!" he hollered. "Overreaction's sure when truth strikes a nerve!" Then he threw up in front of himself and started yelling at the vomit.

A crowd started to gather to watch the two competing protests. And it was about this time that a rumor began to spread. It swept through the mob like wildfire. Someone had uttered a slur! A Christian had called one of the gays a "donut shitter"! No one could believe it. Donut shitter was the worst thing you could say in the English language. People were all staring at each other in disbelief. What kind of person would say such a thing? It was the spark that lit the fire.

The entire mob began to descend upon the Christians and the bridge started to sag and sway in response. There were just too many people on it. Soon the whole structure was creaking. The sound started slowly at first, but before long it began to reverberate across the entire length of the bridge. Then there was a great crashing sound. The side the Christians were on collapsed, and they plummeted down into the dry riverbed below.

The Christians were all killed.

After that the mob scattered. Everyone else survived but the events of that day lived on. People were outraged at what had happened. The entire community was in a state of disbelief. And it just *would not end.* The anger at what went down that day traveled across the city. A crime had been committed. And a price had to be paid. Someone had uttered a slur! And because of this, punishment was due. The Christians would be tried posthumously for the crime so that justice could be served.

The story received worldwide attention, so Larry the Lawyer decided to take up the case. Larry was a lawyer for the ACLU. He was the best attorney they had, and he had recently freed up from a busy schedule defending terrorists and pedophiles. In twenty years Larry had never lost a case. He was so good that the verdict almost seemed like a foregone conclusion. People were all excited – Larry the Lawyer was on the case so everyone knew the ACLU would win.

The trial began with Judge Dover presiding. Larry joined the prosecution and right away he started hammering away at the defense. He called witness after witness. Every Christian on the bridge that day was summoned to appear before the court, but none dared to take the stand. The whispers started in the courtroom and then spread across the city and the world. The Christians were afraid to testify! The jury watched it all go down in awe. No one had ever seen such a brilliant prosecutor.

Larry called many witnesses to support the prosecution's case. But it was the testimony of world-famous fashion designer Gary Gaye that was most damning. "They're guilty!" he cried. "Because people who are like me are good! And people who are not like me are bad! I drove all the way here from Hershey, Pennsylvania! And my butt is sore! I'm tired of riding the Hershey Highway!"

Cheering broke out in the courtroom. "Yay!" people cried. Everyone agreed with Gary. People who were like them were good. And people who were not like them were bad.

At the end of the trial, Larry the Lawyer stood up in front of the court and prepared to deliver his closing arguments. He slicked back his hair with a comb and adjusted his tie. Then he turned to face the jury. "The defendants are guilty!" he declared with a smirk. "These people are pathetic. They are even afraid to appear on the stand in their own defense!" Everyone on the ACLU team was gloating. Larry's strategy seemed foolproof.

The jury deliberated for several hours before returning to the court. Then the foreman stood up and addressed the court. "Judge!" he cried. "We the jury have decided that we are hung!"

The judge was shocked. He lifted up his gavel and was getting ready to slam it down, but all of a sudden a unicorn appeared above the courtroom. The thing was glowing. It was brilliant white – like the teeth of a movie star. People saw it and were mesmerized by its beauty. The unicorn passed through a skylight. Then it glided slowly and effortlessly down to the floor of the court.

"Look at me, everyone!" it cried. "I am the leader of the gays! I am here to spread gaiety and joy. And a few legs too!" The unicorn paused for a moment to admire its own wit. Then it continued, "Can you feel me, people?! Will you?! I stand for freedom! I come for love! And I love to come! I have a message for the court. Judge Ben Dover, I will give it to you! We must not tolerate intolerance! These bigots should be executed! We have all heard the words of the foreman. The jury is hung. And so am I! I am ready to take you for a ride, judge! Ben Dover, I will give you a ride you will not forget! Then after I'm done you can get off!"

"The defendants are already dead!!" cried the judge. "We cannot execute people who are dead! Bailiff! Get this unicorn the hell out of my courtroom!"

Several police officers began wrestling with the unicorn. They were doing their best to drag the thing out of the court, but it was putting up quite a fight.

"These followers of Christ are bothersome!" it cried. "They have a code – a Code of Honor. It is annoying! And inconvenient! Surely, freedom without a such a thing is anarchy. But why can't we all just do whatever we want?! Let us be free! We must all do what is right in our own eyes! I am down on my knees begging you all to get behind me. Listen to me, people. We must all rise up and come together! Oh wait...are you taking me to jail? I'm so excited!!!"

"Put him in solitary!" cried the judge.

"NOOOOOOOOOOOOO!!!"

Artist

Hans was an artist, a *starving* artist, actually – and I was a few moments away from finding out about this again. I had just gotten back to the apartment and a pizza delivery guy was standing in the parking lot all by himself with a box of pizza. He didn't seem to know what to do.

"No answer again?" I asked.

"Yep."

Hans liked to order a pizza whenever he was drunk. But before it arrived he always passed out – usually face down in the hallway by the front door with one outstretched arm clutching a twenty dollar bill. Hans meant well. He *wanted* to pay the pizza guy, but he just couldn't stay awake long enough to do it. Most of the time I bought the pizza off the guy and brought it inside. Hans might have starved without me. He always woke up later and found the pizza. It was the same tonight. "Damn!" he cried. "Where'd this pizza come from?! I love pepperoni pizza!"

I helped Hans get around town too. Whenever he wanted to go somewhere, he asked to borrow Bertha. There was only one problem – Bertha crimped his style. The car just didn't look very cool and this bothered Hans. Artists were all about looks. And Bertha looked *bad.*

"I can't believe I have to drive around in this thing," he complained once.

"You don't," I replied. "Feel free to walk."

It took a lot of chutzpah to complain about stuff people were loaning you for free. But if nothing else, Hans had chutzpah.

Girls loved Hans. They were dying for him. He had the rugged good looks and arrogance they adored. His hair was swept back in a ridiculous pompadour and he had cheekbones that stuck out at crazy angles. Wherever he went, they swooned and keeled over in front of him, dying to have his baby. Hans had a new girlfriend every month. And it always followed the same pattern. The first week he was "in love" and she was "the one." But after that it was all downhill. Week two was good and three was so-so. But by the time week four rolled around, he was looking for an out.

One of these girls was a sexy thing in all black at Club Congress. The place was about to close for the night and Hans had her up against a wall in one corner of the lobby. Hans had his hand up under her miniskirt as a bouncer approached. The bouncer glanced quickly over at him. "Dude!" he announced, "we're closing." And then he paused. He realized that a sex act was in progress and wasn't sure about what to do. But he recovered quickly. "Damn!" he cried. "You guys need to get a room."

Hans and the girl got a room upstairs.

Another one of Hans' monthers was a hot kooky hippie. She was so nutty I couldn't help but like her. The girl carried around a keychain with a lucky rabbit's foot on it. It didn't look like something from a store, though, so one day I decided to ask her about it.

"Hey Flower," I said, "where'd you get the lucky rabbit's foot?"

"Hee hee hee," she giggled. "It's from a rabbit I ran over in Mexico. It was out on the highway when I hit it. I knew it was dead so I cut off the foot on the spot. I guess it's a kind of souvenir."

"Sounds like a pretty *unlucky* rabbit," I said. "Aren't you worried it will turn rotten?"

The hippie seemed confused. This was something she had not yet considered. We both examined the foot. I held it up to my nose and then she did the same. After that we both shrugged. The foot did not seem to have any odor.

"I guess I'll keep using it for a while," she said. "At least until the luck runs out."

Hans liked to make paintings with people in them. This was his art. He painted a lot of paintings. But for some reason he always left out the faces. It was tough to draw a face and his paintings were obviously lacking without them. It seemed weird. And after a while this little detail started to bother everyone. Hans was an artist so how come he couldn't draw a face? We were all worried about it so one day Rocco decided to find out.

"Hey Hans," he asked, "how come you can't draw faces?"

Hans was furious. "I'm an artist!" he cried. "This is great art! What do you know?! You're not an artist! You're a business major. How can a business major understand art?! This is my style! I don't like drawing faces! So I don't draw them! How come no one understands this?!"

Eventually Hans accepted that he could not draw a face. But this put him in a bad spot. It meant that he was no longer an artist. Hans was depressed about this and his self-esteem suffered badly for a few months, but then – he decided to become a famous filmmaker. Lots of guys hoped to become filmmakers. And statistically it was more likely to be kidnapped by an alien. Only a total fool had a plan like that.

Hans learned his craft. He was a quick study and technically he was very good. He could shoot a scene and make it look realistic. The camera was always in the right place. Plus he knew all the angles and the way to cut and paste everything together to make it look good. Hans made a full-length movie. But unfortunately none of the people in it knew how to act. And no one had bothered to write a script. Most of the scenes consisted of his dog bounding around dramatically in slow motion for no particular reason. Occasionally a human would talk, but when it did, the words did not seem relevant or make much sense. And they always came out staccato-style – as if delivered by a robot. The dog was the best actor in the entire film! I had to give Hans credit for one thing, though. He had actually made a finished product. Most people talked a good game. They pretended they were going to do things in life, but then nothing happened and they acted like that was the plan all along. Hans was way out in left field. He loved to boast. And he talked the talk. But he walked the walk too. Hans made stuff happen.

A lot of artists liked to think that they were right-brained – that somehow an inability to understand basic math or science made them more creative. Being bad at one thing made you good at something else. So all you had to do was give up on difficult things and you could become an artistic genius. It made total sense! This was why I studied medieval poetry! But Hans was a fake. He convinced himself he was right-brained and was always asking for help with math, so it was another shock to his self-esteem when he discovered that he was good at making the equipment he used in his films. He even built the spinny rotating thing he used to maneuver the camera into every possible angle. Only an engineer did something like that. It was tough for Hans to admit – but he was a left-brained "artist."

We were watching TV one day when Rocco noticed the spinny rotating thing. "Wow!" he said. "How'd you make that, Hans? It looks pretty complicated."

"I don't know!" Hans cried. "Stop asking me! I'm bad at math!"

And just then a TV commercial came on. It was for Mariachi Madness, a new movie starring the great actor, Johnny Yo-Yo. Johnny was an everyday insurance salesman with a wife, a house and 2.5 kids. He was good at his job and liked people. It was a normal happy life. And there was nothing more terrible than that. As we all sat there watching the trailer, we felt bad for Johnny. He seemed to have some kind of problem in this film – he wasn't trying to be special or anything. Well, one day Johnny's life changed dramatically. A rival salesman tried to kill him to get more territory. He tricked Johnny into eating a radioactive burrito. But instead of killing him, the burrito turned him into a superhero who moonlit as a mariachi singer.

"Wow!" cried Rocco. "Awesome!"

Hans couldn't tear his eyes away. "Oooooooh..." he sighed.

The trailer looked so good that we ran right to the theater to see the film. It was a classic. Johnny wore a cape and flew all around saving people's lives while he sang songs about tasty Mexican food. He was a great singer and after a while his music even started to get popular. His fame grew and grew. So he abandoned his family and moved to Hollywood, where he became a huge celebrity and hooked up with a different girl every night. The film ended tragically. Johnny crashed his motorcycle into a cactus and died trying to break the world land speed record. Then he turned into an angel holding a harp. He sat on a cloud, reflecting upon his life and how great it had been to be crazy and depressed. He had lived every day to the fullest. And it had all been worth it.

Vagina Monologues

I was so excited. The Vagina Monologues were coming to U of A! I had never seen the show before but I knew all about it from Hans. He went out of his way to build it up. "The Vagina Monologues is the greatest sex show ever!" Hans declared. "It's all about vaginas! Every guy should see it!"

We were all looking forward to going to the show together, but the day came and Hans was busy, so me and Rocco wound up going by ourselves. We downed a ton of beer and started hiking across campus to Billy Bob "Catfish" Walker Auditorium. It was the biggest venue on campus. We were staggering around like fools and had to stop and piss several times along the way. But we kept on going. Nothing was going to stop us. We were both really pumped up to see the show.

"I can't wait to see some naked girls!" Rocco cried. "This is gonna be great!"

"Yeah!" I added. "I hope this show is as good as Hans says it is!"

Eventually we made it to Catfish Auditorium. The place was packed and the lights were all turned down really low. We entered the main hall and looked around. Then we walked down a dimly-lit aisle and found a couple seats in the back. A girl on stage was mumbling to herself – I figured it had to be the set up for some kind of sex act, so I did my best to listen. But the stuff she was talking about was really boring. I couldn't make heads or tails out of it so I glanced over at Rocco. He seemed bored too. We both started looking around for hotties. And that was when I realized something – the room was almost entirely female! There were only a few guys and they were all super wimpy-looking. Me and Rocco didn't even have any competition! We were going to get laid for sure! I started looking closer and noticed that most of the girls were dressed like gypsies. I was no dummy. This meant they were probably lesbians. Once I put two and two together I nudged Rocco.

"Hey dude," I whispered. "Look around. We're in luck. This is a *lesbian* sex show."

"I know," Rocco said. "I just saw that too. Awesome."

Just then the girl on stage began to talk about how great it was to be raped by a twenty-four-year-old woman when she was thirteen, and the audience started to clap and cheer. I was puzzled. This somehow seemed wrong to me so I jumped out of my seat. "Rape is baaad!" I cried. "Yagalooga said so! What the hell is wrong with all you people?!"

"Thish shooow suuucks!" Rocco added. "I thought it was a live sex shooow! But all I see is talking and taaaalking!"

A woman with a flattop didn't like what she was hearing, so she turned around and confronted us. "This kind of rape is good!" she cried. "We are rebelling against the oppressive male-dominated patriarchal society!"

"You go, girl!" shrieked a woman up front. "You tell him!" Everyone seemed to agree with the two women. People were all clapping wildly and cries of "Go girl!" began to ring out across the auditorium.

I couldn't believe it. No one in here agreed with the teachings of Yagalooga! I was totally confused. "Uh..." I stammered. "My bad. I guess rape is...*good*?"

"Rape isn't good!" cried the woman in the front. "It's only good when women do it! Don't you know anything?!"

And that was when Rocco stood up, unzipped his pants, and started pissing all over the floor. "Shorry..." he mumbled, "I jush couldn't hooold it any longerrr..."

"Oh my God!" cried the woman with the flattop. "What are you doing?! This is a performance! This is art! You can't pee in here! Stop it! Help! Police! Rape!"

All of a sudden the whole crowd started screaming at us. One of the wimpy guys even stood up. He was staring at his hand and trying to figure out how to make a fist. And it was right about then that Rocco stopped in mid-piss and zipped his pants back up. Then he turned to me. "Hey Jack..." he said. "Follow me. I know a shecret exit..." Rocco started stumbling toward the exit and I was right behind him. We were both wobbling all over the place as we staggered down the aisle, and we were taking a lot of abuse. Rocco kept telling everyone he was "shorry," and we almost fell down a couple times, but somehow we made it to the secret way out. It was a regular door with the word "exit" written on it in big bold letters. Rocco pushed the thing open and we walked outside.

When we got back to the apartment Hans was cracking up. "Ha ha ha!" he laughed. "Did you piss your pants with excitement? I really pulled one over on you guys! That show is just an outlet for jaded women. It's the price we gotta pay for getting laid all the time. We use girls for sex and dump them. Then they go to some cathartic show and let off a little steam. After that we pump them full of booze and everyone gets laid some more. Ha ha ha ha! Girls are funny, huh? They'll die for the first guy that nails them. But it's all downhill after that. They might like the next couple of dudes, but each one means less than the one before. They get watered down! And we get watered up! Ha ha ha ha! Well don't worry. I doubt you guys will get in any trouble. Catfish is really dark so there's no way anyone recognized you."

Punching Cans

Dreamy Coffee Shop was a great place to work. We had the best coffee in the entire universe, and we even had a secret recipe for making drinks. We took giant cans of artificially-colored liquid sugar, poured them into smaller prettier containers, and brought them into the cafe where we used them to flavor drinks. We dumped a ton of sugar into every drink. And people loved it! Dreamy Coffee Shop had a huge supply of these giant sugar cans in the storeroom. It was enough to last for centuries.

I was in the storeroom one day with Esther filling up containers when she gave me a challenge.

"Hey Jack," she said. "I dare you to punch a can."

"No way," I laughed. "Why would I wanna do that?" I didn't see any point in punching a can.

Esther kept prodding me. "Michael punched a can," she said. "How come he can do it but you can't?"

Esther showed me the can Michael punched and the mark he had made. It was a pretty good-sized dent. Michael was a little weasel. I thought about this for a moment. I couldn't be outdone by some weasel. Then I thought about Esther – even in an ugly barista polo shirt she was hot. Next I caught a glimpse of her left boob. It was big! So I decided to punch a can too. I curled my hand up into a fist and slugged the thing. This caused me a little pain but I just pretended it was nothing.

Afterwards, we both examined the results of my effort. I had made a small dent. Esther looked at Michael's can and then she looked at mine. Michael's dent was bigger.

"Looks like Michael is stronger than you," she laughed. "Is that all you got?"

My manhood was being called into question now and I wasn't happy about it. I picked out a new can and stared it down. "You wan' summa dis, bitch?!" I cried. The can didn't say anything. It just sat there. Next I started weaving back and forth like a gangster. I balled up a fist and held it up above my head. I was waving it around, taunting the thing. "What you got, can?!" I screamed. "I'm gon' brang it!" Finally I reared back and belted the thing with all my strength. There was a great big smacking sound. Then the can buckled in. It pinched a knuckle and drew some blood. Pain began to register. And I was pretty sure I had broken a bone. But I just played it off. My dent was bigger than Michael's! I was the winner! So I held up the bloody appendage and began to celebrate.

"Yes!" I cried. "I am the greatest can puncher in the world!"

Esther started cracking up. "Guys are so easy," she laughed. "We can make you do anything. All we have to do is say it the right way."

I began to deflate a little. Then Esther started bragging about all the other guys she had gotten to punch cans. She spun the cans around in the rack to show me. A dozen or more were dented and there was another one with blood. I examined them all. And that was when my pride began to swell. I truly was great. Not one single bastard in all of Dreamy Coffee Shop had been able to top me. Out of all the dents, *mine* was the biggest!

Happy Talk

It was a typical day on campus and me and Rocco were walking to class. I looked around. Everyone was hungover. Some kids still seemed drunk even. People were all lazing around and no one was doing a whole lot of studying. A fiery sun was hovering overhead and it was beating down on people as they wandered about. The campus police were out too. They were riding around on their Segways and ignoring all the drunks. Instead each cop had a hand cupped around his ear. He was hoping to hear something that violated Happy Talk.

Happy Talk was the official name for the new student speech code. It was illegal to say anything that was not considered happy. Everyone liked the new code because we all wanted to be happy. People weren't perfect, though, and sometimes they broke the rules. So whenever this happened, they were brought before *The Panel*. This was a group of the most revered elders in the entire university. There were some old hippies, a few escapees from the mental institution, and a really sleepy guy who could only say one word. It was the job of The Panel to determine the fate of anyone who said something that was not happy.

Me and Rocco were about halfway to class when we saw *him* – a suspicious-looking man of Italian or possibly Middle Eastern descent. He was standing in a big crowd outside the student union, it was a hundred degrees out, and he was wearing a trench coat. The guy was walking along sullenly, grumbling to himself about "infidels" when – all of a sudden – he yanked the coat open, exposing an enormous bomb that was strapped to his chest. Then he screamed something in a foreign language and touched his phone to set the thing off. But nothing happened. A look of astonishment spread across the man's face. A moment later it turned to anger.

"Goddamn AT&T reception!" he bellowed. "How can there be no bars at the University of Arizona!"

A pretty blonde walked up to the man and started stroking his hair. "It's gonna be okay," she cooed. "I understand why you're angry. You're oppressed." But the man was inconsolable. He pushed her aside and started walking away. He was all by himself sulking when Rocco let his emotions get the better of him.

"I can't believe you almost blew us up, dude!" he yelled. "You're a real jerk!" And just then a spam text came in. BOOM! It triggered the man's cellphone and caused the bomb to explode. His face broke into a great big grin as it went off. The explosion sent shrapnel flying everywhere, but as luck would have it no one was hurt. People were all out of range. The blast caused the bomber's head to separate from his body, though. It flew high up into the air. The smiling head was tumbling end over end and moving in slow motion as it rose. It kept going and going, higher and higher. And while it was up there, I started to wonder about things. Did this still count? The bomber had only killed himself. Would he still get the sixty-nine virgins in heaven that all suicide bombers got? I looked around. Somehow, I could sense that everyone else felt the same way. A crowd had gathered. And no one really knew what the fate of the head would be. It was spinning and spinning and hair and blood were flying everywhere. Finally the thing started to come down. Kids all across campus seemed to be pulling for it. All at once a spontaneous chant arose.

"Sixty-nine!"

"Sixty-nine!"

"Sixty-nine!"

The head landed right in one of the campus trash cans. A perfect swish! A three-pointer! The crowd saw this and went crazy. Everyone was cheering. One kid even jumped up onto the trash can. He started doing a funky dance with his butt sticking out. Then he pumped a fist into the air and cried out for joy.

"Haaoooooooooh!!!"

It was a beautiful moment. People had tears in their eyes. We we're all sure the guy was going to get the virgins, but then – I looked over at the library. A guy and girl were up on the fourth floor. And they were performing a sex act in the window. One was munching on a fish taco and the other was gargling a snake. The two of them were really going at it – and they were putting on quite a show. I was confused for a moment. Was this what all the cheering was about? I glanced around for a minute to make sure. And then I just sat there scratching my head. No one had even noticed the suicide bomber! Boy did I feel dumb.

Later on that week, Rocco was called in before The Panel. One of the hippies had witnessed the entire episode from his office in the campus medical marijuana dispensary. And he was not pleased. He felt that Rocco had been disrespectful to the bomber.

"Student," he said, "you're a fratboy, aren't you? I don't like fratboys. We treat everyone *fairly* here at the University of Arizona and I don't think you were being very *fair* the other day. This is a highly respected educational institution! And YOU have violated our speech code – specifically the policy of Happy Talk! We can't have people going around saying things that aren't happy. Calling someone a *jerk* is not a very nice thing to do. What do you have to say for yourself?"

"Sir," Rocco replied, "with all due respect, I hope you realize that I was trying to protect everyone from a TERRORIST! Would you have liked it better if people were killed?"

The hippie looked him over. "I don't like your tone, son," he said. "I think you had better–" And just then a lesbian with a flattop cut him off. She was the leader of The Panel.

"You look familiar, asshole," she said. "Haven't I seen you somewhere before? I know all about your kind. I know what you do at your *parties*! You *used* me! Err...I mean...you *use* women! You only want them for sex! And that's not cool! You got it, punk?"

"What?" Rocco said, confused. "What are you talking about? I never make girls do anything they don't wanna do. And how come you're calling me an asshole? You're violating your own code!"

"We're not students, asshole," said the hippie. "We can talk however we want. It's our job to teach scum like you manners."

The lesbian turned toward the hippie. "Well," she said, "what do you think we should do with him?"

"I've got an idea," he said. "Let's treat him like a..." Then he paused and nudged the guy who could only say one word.

"Dog."

Everyone on The Panel began to chuckle. But the hippie was just getting started. "Damn," he deadpanned. "And if that doesn't work, maybe we could make him eat a..." He nudged the guy again.

"Dog."

The Panel was really laughing now. All the revered elders were cracking up. A mental patient in the back could barely contain himself. "Haaaiieehahahoohoo!" he cackled. "Where ya from, kid? China?"

"Wait!" cried the lesbian. "How about we make him have sex with a..." The hippie elbowed the guy pretty hard this time.

"Dog!!!"

Everyone was busting up now – even Rocco. Sex with dogs brought back fond memories of hazing freshman. He remembered the time they had made a pledge start nailing a fat girl doggy style. Then they blindfolded the kid and swapped the girl out for a dog with a shaved butt. It was a great joke. Everyone thought sex with dogs was funny so The Panel was all laughing hysterically. The lesbian was slapping her knee so hard she burst a shoelace on her combat boot. And the hippie had tears streaming down his face – they soaked into his beard and softened up a few crumbs of leftover vegan meatloaf that he would eat later. The mental patient in the back kept smacking himself in the head and crying out for joy. And the sleepy one-word guy even looked half-awake. "Hahahahahahaha!!!" they all laughed.

It took several minutes for everything to calm down. Then the lesbian paused and tried to stop smiling long enough to address Rocco. "Okay, student," she said, finally, in between hysterical sobs, "you can go back to class now. Just remember to always talk happy."

Preschool Graduation

Uncle Sal's son, Nathan, was graduating from preschool, so Sal called me up and invited me to the ceremony. I guess I felt like I had to go. Graduating from preschool was a big accomplishment! So I hopped into Bertha and drove over to the school to check it out. I ran into Sal in the parking lot. "Man," he complained, "a bum just hit me up for money. Why do people pay these guys? Being rewarded for nothing just trains you to be good at nothing and to expect a reward."

The ceremony was being held in the cafeteria. I walked in and looked around. A troop of show monkeys had been herded up onto the stage, and they were all standing around not knowing what to do. Some smacked each other to pass the time, others fidgeted around, and there was even one boy up front who was proudly showing off a piss circle on his crotch. It was a group of four-year-olds after all so this was all par for the course. Another kid decided to use the moment to dig for gold in his nose. He managed to find something and pulled it out. Then he held the thing up for everyone to see. The applause was slow at first. His mother started to clap. And then his father. But pretty soon all the other parents were joining in. And in no time the sound became a thunderous ovation. A man near the stage whipped out a state-of-the-art camera and started taking pictures. Then another did the same. It took a few seconds but the crowd morphed into a mob of lunatic paparazzi. Everyone was snapping away like mad and flashes were going off all over the place. Photographers were everywhere – they were shooting pictures and yelling for poses. "Show us the booger!" one cried. The piss-circle kid got blinded by all the light. "Mommy..." he mumbled, "where's my trophy..." And then he fell over like a tree and landed on his face. The child's father saw this, whipped out his cell phone, and dialed 911.

An hour and a half later, the paramedics showed up. But the kid's parents had forgotten to bring their lawyers, so everyone just stood around trying to figure out what to do. After a while, one of the paramedics started to get a frustrated look on his face. This was a serious situation so he decided to take a big legal risk and treat the child. First, he looked at the kid's eyes. "The child has eyeballs!" he cried. Then he measured the right arm. And after that he checked the left. "Both arms are the same size!" he yelled. "The kid is gonna be okay!" Everyone breathed a huge sigh a relief. Next he turned to the father. "But I pronounce this man to be dead!" he cried. "Brain dead, that is!" Finally, the paramedic stood up and did a tap dance all the way back to the ambulance. He and his buddies hopped into the thing and drove away.

Imaginary Friend

I have an Imaginary Friend. She's fun! I always have a great time with her. I take her everywhere with me – to the park, into the toilet, I even ogle her while I drive! She's kind of fragile, though, so I always cradle her gently with both hands to make sure she's safe from danger. I pray to her. And whenever I do this, a thumb pops out from each hand and I massage her for luck. Sometimes, when I'm staring at her, I even forget that the outside world exists!

My Imaginary Friend is small and glows whenever I touch her. She glows when other people touch her too. But I don't like that. I don't want any other motherfuckers to get too close to her. *That* always pisses me off. A guy tried to press her home button once and I knocked him out cold! He'll think twice before he does *that* again. I love my Imaginary Friend. She helps me avoid awkward social situations. Whenever I feel depressed about not talking to other humans, I just look at her and she makes me feel better. I stare at her for hours. After that, for some strange reason, I usually feel like killing myself. She's a great communicator. She sends messages to other people for me all day long. And I never have to talk to any of them! It's really great. Everyone should have an Imaginary Friend.

Birthday Party

It was Nathan's birthday and his party was in full swing down at Himmel Park. Everyone was excited. Cousin Tara was there and she had a five-year-old son too. People were having fun but after a while I noticed that they were all whispering. Tara's kid didn't have a dad and everyone seemed worried about this. I couldn't figure out why it mattered! Old school dudes even had a special name for kids without dads – they called them bastards. Basically, old school dudes were a bunch of dumb mean assholes who called people names and discriminated against everyone!

There were a few oddballs at the party. An old man with a bad dye job was standing next to a sagebrush. And he wasn't fooling *anyone*. An inch of gray roots were jutting out from underneath a half-bald slab of black hair. He had to be someone's grandpa. I glanced around some more. It was only noon but one of the dads was all dressed up for a night out at the club. His shirt was so shiny that the sun reflected off of it and caught a nearby sagebrush on fire. A rabbit under the sagebrush was taking a nap and wound up getting cooked alive. The old man saw this and skewered it with a stick. Then he picked the thing up and started to munch on it. I didn't know what was crazier – the old man's taste in snacks or his hair. It looked so fake that someone needed to tell him. But no one did. Instead everyone just snapped pictures in secret, posted them online, and walked around snickering about how clever they were. It was all weirdos at this party – especially the black guy over in the corner who wouldn't stop eating celery.

Cake was served and we all grabbed a piece. This was a routine part of any birthday. But today, a surprising twist had been thrown into the mix. Instead of the standard white cake, this one was black. Immediately a buzz began to ripple through the crowd. A new kind of cake! People were all blown away. Everyone was laughing and dancing around in celebration. It was a winner for sure.

I started making jokes about the cake right away. "American black cake" I called it. Tara repeated my joke. Except when she said it, she whispered the word *black*. And that was when I realized my mistake – a black guy was nearby. You weren't supposed to say the word black around black people. It was racist. And it was against the Policy of Happy Talk too.

I glanced over at the brother. He had just sunk his teeth into a new stalk of celery. But as soon as I looked at him, I realized that I had done a terrible thing. I had *seen* a black person! A sense of horror swept over me. Everyone knew it was racist to *see* a black person. This meant *I* was a racist. Quickly I averted my eyes. Then I glanced around to see if anyone had noticed. I didn't want people to know I was a racist. Next I started to think about the celery thing some more. It was amazing. No matter where I went, whenever I saw black people, they were always eating celery! I was about to point this out when I remembered that it too was racist. It was forbidden. No one was allowed to talk about the food that black people ate. You could only talk about stuff they *didn't* eat. My mouth was open and my lips were quivering. My entire body was trembling. I was a bad person. I couldn't believe I had nearly uttered the word "celery" in the presence of a black man. It had been on the tip of my tongue even. A great sense of shame swept over me and, all of a sudden, my eyes began to dance around to see if anyone was watching. After that I covered my mouth with one hand to stop any sound from coming out. I just couldn't trust myself anymore.

At this point I was starting to feel a little frustrated. Happy Talk was a big part of the Campaign to Make Life Better. Not saying true things helped everyone. We all loved the campaign – it was improving America! But it was a lot of trouble too. It was hard enough to remember which girls I had hit on already and how many beers were in the fridge. And sometimes I had to know stuff for class too. But it was all getting to be too much! How many things could one guy remember! I didn't even know which way was safe to look anymore, so I put on a pair of sunglasses to stop myself from being racist. Then I stuffed a big fat piece of American black cake into my face. This would keep me out of trouble for a while.

I was standing there munching on cake when it hit me – everyone was always trying to help black people, but their condition was worse than ever. No one cared. Whenever blacks complained, people just gave them a new holiday to shut them up. Only one useful thing had ever actually been done – they had been given their own word. And no other group was allowed to say this word. Everyone else had to use a second word that referred back to the first one. This had made black people's lives better.

I looked over at Tara. She was handing a piece of cake to her son. "More cake!" he cried. "I'm hungry, bitch!" Tara gave him the cake. She was the nicest person anyone could ever meet. Her ex was a stringy-haired blond guy with a face that seemed paralyzed. Things hadn't worked out between the two of them. Tara told me the story. Her ex was really tired all the time. Sometimes he was so depressed he couldn't even lift a pencil. The guy refused to apply for any jobs and couldn't even hold his own baby without dropping it. Tara was doing everything and paying for everything, but in the end he forced her to dump him. After that he went on long-term disability for the pencil thing. It was good a guy like that always had some woman or the government to help him out when he was in a jam. Who knew what would happen otherwise? Tara's ex stayed on disability for five years. A pencil sat next to him on the nightstand every night like a thousand pound weight. And nothing much ever got done. But there was still one thing that managed to lift itself up every morning, and it wasn't getting much use. Eventually Tara's ex got tired of being tired, so he bought a plane ticket and went to Thailand. A short time later he came back with a Thai woman. She was his new wife. And she couldn't speak a lick of English or do much of anything so he wound up getting a job.

Inverse Crosswalk

Uncle Sal asked me to drop Nathan off at kindergarten one morning. I was always glad to help out so I hopped into Bertha and drove over to his place. Sal's house wasn't too far from Cho Elementary School. It was within walking distance actually, but children couldn't walk to class because a sex offender was hiding behind every tree along the way. Sex offenders didn't really have any other good options. They couldn't hide *too* close to schools because that was against the law. Trees were just about all they had.

Me and Nathan got into the car. "Jack!" he cried. "Can you play the La La Happy Boys?" The La La Happy Boys were his favorite band. They were a world-famous children's singing group. Everyone loved them. They danced around on stage and sang songs about how special everyone was. I hit play and pretty soon we were both singing along.

> "Oh I am special, so unique
> Thinking about me makes me weep
> Candy is dandy it gives me health
> I am the hero of myself
> I'm perfect I never misbehave
> Oh other people should be my slave!
> Yeah other people should be my slave!"

We were driving along when I spotted a sex offender up in the branches of a tree. He had one hand on a pair of binoculars and the other in his pants. "Hey pervert!" I shouted. "What are you doing up there?!" My yelling startled the guy. He fell down a couple of branches and impaled a knothole with his engorged member. It was an ugly scene and the paramedics had to be called in. The man recovered eventually but the tree wasn't quite as lucky. It had lost its innocence – forever.

Sex offenders weren't too difficult to spot. Besides the tree thing, they usually wore trench coats or Arizona State University gear. That was what I had read on the Internet. Sex offenders were a big problem nowadays. They were multiplying exponentially and lurking around after children everywhere, but paying attention to kids was a lot of trouble. It took *energy*. And no one ever really knew what a kid might do, so it was easier just to pay other people to watch it. This freed up a lot of time for checking behind trees.

We made it to the school and parked. To get a child from the parking lot to the school you had to cross a street, and to make things easier a crosswalk was painted on the road as a guide. We put on our government-approved walking helmets and got ready to cross – but then I looked around. Parents and children were crossing everywhere *except* at the designated spot. I thought about this for a moment. It was only fair. This was America! And we were all free! It wasn't right for a free people to have to use a crosswalk! Gazing up and down the street, I felt a sudden sense of pride. Tears began to well up in my eyes. It was beautiful – like a one-lane road in Mexico with cars going in both directions. People were all wearing their walking helmets and they were darting back and forth across the street like so many suicidal quail. I grabbed Nathan's hand and we stepped off the curb and out into the street.

Standing randomly in the middle of the road was a crossing guard in a trench coat. "Behold!" he cried and then he motioned to the white paint. "You have entered the inverse crosswalk! An invisible laser covers the space in between those two white lines with a beam of death! Anyone who enters will be incinerated! Instantly! Enjoy your trip! And let freedom ring!"

The two of us strolled happily across the inverse crosswalk, and once we were on the other side of the street we were surprised by a woman who handed Nathan a trophy.

"This is for Nathan!" she cried.

"Thanks," I said. "What's it for?" I had no idea that Nathan had won a trophy.

"Haaaiieehahahoohoo!!!" she cackled. "We give every child who arrives at school on Monday a trophy. We hand out trophies on Tuesday, Wednesday and

Friday too. Today is sharpen-a-pencil day! They get one for that also! Better bring a sack if you're picking him up!"

I glanced at the school office. There was a giant stack of trophies inside. They had thousands of them! A guy with a hammer was in there and he was busy making more. The trophies all looked so shiny. I was just staring at them, completely mesmerized, when all of a sudden I became distracted. There was a commotion out in the street. A pair of five-year-old twins were crossing the road and one was bending down to pick something up. His mother realized what he was doing and a look of horror spread across her face. "Nooooooo!!!" she cried. "Don't do it!!!" But the boy paid her no mind. He picked up the object and stood there, holding it in his hand. At this point I realized just how serious the situation was – the child was holding a *peanut*. My mind began to race. Where had the peanut come from? And how had it gotten so close to a school? I racked my brain and put two and two together – this was the work of *terrorists!*

The kid's hand swelled up like a balloon. And then it exploded. He collapsed to the ground in obvious pain, twitched around for a few moments, and died. His brother witnessed the entire tragedy and it was all just too much for him to take. He pulled an AK-47 out of his backpack and ran through the school grounds mowing down anyone who crossed his path.

"Eat lead, bastards!!!" he shouted. "I'm special!!!"

"We understand your pain!" people cried as they were shot. Some even jumped into his path, sacrificing themselves so he could feel better. Everyone wanted to help – all except for one very nice-looking young woman. She didn't like what she was seeing. "You can't shoot in here!" she cried. "This is a gun-free zone!" And at that moment a bullet hit her right between the eyes. She crumpled to the ground and blood began to dribble slowly out of the hole in her forehead.

It all went down pretty fast. Altogether the boy killed thirteen people and no one even had time to react. But eventually the kid just ran out of bullets, so he sat down in the teachers' lounge and started playing Grand Theft Auto. When the teachers all realized what had happened, they were shocked but then – a buzz began to travel up and down the hallways of the school. It grew and grew. And pretty soon all the teachers were smiling. Their students never learned much since they spent all their time focusing on the kids whose parents didn't care, but finally – one of their own was good at something! Never before had a five-year-old notched so many kills.

"Yes!" cried the principal when she heard the final tally. "It's a record!"

After that everyone started to chant.

"We're number one!"

"We're number one!"

"We're number one!"

There was a great celebration and people were all running around dancing and singing. It was an amazing day. But every good thing had to come to an end. The boy was arrested in the aftermath and no one could decide what to do with him. He was just so *young*. It didn't seem right to haul him off to jail, so a child psychology expert was brought in. After conducting a thorough examination, he determined that the rampage was all caused by a self-esteem problem. So the school made the boy a special trophy – one with a gun on top and the number 13 engraved on a special commemorative plaque. Everyone was excited about this. People were all slapping each other on the back and congratulating themselves.

Classes went on as scheduled that morning since it was anti-bullying day. Anyone who ditched was sure to find themselves on the list of non-attendees on the school website. I came back after school and picked Nathan up. Then we hopped into Bertha. With great caution I pulled out into the street. I glanced around. There were just too many quail. They were everywhere! Finally I started to drive. I was dodging them left and right when – all of a sudden – one darted out into traffic from behind a van. It didn't even bother to look. The woman just hit the street blind, in full stride. Finally, at the last moment, she saw me. "Aaaaaaaaaaagghh!" she cried. I slammed on the brakes and saved her life. To show her appreciation she flipped me the bird and kept walking. It was all an unfortunate misunderstanding. Cars had to use the inverse crosswalk too – it doubled as a street after all. And there just wasn't any other good place for them to go. They were too big for the sidewalk and couldn't fit in a bag. I managed to weave my way through the rest of the quail somehow and cruised back to Uncle Sal's house. The two of us cracked open a couple beers and had a good laugh about the crazy day at school.

Bad Boy Factory

A guy in tighty-whitey underwear and a partially torn cape was sitting in the U of A library, out in the open, surfing porn on a computer. I saw him and right away I was confused.

"Why are you looking at porn here?" I asked. "You can't polish the Pope in front of everyone. What's your goal?"

The guy didn't want to talk. Instead he just pointed at an ad on the wall next to one of the computers. I looked at the note. It was for some type of job opening.

Wanted: Porn Surfer

Seeking graduates of Bad Boy Factory to fill positions surfing porn on library computers.

What is the Bad Boy Factory?

The Bad Boy Factory is where most children are raised nowadays. This place does not teach manners or the difference between right and wrong. When one child spits on another, they pretend not to notice. And if a kid doesn't eat, they throw his lunch away so the parents won't worry. The Factory's job is to take possession of children for a period of time and return them alive.

Why was the Bad Boy Factory Created?

The Bad Boy Factory was created to make life easier for people. Once every generation civilization is invaded by barbarians. And these troublesome creatures come with a built-in chip to turn their parents into grownups. They are always pushing the boundaries, trying to see what they can get away with. A hot pot on the stove is adventure. And rocks are food. Parents have to constantly teach them what to do and what not to do, so they can learn. This deactivates the chip and also trains the parents to be grownups. A grownup is someone who always does the right thing for the next generation. Being a grownup isn't always fun. It just feels better at the end of the day.

Is the Bad Boy Factory good?

Of course! Well, except that many children nowadays have never been told "no." Their Bad Boy Chip has not been deactivated by learning boundaries. And their parents have never figured out how to become grownups. When a chip is still active, a kid keeps on doing bad things to get attention until something goes wrong. Sometimes he even winds up in a library surfing porn.

All of a sudden I was pissed off. I looked at the surfer. "Hey asshole," I said. "This computer is MINE! Get off! It's my turn!"

"Fuck you!" he countered. "No way!"

SHART

I was in San Francisco on vacation and I was so excited. I was about to walk into Stoned Hippies Artistic Recreational Teahouse. The name was a mouthful, so everyone just called the place SHART. It was the most famous teahouse in the entire world – the great hippie temple of wisdom. This was where counterculture heroes had first planned the Campaign to Make Life Better. They had smoked pot, dropped acid, and outsmarted a lot of ancient dudes by realizing that "if it feels good, do it." They had changed the world. It didn't take long before people began to act upon every impulse. And no one figured that anything could go wrong with this.

Nowadays people came from every corner of the globe to feel the vibe of the Teahouse. They wanted to experience the great and historical SHART that had given birth to the counterculture. The place was famous in a lot of ways. The popular singer Stinkie Hairpie had even overdosed here. She smoked too many dried grasshoppers one night and then passed out and drowned in the toilet. This type of death automatically qualified someone as a rock star. Stinkie was a virtual unknown before the accident, selling only 69 records, but afterwards she sold millions and became a household name. SHART was responsible for the legacy of Stinkie Hairpie.

Bars and cafes were a dime a dozen. There were a lot of stinky old holes around Haight and Ashbury – but there was only one SHART. I stepped into the place and looked around. Right away I realized that today was a special day. Everything was half price to celebrate the outlawing of sugar. The City Council of San Francisco had just passed a new law – no one was allowed to buy or sell sugar or any product that contained it. Sugar was bad for you. It seemed good at the moment and it gave you a temporary happy feeling, but the side effects were all bad. Altogether it had been a productive week for the City Council. They had also legalized all drugs. People wanted to take drugs, and there was no way to stop them, so a new law was passed to allow for this. Everyone was happy about these new legislative accomplishments. A lot of progress had been made.

I glanced around the cafe. People all had their own unique style. Wherever I looked there were ABNs (anything but normals). Everyone looked cool! It didn't take any skill to have a look, but it was a good way to get attention. People hanging out in the back had giant African hoops stretching out their earlobes. And none of them were from Africa. They were all white. One kid had even managed to fit a salad plate into his. The thing still had a little ranch dressing on it, and some parsley up near the edge. Another guy had his neck all stretched out giraffe-style with golden African neck rings. This had seemed like a good idea to him one day when he was high. But now he wasn't so sure. "My neck itches," he complained. Then he started looking around. "I have a toothpick. Can someone scratch my neck for me? If I take these rings off, my spine will collapse."

Everyone pretended not to hear him.

I couldn't make heads or tails out of the whole scene. Everyone was trying to be the most unique person in the world, but they all had a similar style. The more people tried to look different, the more they all seemed to look the same.

I got in line and waited to place my order. After a few minutes it was my turn, so I walked towards the cashier. I was all set to order a certified organic, gluten-free, non-GMO, kosher, Vegan brownie with no preservatives, artificial ingredients, refined sugars or proteins, but when I stepped up to the counter I was rudely interrupted. A white woman with dreadlocks cut sideways through the line and pushed me.

"Out of my way, *normal*," she sneered. "I'm headed down to the show."

"What show?" I asked. "What's going on?" But the woman couldn't be bothered. She just kept moving, zipped past a sign, and disappeared down a flight of stairs. I looked at the sign.

"Inventor of feminism to speak at 3 PM in basement."

The inventor of feminism! I didn't even know who that was, but I was excited to see her. I was sure she would say a lot of important stuff. Feminism had done so many great things for women. It had freed them from the bondage of the home and given them exciting fulfilling lives. I grabbed my brownie and followed the dreadlock woman down a dungeon-like flight of stairs into a dreary old basement. The lights were all turned down low, but the speaker was lit up under a great big spotlight on stage. I took a good look. Then I dropped my brownie and stood there with my mouth open. I couldn't believe what I was seeing – the inventor of feminism was a man! He was old. The guy had to be at least seventy. He was dressed in a black turtleneck with a long unruly beard, and he spoke with a ridiculous French accent. The man was making eye contact with everyone and gesturing around wildly, exaggerating every word that came out of his mouth. I recovered from my initial shock and grabbed a seat at the back of the room.

"I love all zee wo*man*!" the speaker cried. "Zee man and zee wo*man* are eegzact*lee* zee same! On*lee* zee se*xist* socie*tee* eez responsi*boll* for zee differ*once*! Zee tradition*al* role for zee wo*man* eez horri*boll*! Eet eez slave*ry*!"

Then he opened up a cage next to him and two birds walked out.

"Voi*la*!" he cried. "I geev you zee cassowa*ry*!"

A male and a female cassowary walked out onto the stage. The male bird busted a grumpy on the floor. Then the female kicked it in the head. The thing fell to the ground in obvious pain – but with a smile on its face. The crowd loved it. People were all nodding and clapping excitedly at the two birds. And they couldn't get enough of the speaker. He owned them. The guy was on a roll and he knew it. He looked around for a moment and then paused dramatically, teasing the audience, as he prepared to deliver the final line of his speech. A beret sat cockeyed on his oversized skull. He pushed it up slowly with his left hand and steeled his gaze. And at that moment the male cassowary sat down on an egg.

"And zees!" he cried. "Eez why zee wo*man* shood be zee man and zee man shood be zee wo*man*!!!"

The crowd heard this and burst into applause. Women jumped up and began hugging him. A college girl lifted up her shirt, exposing a pair of large nicely-shaped breasts. "Sign them!" she cried. He did. And then he got her number. The scene was mad. It went on like this for quite a while and then the audience began to slowly filter out. A few minutes later everyone was gone. I picked my brownie up off the floor, took a bite, and then spit it out. The speaker had started to pack up his things, and we were the only two people left in the room, so I walked over and struck up a conversation.

"Interesting speech," I said. "I'm sorry. I didn't catch your name..."

This seemed to offend him. "You do not know?!" he cried. "Zey call me Jacques de la Mer*de*. I am zee per*son* who do zees femeen*eezm* for zee man. I cre*ate* zees revolu*tion*! I make all zee pee*poll* so hap*pee*!"

"What do you mean?" I asked. "How have you made everyone happy?"

"Why, I geev zee pee*poll* what zey want! Zee wo*man*, zey sec*ret* want to be zee man. And zee man, zey sec*ret* want to be zee tod*dler*. You see! I do zees! Now, zey all so hap*pee*!"

"Awesome! I've always wanted to suck on a boob and get mollycoddled all day. That's my dream! You are pretty cool, dude!"

"Ah, you are smart like moi. Zee wo*man*, zey all sear*ching* for zee man zey ad*mire*. And zee man, he want to have zees admira*tion*, zees res*pect*. Zee man is al*ways* succee*ding* when he eez ha*ving* zee responsibili*tee* and zee motiva*tion*. But eez trou*ble*!!! Eez bet*tah* to be zee tod*dler*. I am hel*ping* zee pee*poll* to a*chieve* zees! I am do*ing* so ma*nee* of zee trick. You are pop*ping* zee ho at universi*tee*, no? I make zee Pill for zee wo*man*. So no ba*bee*. I geev you zee ho! Zees eez zee dream for zee man! Zee wo*man*, zey all ha*ving* sex like man now! In zee old day, when zee man make zee *woman* weef bun een *oven*, he must mar*ree*. But now eez great! We kill zee ba*bee*! Be*fore* we are li*ving* zee dream of zee wo*man*. Zey are wan*ting* to be weef on*lee* zee one guy. But zee man, he eez sec*ret* wan*ting* to have zee ha*rem*! We are clo*ser* zan ever to zees! Soon we are all pop*ping* zee ho! I geev zees dream to you!"

"Yeah! You nailed it, French guy! People aren't supposed to be tied down to one person! That's what I've always said. Playing the field is natural – it's like ripping a good fart! But...wait a minute. What if my grandma was right? She always said I should keep it in my pants."

"Zees eez ab*suuurd*! Zee grandmo*zer* does not know any*sing*! Zee pee*poll* are free now! Some*times* zere are e*ven* zee crazy one who mar*ree*. I am also ta*king* zee wife. But eez bet*tah* now! Every*sing* eez half! I ne*vah* do more zan half of any*sing*! Een zee old day, zee man and zee wo*man*, zey are dy*ing* for each ozer. Zey have zees horri*boll* obliga*tion* for each ozer. But I am chan*ging* all zees! I make zee cut*ting* so ea*zee*! Zee pee*poll* are no lon*ger* depen*ding* on each ozer. Every*sing* eez half! And I ne*vah* do no*sing* be*cause* I am do*ing* all zee work dur*ing* zee sex! I am mov*ing* back and fors weef zee hip! Zees eez zee half I do!"

"Tell me about it, dude! Bustin' a nut is hard work! Girls just lie there like they're a dead fish or somethin'! And then they want us to go shoppin' with 'em later. Damn! I'm tired after I hit it! I just wanna chill and watch some Arizona basketball. I wish girls would turn into a pizza and beer after sex, but they're all crazy anyhow so who cares? How come you got married anyway, Jacques? I thought feminists were against marriage."

"Oh, but of course I am mar*ried*! I have zee new tro*phee*! I am mar*ried* for zee time num*ber* four last week. When*evah* my wife turn for*tee*, I am – how you say? – tra*ding* her een for new mo*del*! My new wife, she eez sirty-*two*. She eez good for eight year toge*zer*! I keep her un*less* she eez do*ing* too much complain*ing*. Zee man, he eez not want*ing* to hear zee criti*cal* sing, you see. I am per*fect*. I have no flaw! Part of zees femeen*eezm* for zee man eez zee non-judgmen*tal* sin*king*."

"Sinking? What do you mean by sinking?"

"You know, Ameri*can*. Sink*ing* weef zee brain. You have brain, no?"

"Oh. You mean *thinking*. Thinking starts with a t-h, dude, not an s. What about kids? You got any kids?"

"Oh yes! I have some here. And some zere. I sank God for zee abor*tion*. Wiz*out* zees I will have ma*nee* more! I am not sure zee to*tal* num*ber* I have...but zey are great crea*tures*, zeez child*ren*. Zey are like zee weed. Zey grow wiz*out* wa*ter*. Some are in zee jail. And some are free. I am some*times* hear*ing* from zem..."

"Wow. So how come you decided to start feminism anyhow, Jacques? I'm just curious."

"I ne*vah* tell you."

"I'll buy you a bottle of wine."

"Okay. I tell. Eet eez for zees rich – how you say? – trust fund ba*bee*. Zees guy eez bored. He eez ho*ping* to get more of zee sing be*tween* zee leg from zee la*dee*. He want to make zee life ea*zee*. Zees man is buy*ing* for me one crois*sant*."

"That's it? A trust fund baby bought you a croissant and you started feminism? Seriously???"

"And zee wine. He eez gee*ving* to me zee wine. For zees I make zee pro*mise* to do zee femeen*eezm* for zee man."

"Damn. Well, how'd you do it?"

"Oh zees eez sim*ple*, Ameri*can*. Zee wo*man*, zey are gulli*boll* for zee man. Zey want to be*lieve* us. Zey want to eat zee ap*ple*. Zey love me. So I say to zem, 'Zees eez un*fair*. Every*sing* eez un*fair*.' And zey fol*low*. Zey also like zee trick weef zee bird."

Passive-Aggressive Man

A new kind of man was spreading all across America, so a new superhero was created. His name was Passive-Aggressive Man. He was male but had curly pink hair and bright pink nail polish. His parents had divorced when he was little and not much had changed since then. Passive-Aggressive Man was 35 years old now and still lived in his mom's basement. Every day he woke up and put on a superhero outfit that consisted of dirty tighty-whitey underwear and a partially torn cape with a radiation symbol on it. He was always begging his mom to fix the cape, but somehow or another she never got around to it. Passive-Aggressive Man had lips that were permanently pursed, so it always looked like he was sucking on a lemon. He was a man on a mission. His goal was to make everyone else's lips look just like his.

Passive-Aggressive Man was sitting on his mom's couch in the basement one day. He had a lot of fond memories of that couch from childhood. He used to wake up on it every day to the family dog pissing on his head. But today he was just sitting there laughing to himself.

"Ha HA!" he cried. "I have foiled my friend! My diabolical scheme has run its course!"

Passive-Aggressive Man only had one friend. He had met him last year through an ad on Craigslist and two days ago he ran into him at the mall. "I'll call you," he said to his friend. But he never called. Instead, his friend called *him* and left a message. Passive-Aggressive Man listened to the message and deleted it. The next day he saw his friend again.

"I called you," his friend said. "Did you get my message?"

Passive-Aggressive Man acted confused. "What?!" he said. "Did you call me? I never got the message. AT&T must have some problem." The next time he saw his friend, his friend's lips were pursed too. Passive-Aggressive Man had succeeded.

His friend liked to make plans with him. Passive-Aggressive Man always agreed to the plan but in the end he usually flaked. A plan was just an option to do something and Passive-Aggressive Man's friend was too dumb to know this. He thought a plan meant that people had agreed to meet. Passive-Aggressive Man had duped his friend many times. He had a big bag full of tricks and was still smiling about the one he pulled last December.

"Hi friend," he said. "What would you like for Christmas?"

"I don't know," his friend replied.

But later on his friend started to feel guilty since he hadn't bought anything for Passive-Aggressive Man. So he went shopping, picked out a pack of new tighty-whitey underwear, and gave it to him a couple days early. Passive-Aggressive Man took the gift and went home. "There's one born every minute!" he laughed. Passive-Aggressive Man didn't have any intention of getting his friend a gift. Instead, he returned the underwear and used the money to buy some pot. Then he went into the basement, got stoned, and watched My Little Pony.

While he was in the basement, Passive-Aggressive Man heard the neighbor's dog barking, so he grabbed his phone and called the police. "Hello Mr. Policeman," he said. "My neighbor's dog is barking too much. Can you put a stop to this?" The policeman forwarded his complaint to the Passive-Aggressive Complaints Department and mailed a $100 ticket to the neighbor.

After that Passive-Aggressive Man hopped into his car and started driving to work. He was a great driver so he spent most of his time honking at other people. One of his superhero duties was to point out the mistakes of others from inside the cocoon of his own car. Passive-Aggressive Man even had a super skill. He could pick boogers and drive at the same time. And whenever he picked one, it turned bright pink and became magical. Then he ate it. This skill gave him the ability to repulse any nearby person who was watching. It was one of the many tricks he had for repulsing people. Passive-Aggressive Man kept driving and honking, and finally he made it to his job. He worked at a magic store in El Con Mall. It was right next to a hotdog stand. Passive-Aggressive Man didn't like the guy who worked at the hotdog stand, so he never missed a chance to snub him. His favorite trick was to look in hotdog guy's direction and then turn his head away quickly as soon as hotdog guy noticed. His goal was to *get* hotdog guy. Passive-Aggressive Man even created a fake email address and sent him a mean email.

Hi Hotdog Guy,

You are dumb! You need to stop sucking on those hotdogs when no one is looking! Loser!

Thanks in advance,

Mr. Awesome

After he was done working for the day, Passive-Aggressive Man went home and fought with people on the Internet. It was amazing how many people were wrong. And the best way to co-opt them was by hiding behind a computer and insulting them until they agreed with his point of view. He posted a lot of good disses online. And a lot of people wound up with pursed lips.

Passive-Aggressive Man woke up early the next morning. "Today," he declared, "I will fix one problem!" He was still wearing the tighty-whities and cape from the night before, so he was all ready for action. Passive-Aggressive Man got into his car and drove over to U of A. Then he climbed up onto the roof of the student union. It didn't take long for people to notice. A crowd began to gather.

"I am a superhero!" he cried. "I can fly!"

A kid in the crowd was skeptical. "No way, dude!" he yelled. "Humans can't fly. If you're a superhero, then prove it! Jump!"

"I can fly!" Passive-Aggressive Man cried. "Really! I can! Watch me!"

Passive-Aggressive Man took a few steps back. He stretched both arms out in front of his body to help with aerodynamics. Then he got a good running start and leaped off the edge of the building. He flew straight down to the ground and smacked into the pavement. Splat! Passive-Aggressive Man's head cracked open like a watermelon and juice and seeds began to dribble out of the skull. He was dead. Superheroes weren't supposed to die, though, so no one really knew what to do. Finally, the skeptical kid walked up and kicked his body to make sure he was done. "Dumbass..." he muttered. "Told you humans couldn't fly."

A few days later the funeral was held. Passive-Aggressive Man's mom showed up and so did the guy from Craigslist. He was the first one to speak.

"I'm gonna miss my friend," he wailed. "Whenever he wasn't making mean comments disguised as jokes, he was a really good guy."

Next it was his mom's turn.

"He was the best son a mom could have ever asked for!" she sobbed. "I gave him everything and told him he was special every day! What did I do wrong?!"

After that, the two of them walked up and paid their last respects to the body. Once Passive-Aggressive Man's mom and the guy from Craigslist were finished, a man sealed the casket in lead and lowered it into the ground. Then he stamped a bright purple radiation symbol onto the headstone. "It's a warnin'," he cried, "to all the people that's still alive! Passive aggressive is the worst radiation in the world! And we don't want nobody else to catch it!"

Burning Man

I decided to go to the annual Burning Man festival, so I hopped into Bertha and drove for miles and miles through the most horrendous, godforsaken, barren desert on earth. They called it Nevada. And things were afraid to grow in this place. There was nothing but dirt as far as the eye could see – and even the dirt didn't want to be here. The stuff was swirling around, forming itself into dust devils, and trying to attach to some host and escape. After many hours of driving through this endless-nothing, I arrived at the entrance, and that was where a topless Martian woman greeted me. Her entire body was painted green, but all I could see was a set of big green knockers. The Martian's rack was amazing – it did not even move as she walked! Her doctor had done an absolutely masterful job.

The Martian walked up to my car. "Hello," she said. "Do you. Have. A ticket?"

"Yeah," I said. "Are you from Mars?"

"Yes," she replied. "Welcome home. You are. At. Burning Man."

The Martian woman took my ticket and let me in. The sun had just set and the horizon was glowing with orange and red flames. I was excited so I hit the gas and followed the signs down a dusty road toward my buddy Zabo's camp. I looked around as I drove. Burning Man was one great big shantytown. Random tents and campers were scattered all about, and wherever I looked there was someone naked or crazy. People were high and they were all stumbling around, tripping over each other. Laundry lines were strewn about everywhere as if hung by a drunken spider. It was just one big jumble of chaos and the only thing that seemed to make sense were the streets – they were all laid out in a sensible grid with numbers going one way and letters the other. I kept driving. A kid was passed out naked, face down, in the middle of G street. I honked at him to move but he didn't even budge. After that I observed him for a few moments – his lungs were going up and down so I decided he was still alive. I paused and wondered if I should stop to help, but then I snapped to my senses, spun the wheel, and drove on by. It was party time! And all these other bastards could take care of themselves!

The whole city was on fire with light. It was a burning jewel. There were lights and art and colors as far as the eye could see. This place was *something*! And everyone was wearing some kind of costume or nothing at all. I looked around. People were all special and they were trying to look as ridiculous as possible. Some were on foot and others rode around on crazy art cars or well-decorated bikes. One of these art cars was a purple school bus with giant speakers blasting techno out the windows. The thing cruised by and kicked up a huge cloud of dust. For a moment I couldn't even see, but then the cloud settled and I got a good look at people's faces. Everyone on the thing was high. They were all dancing around and yelling as if today was their last day on earth. I saw my buddy Bam on the bus and waved. He couldn't see me. Eventually I made it to Zabo's camp and parked. Everyone slept during the day at Burning Man, but once the sky turned black, it was on. People were just starting to stir, so I got a chance to meet a few of the other "burners" at camp. They were all friendly and did their best to make me feel welcome. Zabo even woke up and popped his head out of a tent. "Jack!" he cried as soon as he saw me. "You made it!" Zabo was a really macho straight guy – maybe the last actual man in America. But here he was all decked out in a pink tutu. The last man was dead too.

I set up my tent and organized everything. Then I decided to check out all the art and lights, and before long I was wandering around out on the Playa. This was the open area in the middle of the city. A fifty-foot-high mechanical flower was cruising around, entertaining everyone with techno, and some half-naked zombies were trudging along after it in a stupor. Burning Man was an orgy for the eyes. I just stood there for a moment taking it all in, and then I continued on my way. There were idiots to my left and more to my right. I couldn't decide which one was the best – and then I saw *him*. A bald old man was standing out in the open where everyone could see him, and he was trying to be sexy, doing some kind of naked dance with a blue scarf. *This* was the greatest idiot of them all. I watched the old man and felt a sudden pang of jealousy. It looked like he had found Zong Zong Boogaloo. I wanted to find it too. Deep down I hoped that I could be as crazy as him.

Back at camp, I saw the water truck coming towards me. Its job was to circle the makeshift city and spray water onto the dirt streets in a hapless attempt to slow down all the dust. A group of naked people were chasing after the thing and receiving a free shower. I was talking to a hippie chick as the truck approached. She liked me. But I wasn't really into hippies. I always figured the girl should be cleaner than the guy. The hippie was very friendly, though. She offered me a blue pill. "It will make you feel good," she promised. "Just try it." This sounded cool so I popped the thing into my mouth and downed it with a beer. Then I jumped up and sprinted after the water truck, tearing my clothes off as I ran. It was hot out and I was ready for a shower.

"Bye!" I called back to the hippie. "Thanks for the stuff!"

"Wait!" she cried. The girl was sweet. She wanted me to stay and talk to her some more. But I was off.

I caught up to the truck in no time and when I did, a powerful stream of water hit me. It was quite a shock and I shuddered at the first blast. I just wasn't expecting it to be so *cold*. The stuff felt like liquid ice. It was pure pain but I just couldn't stop running after that truck. I was with five random girls, chasing after the thing, catching ice cold blasts of H2O and enjoying myself. I can't say as much for the girls, though – women all looked like wet cats at Burning Man. They liked the luxuries. Civilization was men on a mission, making creature comforts for women, but Burning Man didn't have any of that. I chased that truck a good long time – a mile or so at least. Finally, I was the only one still running. I couldn't get any cleaner or colder so I decided to stop.

I was the only one around now and I was way out on the outskirts of the city. I looked down at my feet. They were covered in a kind of gray goo from all the mud. Then I noticed Barney. He had retreated back into the forest of hair surrounding him. "Fuck..." I muttered. Barney was the smallest he had ever been! His skin was all wrinkled up like a Shar-Pei and his head was the size of a tiny mushroom – the kind you saw in overpriced Thai food. I couldn't believe it. This was just *great*. It was my first time naked in public and Barney was super small. I was so embarrassed. I paused for a moment and prayed for Barney to be bigger.

I started heading back to camp and the sun began to heat me up. Pretty soon I wasn't cold anymore. I forgot I was naked and started scoping out campsites as I walked by. Burning Man was a feast for the eyes. Everyone had something crazy going on and I didn't want to miss anything. I was walking along and everything was going smoothly, but then something unexpected came up. Barney awoke from a deep slumber and began to rise out of the forest around him. He grew and grew. A great missile was preparing for launch. The tiny mushroom was gone and in its place was the helmet of a fearsome warrior. Barney began to darken into his all-business color. He was a purple mercenary now and he was ready for action. It was all very bad timing and I couldn't figure out why it was happening. I wasn't in middle school anymore so it didn't make any sense. But then it hit me. The blue pill was Viagra! I had been tricked by the hippie.

A pretty girl was attending to a clothing line at her site. She looked nice – so nice in fact that she didn't seem to belong at Burning Man. The girl was about to smile at me, but then she noticed that I was naked and standing at attention. And at that moment her eyes popped out of her skull and she recoiled in terror. All the blood drained from her face as she spun around and ducked into a tent. A finger shot out through the zipper. "Sex offender!" she cried. "Help! There is a sex offender on the loose!" A pretty girl was in danger so guys started popping out of the woodwork all over the place. There were dozens of them and in no time a lynch mob began to form. "I'll save you!" one cried. Another grabbed an axe and began to stroke it with an evil grin. A third started smacking two tin cans together rhythmically. All at once they began to chant.

"Get him!"

"Get him!"

"Get him!"

In an instant the entire mob began to join in the chant. And at that moment a kid with a Mohawk stood up and started to pound his chest.

"Kill him!" he yelled. "He's a sex offender!"

"Huh?" I said. "What did I do? What's up?"

All at once the entire crowd began to descend upon me, so I decided to turn tail and run. I started sprinting away as fast as I could – a mad pack of hippies was chasing me, but they had all smoked too much pot and not a one of them had any lungs. Most were choking and gasping after a few steps. They quit running and started to whip out bongs and suck on the things as if they were oxygen tanks. But I just kept on going. I had to get out of there. I ran and ran – past campsite after campsite, down street after street, and pretty soon it was all a blur. I just kept going and going. And somehow – I made it back to my tent.

A naked woman was a beautiful thing. Guys would sit around forever drawing one or chipping away at a sculpture, trying to get it just right. But a naked man? That was different. A naked man was a threat! It was something no one really wanted to see, so I grabbed some clothes, got dressed, and put on a big wizard hat and cloak as a disguise. Then I sat down and cracked open a beer. I decided to kick back and relax for a while because this place was *way too crazy*. I needed a little time to collect myself and gather my senses since we were all planning to go out later.

Zabo had a special Burning Man wallet with an uncountable number of secret pockets. And each pocket was filled with a different drug. He had taken each drug many times, but somehow his brain was still intact and he was able to keep all the pockets straight. Darkness descended upon the Playa. And as soon as it did, Zabo whipped out the wallet. Then he started flipping through the thing like a madman. His hands were moving around lightning fast, opening up this pocket and that – not even a magician was as quick as him. Finally, after a few seconds, he found what he was after. Zabo pulled a small object out of one of the pockets and cradled it gently in his palm.

"Who wants some E?" he asked, looking around. "This is the good stuff. Jack, you want some?"

"Sure," I said. "I'll try it." It seemed like a requirement to be part of the group.

I put the ecstasy on my tongue. Then I swallowed it. Out of the corner of my eye I noticed Billy. He was watching to make sure it actually went down my throat.

We got on our bikes after that and started riding across the Playa. Random art was strewn about all over the place. A life-sized Barbie doll was lying dead on the ground with its legs spread and a knife in its chest. Nearby was a giant 5-foot-tall ashtray. A kid next to it was working hard, doing his best to light a bong. But the wind kept blowing and blowing and the lighter kept going out. The kid was getting frustrated. "Cigarettes cause cancer!" he cried. "Pot rules!" Wind and dust were swirling around us like crazy. We were all wearing goggles and dusk masks, but still I wound up with vertigo. We were cruising along when, suddenly, I fell off my bike and landed hard on the cracked mud below. Zabo and Billy helped me up. Bam and Hana were there too. I got back on my feet and just stood there for a moment. The ecstasy was starting to kick in so, all of a sudden, I was overcome with a great feeling of fake, chemically-induced love. I started hugging everyone. "I love you guys!" I cried. "We're all gonna be friends forever!" And then I looked around the Playa. Everything was calm and perfect. The world was a beautiful, peaceful place. People were nice and they all cared about each other. Humans were all about love and I loved them all! We were *all* special – like the petals of a flower. Then I started thinking about flowers. There was one type in particular I liked. It had a yellow center and pretty white petals. I was thinking and thinking, racking my brain, as I tried to remember what the thing was called. It was on the tip of my tongue even. I was standing there dreamily, trying to recall it – and that was when Zabo brought me back to earth. "Hey spacehead!" he cried. "Let's get going!" After that we all laughed off the crash and decided to move on.

It was about then that a noise across the way caught our attention. We heard the sound of a thousand jets. Peddling along, we crept up on it, and the closer we got the louder the noise became. In no time it turned into an insanely loud din.

Finally, we went around a corner and discovered the source – a campfire. We all stared at the thing in disbelief. Who knew a campfire could be so loud? The flames danced around mesmerizing us for a while. And then we were off again.

We wandered around some more and stumbled upon a great big sparkling ball of light. It was a round ten-foot-high structure covered with hundreds of small video screens – and each screen was flashing a different solid color, one after another, in an ever-repeating pattern. The ball was magical. Some unseen force drew us in and forced us to gaze at it. After a few seconds, the sequence of lights became obvious: Red. Yellow. Green. Blue. Red. Yellow. Green. Blue. But the display was hypnotizing and as soon as one color appeared, we all just stood there, waiting desperately for it to turn into the next. Eventually the new color showed up, and then it too captivated us in the same mysterious way. The magic ball owned us and there just never seemed to be a good point to break away. Finally, after a few hours, I pulled my Imaginary Friend out of my pocket and we all walked off. As we did, I glanced back at the art. People were just standing there, looking at it for no reason. I couldn't believe how stupid they all were. "Buncha dumb monkeys…" I muttered. "Staring at screens…"

Walking around, we ran into a guy who had fashioned an eight-foot-high cross for himself out of two planks of wood. He was standing on an empty crate in front of the thing, mocking Jesus and pretending to be crucified. This was his plan to get laid. A couple girls were heading in his direction so he decided to turn it up a notch.

"Ooooh, the pain in my hands!" he cried. "Please help me sexy ladies! I will turn water into wine for whomever shall free me from this cross! Don't make me wait until Sunday!"

The girls just ignored him. The mocker's skit didn't seem to be going very well, but then a couple white guys with dreadlocks saw him and they couldn't stop laughing.

"Ha ha, bro!" one yelled. "Look! It's Jesus! He's back. And they're crucifying him again! Awesome!"

The dreadlock guys and the mocker were all hamming it up, laughing about how clever they were when, out of nowhere, a preacher appeared. He had a Bible in one hand as he approached the mocker.

"Please Lord!" he cried, looking the mocker in the eye. "Forgive this man for his sins! He knows not what he does!"

We were all really offended to see a preacher at Burning Man. This bastard had some nerve! How could such a closed-minded person dare to join all the open-minded ones?! It just didn't make any sense. The mocker's mouth hung open for a second when he saw the guy, but he recovered quickly. Then a cynical look swept over his face.

"I know exactly what I'm doing you old fool!" he yelled. "I'm dissin' your pretend hero. And I like sin! It makes me feel good!"

When the preacher heard this, he shook his head in sadness. Then he raised both arms up towards the sky. "Lord, I ask you to–" And at that moment one of the dreadlock guys cracked him over the head with a plank of wood.

"Ha ha ha ha!" he laughed. "Hey preacher, I ask *you* to – shut up!"

"I've got an idea," the other dreadlock guy said. "Let's crucify him!"

The two of them picked the preacher up off the ground. He was bleeding now, but the first guy managed to get him up on the crate while the second one laughed.

"I don't have any nails," he chuckled. "Hey, maybe I should use this?"

The guy whipped a knife out of his pocket. Then he pulled his arm back. He was all set to jab the knife into the preacher's hand, but suddenly I realized what was happening and snapped to my senses.

"Hey!" I yelled. "What do you think you're doing?!"

"Yeah!" Billy cried. "Leave him alone!"

I ran up and grabbed the dreadlock guy's arm. Then he dropped the knife and took off running with his buddy. "Fuck you guys!" he yelled as he ran. "Assholes! You just helped an evil dude!"

No one knew what to do with the preacher. He wasn't injured too badly, but Burning Man was not a good place for him to be.

"You better get out of here," I warned. "You're gonna get killed."

The preacher took off running too. "You know what sin is?" he blurted out as he stumbled off. "It's stuff that feels good at the moment but turns out bad later. Your choice. Either you own it or it owns you!"

After that we all just stood there, stunned. Everything had happened so fast and it was hard to know what to make of it all. But things changed pretty quickly at Burning Man and we were easily distracted. We walked along for another block or so and then we came across a couple of half-naked lesbians making out in the middle of the street. Two guys on bikes were riding towards each other from opposite directions – and they were both gawking at the girls. The bikes hit head on and the guys fell to the ground, dazed but smiling. Billy seemed dazed too. He was in a trance and couldn't keep his eyes off the two lovebirds. Girls didn't like Billy looking at their nakedness, though, since he had a big belly and the red hair of a clown. Women wanted to be ogled by good-looking guys – and lesbians were no different. There wasn't really any such thing as a lesbian anyway. All it took was one good guy and they would turn straight. One of the girls peered at us out of the corner of her eye. Then she shot Billy a look. This irritated him. "Why are girls walking around naked if they don't want anyone to look at them?" he complained. "It doesn't make any sense." But a minute later he was laughing again.

We checked out the whole scene. There were a few hotties walking around in various states of undress. But for every pretty girl, our eyes were stung by dozens of ugly old ones and worse yet – naked dudes. Some of these guys went bottomless, wearing only a shirt to hide an oversized belly. This style was known as "shirt-cocker." One shirt-cocker had just used the toilet and he was strolling around, holding in his gut and doing his best to look cool. Everyone was snickering at him behind his back, though – he had a bright red ring on his ass from dropping a load.

Later on that night we went to an outdoor dance club where the world-famous deejay Zip Zop was doing a set. Zip Zop was a big crowd-pleaser. Everyone loved him. We danced for hours and hours – and the music just never seemed to stop. It was great fun, the ecstasy kept us all going strong, and for a while it even seemed like the night might last forever. It was *perfect*. Blasts of fire were shooting through the air above the crowd and it was all part of the show. One soared right over our heads. It lit up the club, turning faces orange and creating smiles as it went. Everyone was cheering. The temperature had dropped and the flames warmed us all up. They seemed close enough to touch even, so I reached out and tried to grab one. But the thing was too far away – it was just out of reach. After that a bottle of whiskey began to make its way through the crowd. Zip Zop was spinning tunes up in a booth, so I took a big swig and passed the booze up to him. He downed the last of it and kept going.

Sometime later, I climbed up onto the platform surrounding the club. It was a good thirty feet in the air and people were all jumping around and dancing on the thing. It was a deathtrap with no guardrail for sure, but no one seemed to care and *somehow* no one had fallen or died. I looked all around. The view was spectacular! I could see all of Black Rock City. My hands were waving around to the music and my feet just wouldn't stop. I gazed around at the sky and the crowd, enjoying it all. This place was amazing! I had a great view of Opposite World down below and the whole anything-goes vibe of Burning Man. It was all the reverse of traditional America, so I broke out in a great big smile. We had finally defeated the forces of evil! I glanced all around. There were ABNs wherever I looked – you were either anything-but-normal here or you were nothing. All of a sudden my eyes focused on a hottie down below. A young topless blonde had a spaced-out kid dancing all around her. The kid kept hugging her and for some reason this seemed to annoy her. Guys everywhere had on skirts. And there was even one girl pretending to be a dude. She was walking around wearing a wrinkled up old 7-11 hotdog as a shlong. I took a deep breath, choked on some dust, and soaked up the vibe. Burning Man was quite a scene. It was beautiful! A tear formed at the corner of my eye. Inside was a ray of sunshine. It rolled off my cheek and fell slowly down toward the crowd below. Then it hit the ground. The tear burst into a cloud of love and filled the world. I couldn't believe it! The dream had been achieved! This was the perfect place. I had finally found Zong Zong Boogaloo!

Several hours later we left the club, but walking down the block we were punched in the face by a horrendous odor. The stench was unbelievable. It was so bad that we just had to find out what it was, so right away we started following the smell. We tracked it down street after street. On we marched. We just kept going and going. And then, suddenly, we found ourselves standing in front of a crowd. A few dozen people were gathered around in a circle and strange cries were coming from somewhere in the middle. We moved in closer and closer, trying to get a better view. What was happening? What was this strange mystery odor? We just couldn't wait to find out. Finally, the five of us pushed through the crowd and came upon the scene. A man was lying flat on his back with his legs high in the air – and he was giving birth to a baby!

The man was pushing hard. He was grunting and groaning. And in between every grunt he was doing a lot of bitching and moaning. "Shit!" he whined. "What a load of crap!" The birth was taking a long time and the guy looked pretty worn out. People were all starting to get irritated about it too. They were beginning to wonder if he could actually pull it off.

An old hippie woman started complaining. "This bitch ain't got what it takes!" she griped. "He cain't have no baby!"

A Seattle hipster was standing next to the hippie. "Hot damn!" he cried. "This dude does not have the cojones to finish the job!" Then he twirled his ironic mustache a few times and shot himself in the head.

The pregnant man seemed sure to fail. He was lying there exhausted and people were all beginning to lose faith in him, but then suddenly he grabbed both butt cheeks and pulled them apart as wide as he could. "This suuuuucks!" he wailed. And then a baby popped out.

The crowd let out a huge cheer. At first, the baby got tangled up in the new dad's ass hair. But as luck would have it, one of the bystanders was carrying a sword – and he was a quick-thinking to boot! The guy whipped it out and slashed the kid free. He saved the day. The baby just lay there on the ground for a few seconds, and then it started to cry. And at that point someone handed the new dad a beer. He guzzled the thing and let out a proud belch. And with good reason – he was the first man to have a baby. It was about time.

The sun was starting to come up so I decided to head home and crash. I'd had enough excitement for one night. It was a great time but life was a kind of mirage. An illusion could seem real from far away. Even up close it was hard to tell the difference, but then one day you looked around and nothing was real. You were standing all alone in a barren desert and everything that seemed like something was really nothing. This place was missing all the trees. There just weren't any at

Burning Man – and what was life without them? Trees were all we had. You had to plant one in good soil to get it started. And solid roots kept the thing alive. It needed daily sustenance and only one thing really mattered in the end. What did it produce? What kept the whole cycle going? You had to judge the thing by its fruit.

The next morning I woke up in an oven. The rays of an infernal sun were baking the tent and buckets of sweat were pouring out of my body. I felt the pain of the Walmart chicken under a heat lamp. I was worn out from the night before and just didn't feel like getting up. But I had to. I didn't have any other choice because one more minute in that thing and I might have died. In a slow and agonizing manner I managed to get up and drag my weary body out of the tent. Then I saw Zabo. He was sitting all by himself in a camping chair.

"Bam died last night," he said. "He got into an argument with Hana." And then he told me the whole ugly story. Something had gone terribly wrong. The two of them had gotten into a bloody, knock-down, drag-out fight and I had slept through it all. Hana had disrespected Bam in front of everyone and this started an argument that turned into a physical fight. Eventually, the two of them were separated and Bam ran off. A mile away and an hour later, across the Playa, he died. Bam's heart stopped in the middle of a confused scene full of random people. He was only twenty-seven. Bam's body had seen a lot of drugs over the course of those twenty-seven years – his face told the story – but still, we were all shocked. Twenty-seven-year-olds weren't supposed to die. Everyone acted sad about Bam, but no one left the show – the big drugs and lights party only happened once a year, tickets were expensive, and no one wanted to miss anything. All of a sudden Burning Man didn't feel like Zong Zong Boogaloo anymore.

You never knew when your number was going to come up. There wasn't much you could do about it so it didn't make sense to worry, but once you were gone – you were gone. And all people had left was the memory of how you had treated them back when you were still alive.

Anti-PI Conference

Zachary Zero was driving around in his Lexus with the top down. "I am smart!" he cried. "Because scientists cannot prove god exists!" Everyone knew that not believing in god made people smarter. It was common knowledge. But no one really knew why. "There's no god!" Zachary yelled and then hit himself in the head. "So I can do whatever I want!"

Zachary was on his way to the Anti-PI Conference. Whenever atheists weren't busy reminding people how smart they were, they spent their time trying to figure out the last digit of PI. And this was why the Anti-PI Conference was created. It was in Paris this year. The conference gave lots of smart people the chance to showcase their intellects by railing against PI. Everyone got up on a soapbox. PI was irrational and they were all determined to destroy it.

The Anti-PI Conference was popular with all of the great intellectuals of the day. Everyone hated PI. But even at this amazing unifying event there was discord and some people went to extremes just to get attention for themselves.

The Zeroists were a major force at the conference. Zeroists did not believe in any number except for the number zero. Only nothing was something to them, so every year they attended the conference in protest. Their leader was Zachary Zero.

The Zeroists' main rivals were the Nothingers. Not to be outdone by Zeroists, the Nothingers believed in nothing at all. They did not believe in numbers or even the fact that humans or the universe existed. Their leader was Nendrick Nothing.

The Anti-PI Conference had been held in San Francisco last year, and it was marred by an ugly altercation between the Zeroists and the Nothingers. Nendrick Nothing had pulled out his soapbox and stood on it in the middle of the room. "Why are we all here?" he shouted. "We are here but we are not here – if you know what I mean. We do not even exist! And none of this is happening!"

Zachary Zero took offense to hearing this. The two had a long sordid history of quarreling with each other. "Of course we are here, Nendrick," he replied. "We are here to protest the absurdity of PI! And we, the Zeroists, also reject all other numbers. We do not believe in anything except the number zero!"

"Zero?" said Nendrick Nothing. "Zero is not even a number. Even if numbers existed, it would not be a number. How can you support something that does not exist? Everything is nothing! And nothing is everything! You are a fool!"

"You are wrong!" cried Zachary Zero. "Zero is the most important number of all! In fact, it is the *only* number!"

Nendrick covered his ears. "I can't hear *youuu*..." he taunted. "You don't exist."

"But–"

After that Nendrick Nothing started to sing like a little boy tormenting his sister. "La la la la," he sang. "I can't hear *youuu*, Zachary. La la la la..."

Zachary Zero had heard enough. He reared back and slugged Nendrick Nothing in the mouth. It was a good solid punch and it made a nice smacking sound. Right away blood began to drip from Nendrick's lip and a tear formed in his eye. "Did you feel THAT?!" Zachary yelled. "Do you exist NOW? Does PAIN exist? Would you like to exist a little MORE, Nendrick? I really ZEROED in on nothing there, now, didn't I? Ha!"

After that, there was a huge brawl. Zeroists and Nothingers were all throwing chairs and knocking down tables. It was beautiful. Zachary Zero even managed to lose his keys somehow in the middle of it all. Things were really starting to get out of control, so the chairman of the conference got on the mic.

"Brothers!" he cried. "Why do we fight each other? We are here for one purpose! One cause! We hate PI. And we must remain united in our effort to destroy this evil number! Do not lose your focus! We are one! And we must fight together as one! We must overcome this irrational force in our midst!"

Once the chairman had spoken, everything calmed down. The fighting stopped and then everyone sat back down and renewed their vow to destroy the evil number. Thousands of people were in attendance and this was how it always went at the Anti-PI Conference. Things weren't always smooth. But that's just the way it was – everyone had an axe to grind. A lot of people went through life consumed by an irrational hatred of PI. They never even gave it a chance. And once something became the popular opinion, all bets were off and no one bothered to think after that.

All of a sudden, Nendrick Nothing jumped up from his chair. "Hey everyone!" he yelled. "I know what the last digit of PI is!" People were stunned. They all stopped what they were doing and waited for him to finish. "The last digit of PI is 'q'!" he cried. "And no one can prove me wrong!"

Underneath the table where he was sitting, Zachary Zero began to slowly ball his hand up into a fist. But then he realized he had lost his keys. He remembered having them before the brawl, so he knew they had to be somewhere in the conference room. Zachary glanced around for a few seconds but quickly gave up. "Pfft!" he snorted. "This room is too dark. I can't find anything in here. I better go outside and look in a more comfortable area!" It was noon and the sun was shining, so he walked outdoors and started scrounging around for his keys under a bush. But he never found them.

Seven Deadly Sins (by Jacques de la Merde)

I have some*sing* to share weef all zee pee*poll*! I am discover*ing* zee great sing! Sin! Sin eez not on*lee* zee descrip*tion* of zee deli*cious* choco*late*. Eet eez also for zee fun ac*tion*! I must tell everybo*dee* about zee se*ven* great sin! I am lo*ving* zee glutto*nee*, lust, greed, en*vee*, an*ger*, pride and sloss! Zeez are zee sing zat make me so hap*pee*!

Zee glutto*nee* eez so great! All zee time, I am ea*ting* and drin*king* so ma*nee* of zee sing! Zees eez zee life! I am ta*king* and I am stof*fing* zee face weef zee wine and zee cheese. And al*ways* I am wan*ting* more! Eet eez so disgus*ting* een zee great way! Zere eez no*sing* like zee fee*ling* af*ter* zee all-you-can-eat buf*fet*! Who need zee self-con*trol*?! Zees eez for zee fool! Zees eez not to co*ver* be*cause* I am unhap*pee*! Non! We all have zee hole. I am ta*king* zee ga*ping* hole in zee cen*ter* of zee soul and I am fil*ling* eet weef zee food. And once I fi*nish* zee food, I am drin*king* zee wine and smo*king* zee grass! I am so hap*pee* for zee great hole!

Zee next sin eez see lust. Once I am so sick and so drunk and high, zees eez when I see zee women! I am seeing zee curve of zee breast and zee buttock. And I must grab eet! At zees time, I cannot sink of zee ozer sing. I must taste zee ladee! Zee wine help me to focus on zees. I onlee want to satisfy zee snake! I am having so manee babee and disease from zees. But eez no problem. Onlee zee strong snake can make zee babee! I am taking Viagra and having zee strong snake! Zee snake eez like zee brain for moi! I am sinking weef zee snake and using all zee time for zee snake! And always I want more! But sometime, zere eez zee sing I cannot have. Sometime, zee woman eez not geeving zee sing between zee leg. And zees eez terriboll! Zees eez when I am watching zee great porn of zee gay Laotian midget on zee computer! Eet eez so exciting!

After zees eez zee greed. Sometime zere eez zee sing on zee TV I like. I am seeing zee commercial and I am sinking about zees sing and zat sing. I want all zee sing! I like zee shinee object! And zee sing are bettah zan zee peepoll! Zey are nevah doing zee talking zat eez different from moi! I forget zee peepoll! I am always grabbing and grabbing! And I nevah geev nosing! I keep eet all! I am sinking onlee of zee self and zere are no ozer peepoll! I am zee onlee peepoll! Zee greed eez zee way to get more and more! Eet eez helping me to succeed! I am showing off all zee sing and proving I am so great!

One day een zee future I will be having everysing! Until zees day I am feeling zee sin zey call envee. When I am not having everysing, I feel zees envee. I am jealous. I see zee ozer peepoll weef zee sing and I resent zem! I feel great pleasure when zey fail! I live for zees! And when I see zem in miseree, I laugh! Ha HA! Whenevah zere is zee person good at somesing, I pretend zey are nosing! Even eef zey are zee friend! I spit on zem! Peuh! I tell you zee secret of zee life – zee happee peepoll, zey get zee happeeness by making zee ozer peepoll happee. And zee unhappee peepoll, zey get zee happeeness by making zee ozer peepoll unhappee. I am so happee!

All of zees is causing zee sin of zee anger. When I am angree, I am burning like zee fire. I am burning and burning! And I nevah quit! Zee more I am feeling zee anger, zee more I burn! And zee more I am burning, zee more I am angree. Zees eez zee good feeling! Eet eez like zee fire wizout control. I cannot stop eet. Zere eez no person who can stop eet! Eef some person cross me, I nevah forgeev! And I nevah forget! I hold zee grudge forevah! I hate zat person! Everee morning I am waking and writing zee list. I must remember all zee peepoll I am having zee grudge for! Sometime, I am exploding because I am so angree. I ruin zee relation. But zee peepoll must accept zees! I cannot change! I am living zee golden rule! I do unto ozer peepoll zee way I want! And zey do unto me zee way I want!

I am zee onlee person een zee world! And I am sinking always of zee self! Zee peepoll all adore zee name Jacques de la Merde! And I allow zem to geev me zees worship! I am nevah making zee mistake so I am nevah having to correct zee mistake!

I have zee great pride! Zees eez zee reason I am so good at zee ozer deadlee sin! Zee pride eez zee root of zees success! Eet eez zee reason I keep zee ozer sin so strong! Zere eez no reason for changing perfection!

Since I am zee greatest, I refuse to do anysing! I am zee great sloss! Responsibilitee eez for zee fool! And I am shirking zees! Zee ozer peepoll must do zee work! I am good at zee rest and zee relaxation! Zee eazee life! Zee diligent peepoll do zee planning. And zey are working like zee ant. Zees hard work eez making for zee good feeling after. But I cannot wait for zees! I want zee good feeling at zee momont! Sloss is zee great sin! I am moving slowlee like zee sloss monkey! And I am sinking slowlee weef zee brain like zee sloss monkey! Whenevah zere eez zee person who disagree weef zee sing I am saying, I nevah listen! Zees eez because I know all zee sing alreadee!

I love sin! Zee self-control eez so horriboll! Wizout zees I am free! And I do all zee great sin! All zee time! I do everysing zat I am feeling whenevah I am feeling eet! And zee more sin I am doing, zee more I am wanting! Zee great sin are all feeding off each ozer! And zee gaping hole in zee center off zee soul eez growing! Eet eez incrediboll! I am so happee!

Poly Sci I

It was time for political science class. I was sitting in my seat ready to soak up knowledge when a guy I had never seen before walked in and stood at the front of the room.

"Hello class," he said. "I'm glad to be joining you. The regular professor has decided to take the week off to play golf with his buddies. Today we're going to talk about a very important topic: Why Republicans are racist. I know. I know. It's an obvious thing that we all just take for granted. But I want to make sure you all *get* it. So listen up. People all recognize when someone looks different, right? We can't help that. But what makes someone racist is when they actually treat people differently. This is why Republicans are racist! They actually support different standards for different people based on race! Can you believe it?! You see that black guy in the back of the classroom? He doesn't have to score as high as everyone else to get into college. Is that condescending or what?! And kids who go to schools that are too advanced for them have a higher dropout rate! But Republicans don't care! They want black people to fail!"

Everyone turned around and looked at the black guy. He seemed a little embarrassed to be singled out. "Damn," he muttered, "I guess graduating is the most important thing."

"And look at this Asian girl in the front row," the lecturer continued. "Her English sucks, right?" A few people started to snicker. It was true. Her English did suck. "Well it doesn't matter if she only came to America a few years ago. Some schools actually hold her to a *higher* standard. How are the best and the brightest supposed to succeed when we punish new immigrants based on race! Fucking Republicans!"

The Asian girl didn't like being singled out either. She stood up. "My Engrish not suck, bastald!" she yelled. "What you tark about?!"

"Okay," the lecturer said, shaking his head, "looks like some people are having a little trouble with the obvious. This country is still mostly white, though. So the testing standard is based on white people." He had his eye on me now. "I can't believe anyone could top the score of this guy," he said, sarcastically. "Look at that swollen up mug. I'll bet he's still drunk from the night before!"

Everyone started laughing. "What?" I said. "Last night was cheap drinks at Wildcat House. It was a good deal."

"And what about SBV?" he continued. "You know – the Scheme to Buy Votes. There's an entire segment of the population Republicans have plotted to keep poor. They give them free money – just enough to stay alive! Republicans want to keep all these people hooked so they will vote for them! What kind of bullshit is that? They've been sbaving us all for years! Well, we need to give people hope and put a can-do look on their face! People need to work and feel useful. Republicans suck! They love us like a parent who gives their kid ice cream for breakfast! These guys are the enablers of poverty and victimhood! Oh and I'm sure it's just a coincidence that they targeted a lot of black people with their plan. It has nothing to do with their being evil and racist! Yeah, right! Goddamn evil racist Republicans!"

Everyone was looking around at each other, shrugging. We all knew Republicans were evil. But no one knew it was this bad.

"And what about the Emancipation Proclamation?" the lecturer cried. "This was done by the famous Democrat, Abraham Lincoln. He freed the slaves in the bloodiest war in American history! Republicans wouldn't have done it! They ran the South the whole separate-but-equal era! George Wallace and his Republican buddies thought Jim Crow laws were cool! And they refused to change until the famous Democrat, Dwight D. Eisenhower, sent troops into schools in Arkansas to enforce desegregation!"

The black guy in the back stood up. "Fuck Republicans!" he yelled. "They made Rosa Parks sit in the back!"

"Yeah!" cried the Asian girl. "Lepubrican suck!"

After that a lot of other kids stood up and started yelling things. Everyone was dissing Republicans. I thought about getting up too but I was still drunk from the night before and standing up seemed like way too much trouble.

"Okay," the lecturer said, finally, "I'm glad you all understand now. And don't get me wrong. Democrats have done bad things too. Some of them are racist, but they aren't so tricky about it. We'll talk about Democrats next time. Well, thanks for letting me teach you today. It has been a pleasure. I'll see you all again on Thursday."

Poly Sci II

The lecturer walked into class and right away his eyes started darting all around. He was just itching for something to complain about. The guy seemed really irritated. Finally, once everyone was sitting down, he took a deep breath and launched into a tirade.

"We're going to talk about Democrats today!" he cried. "These guys are the biggest bunch of inarticulate dunces I've ever seen in my entire life! They hate everything new! And they think they can just bludgeon everything into place. What kind of idiot does surgery with a sledgehammer?! They love their Bibles, right? Well, how come they've never read them?! Don't they know a gentle tongue can break hard bones?! You gotta explain stuff to people. Bludgeoning just creates the backlash! When you tell an arrested adolescent not to do something that just makes him want to do the opposite. Democrats want to stop abortions?! Well, good luck with that! How about you, young lady?" He was looking at the girl with the bad English again. "You're gonna have an abortion, aren't you? It's your right! And all just because Democrats told you not to?"

I was sober today and this guy was crazy. I didn't like him. Democrats were cool – they were good guys. And Mi-ho was hot. I had heard just about enough so I stood up. "Hey!" I cried. "Stop picking on Mi-ho! Who the hell do you think you are?!"

"I'll tell you who I am!" he yelled. "I'm the substitute lecturer! That's who I am! I ain't some nobody, drunk college kid! They pay me ten bucks an hour to teach you clowns! Now sit down and listen to my lecture!"

"Fuck you!" I yelled. "If we're clowns, then you're a mime! You're worse! And I ain't sittin' down! You can't make me!"

"Okay," he said, "then don't sit down. And don't listen to my lecture."

"No way am I doing what you want," I cried. This guy was an asshole. He didn't want me to sit down and listen. So I sat down and started listening.

"You see how this works," the lecturer said. "We're a whole country full of toddlers. How can people learn anything if they never listen to what anyone else has to say? When are we all going to grow up?"

Mi-ho was mad again. She jumped up. "You no want us risten!" she yelled. "Fuck you, mime! We crown! And you mime! Fuck Democlat too!"

"Yeah!" said the black guy in the back, standing up. "Fuck Democrats!"

Just then, a kid with blue hair and a handlebar mustache started walking down the aisle. "My political party is the best!" he cried. "I never listen to the other guys because they're brainwashed!"

"That's funny," the lecturer said, "I guess *brainwashed* must have a different meaning nowadays. I thought that was what happened when you only listened to one side."

After that, everybody jumped up and started yelling terrible things about Democrats. The lecturer just stood there, taking it all in.

"Well, now you guys know all about the two parties," he said. "We have the bludgeoners and the enablers. And one more thing. Don't forget that a politician only has one job – to get reelected. Thanks for letting me teach you again today. I had a great time. The regular professor will be back next week once he's done playing golf."

The professor came back the next week. He had a nice tan and seemed very refreshed as he walked into the room. "How is everyone?" he asked. "I hope you all had a nice week off. I know I did. And please accept my apologies for canceling class. But every year I have to participate in the professors' golf tournament."

One kid raised his hand. "What do you mean 'week off'?" he asked. "We had a substitute lecturer last week."

"What?" the professor replied, dumbfounded. "Didn't you see the note I put on the door to cancel class? I didn't schedule anyone to be here. You must be joking. Ha ha. I guess you're just pulling my leg. Well, where were we anyhow? We were going over all the terrible things America has done, right? We enslaved the blacks, killed the Indians, and took Mexico's land. How have we oppressed Asians? Is there anyone here who can tell me about Hiroshima? How come so many immigrants want to come to this country anyway? I don't get it. We're a bunch of dirty rotten imbeciles. There must be something I'm missing..."

Tequila Drinking Contest

We were at a house party and there were no hot girls. I was totally bored so I started bragging about my tequila drinking ability.

"I am the greatest tequila drinking champion in the world!" I boasted. "I can drink more than anyone! And no one can beat me!"

A guy overheard me and he was bored too. "No way, dude!" he cried. "I can out drink you any day!"

It was on.

My buddy Smurf plopped a brand new bottle of Patron down onto the kitchen table, I grabbed a seat at one end of the table, and the guy sat down at the other. After that we began to stare each other down like two cage fighters. I was ready but the other guy was nervous from the get-go so I knew I would win. Words didn't mean much. It seemed like most people talked with their eyes – and his were saying he was sorry he'd ever opened up his trap. But he couldn't quit now without losing face.

The bottle was sitting on the table along with two glasses that looked like they came from a cheap motel. I cracked open the tequila. Then we each grabbed a glass. First I did a shot and then I slid the bottle over to the guy. He drank one, too, and did his best to act cocky. "Bring it, dude!" he smirked. The two of us started slamming shots, sliding the bottle back and forth after every turn.

Things got ugly fast. Before long, we were pouring double and triple shots, matching whatever the other had done. But after a few rounds of this I began to lose patience. The guy drank his shot and then I was up. I didn't even wait a second. I slammed mine and pushed the bottle back over to him. The pressure was on now. The first time I did this he matched me, downing his right away. But the next time he was slower. I kept at it. With each turn the guy was taking longer and longer to man up until, finally, the big moment arrived – the bottle was staring him in the face and he was afraid to move. I sized him up. His mug was pale and sick and his eyes were dancing all around the room. He was afraid to look at me. The bastard's mouth was all zipped up now and he was just sitting there quietly, wondering when his period would come. He looked like he wanted to die. I owned this bitch. But there was no reason to torment him. "I have defeated another worthy challenger!" I cried, letting him off the hook. "He was an honorable opponent! But no one can beat the greatest tequila drinking champion in the world!"

The guy took the opportunity to leave the table. He got up, ran to the bathroom, and stayed in there a good ten minutes. I was so proud! The contest was over and I was the winner! My buddies all started yelling and everyone at the party was congratulating me. I was feeling pretty good about myself. I was the Man! To celebrate, I grabbed the bottle and dumped the rest of it into the motel glass. I got a good eight ounces in there. Then I sucked it all down in one great big greedy gulp. The stuff tasted horrible – it was like battery acid mixed with urine, but somehow I managed to choke it all down. I just had to show everyone how great I was. I felt even prouder now, but instead of cheers my latest feat was met by a room full of groans. Everyone knew it was bad to drink that much tequila all at once. I was alright for a minute or so, but then someone slapped a kaleidoscope over my head and the whole room started to spin. I stood up and began to stagger around. Something was wrong with this room. I glanced around. The floor wasn't level. And there were two of everything where only one had been before. After that the whole house started throbbing back and forth.

It was my turn now.

My vanquished foe was still in the bathroom so I stumbled toward the backyard. I threw open the door and lurched outside. Then I hurled a beautiful rainbow arc of vomit high up into the warm night air. Matt and Smurf were hot on my tail. They found me in the yard and started busting on me right away.

"Go champion!" Matt yelled. "You're the greatest!"

"Dude!" Smurf cried. "You still thirsty? I got another bottle!"

"F-f-fuck!" I stuttered. They were pissing me off, but I could only spit out one word at a time. "B-bastards. Yeah. Watch. Me. Puke."

Matt and Smurf heard this. Then they turned to each other and exploded in laughter. It was the most hilarious thing they had ever seen. Their buddy was all hunched over, chucking up his lunch, and trying to dis them at the same time. Neither one could stop laughing. It was just *great.* I had done an excellent job of entertaining everyone. And that one didn't die for at least a year. Any time we were all hanging out and there was a lull in the conversation, Matt would look around at everyone, his eyes would start to sparkle, and then he would deliver the line, "F-f-fuck! B-bastards. Yeah. Watch. Me. Puke." After that everyone would start busting up. I always cracked up too. I had to. If you couldn't laugh at yourself, you really weren't worth much.

A tequila drinking contest was a funny thing. When you lost, you lost. And when you won, you lost. But the bystanders all won. Everyone loved a trainwreck.

The Program to Increase Speaking Skills

The University of Arizona was offering an exciting new class. Many people realized that men did not talk as much as women and that this was an artificial problem caused by the sexist society, so to fix it all, the Program to Increase Speaking Skills (PISS) was established. Schools all across the land were beginning to let students major in PISS.

Guys were all improving their speaking skills, and the old sexist society was quickly being exposed as a fraud perpetrated by the Man. America was changing! Men *could* communicate as much *and* as frequently as women. PISS had been difficult for men to master, though, and not everyone could do it. It was complicated. There was a time to zip it and a time to let it all hang out, you had to hold yourself correctly, and it was important to keep your head pointed in the right direction. But as long as a guy remembered all of this and relaxed, everything was sure to come out alright.

All across campus males were working to increase their speaking skills. We were learning how to vocalize ourselves more frequently and evidence of the program's success was all around. Men were emitting a far greater number of sounds than they had in the past. Most of the new sounds consisted of grunts and guttural moans – but these still counted. All over Tucson, people were excited but there was still work to be done. Local employers were disappointed because a lot of U of A kids were graduating and didn't know PISS.

The class valedictorian, Sven, was a graduate of PISS. He was also a jar-denier. Sven refused to open any type of jar since this activity had always been done by men in the past. Opening jars was considered sexist and degrading, so jar-deniers were popping up everywhere. Women were unable to open jars, and now men were refusing to do it too, so the task fell upon machines. A company in China had even become rich by selling an automatic jar opening machine, and people were all happy about this because now no one had to do anything anymore. Everyone knew this was a great solution.

Sven gave the commencement address at U of A last year. It was an amazing speech that no one would ever forget. "They said we couldn't do it!" he cried. "They told us PISS would miss its mark! But let me tell you about the education I have received here at the University of Arizona. It is full of PISS! PISS is good! I am standing here before you today as class valedictorian, and I am proud to say I have been totally immersed in PISS. They said we would only practice PISS on girls when we were drunk to get laid! Well, what a lie that turned out to be! Arizona has graduated thousands of men who are experts at PISS! And we have been diving into PISS with our neighbors, our grandmothers, and even the family dog! The University of Arizona has been showering the community with a continuous stream of PISS!"

A girl in the front row couldn't contain herself. "I love you, Sven!" she cried. Then she jumped up and ran towards the stage with her mouth hanging open in awe.

"I love you too!" Sven replied. "Stand right there and I will give you a golden shower of words! You will receive a taste of PISS!" Then he reached into his pants and whipped out a long poem he had copied down from a dumb old book. After that he recited it to the girl.

"Your navel," he said, "is like a rounded goblet that never lacks wine. And your waist is a mound of wheat encircled by lilies. Your breasts are like two fawns, like twin fawns of a gazelle. And your neck is an ivory tower. Your hair is like a flock of hungry goats. And your breasts like clusters of fruit. I will climb the tree. I will take a hold of its fruit!"

"Oh Sven!" she cried. "You are a master of PISS!"

"No," he replied, "I only have a bachelor's. It will be another two years until I get my master's degree."

Golden Years

Grandma Inhofe was ready to make a change. She was getting old and everyone was too busy to take care of her. "My family all done gave up on me," she complained. "I'm gettin' up there and they don't care no more, so I gotta move into a nursing home. Good thing Medicaid come along. Back when I was in college, President Lyndon Johnson made up Medicaid. It was all part of the Grate Society. He gave people free money and they all voted for him. Medicaid was supposed to help poor folk, but things got a way of gettin' all changed up, and now it's used mostly by old queefers like me. The government pays for us to hang around in nursin' homes 'cause our families are all too busy. I'm so glad they're takin' care of me. Don't know what I woulda done otherwise. I woulda probably died out on the street or somethin'. The Grate Society seems to a gone exactly as planned. Don't nobody rely on nobody no more! And since people don't rely on no one, they don't bother havin' no manners. Without manners, they just spend all their time gratin' on each other and gettin' on my last nerve. But at least I got someplace to sleep!"

A brochure for a nursing home had just arrived in Grandma's mailbox. At first glance it looked like a vacation ad. Grandma picked the thing up and looked at it. "Enjoy the golden years!" it blared. "Live life to the fullest at Sunny Day Nursing Home!" Below that was a photo of a Sunny Day nurse. He had a crooked smile and a neck tattoo and was keeping himself busy sweeping dust under a rug. There was a quote underneath the picture. "Trust your loved ones with us!" it said. "You can keep money and valuables in their rooms! We clean them out from time to time!"

The brochure also featured a picture of one of the residents. Her arm had been amputated at the elbow but she was still happily waving the nub. "Hi, I'm Loretta Smith," it said. "I have Alzheimer's. When they first brought me here, I was a troublemaker. I had a bad rash that was hard to manage. But Sunny Day took care of it! They amputated my arm and that got rid of the rash! Now I spend most of my time looking at this bird." Loretta was staring at an empty birdcage in the picture. It was once the home of a bald eagle. The bird had escaped a long time ago but no one ever bothered to tell Loretta.

Doritoed

I had rummaged through all the cupboards, searched the entire refrigerator, and checked under each and every cushion on the couch, but I could only find one thing to eat – a bag of Doritos Nacho Cheese Tortilla Chips. Chips weren't a meal, though, so this bummed me out because I was feeling lazy and didn't want to go anywhere for food. I didn't know what to eat for dinner. But then a truly amazing idea hit me – I could just eat the chips! This got me all excited. Chips for dinner was something I had never tried before. Doritos tasted great. One chip was *awesome*. So an entire bag was sure to be pure ecstasy! All of a sudden my mouth started watering. I could barely wait to start.

My parents had never let me try anything like this when I was growing up. But they were *old*. What did they know! I was a college student now and *nobody* could tell me what to do! I did *whatever* I wanted to do *whenever* I wanted to do it! I grabbed the bag of chips and looked at the paragraph of ingredients on the back. Then I sat down and scratched my head. There was a lot of stuff in a Dorito. I had no idea they were so complicated. Next I looked at the nutritional chart. It was all zeros. Now I knew I was doing the right thing. Nutritious stuff always tasted bad so any food with no nutrition was bound to be good. This was going to be the best meal I had ever had!

I unfolded a paper napkin and placed it on my lap. I put a fork on my left and a knife on my right. Then I popped open the bag. I held the first chip up and lowered the thing slowly into my mouth. How delicious it was! I savored the bizarre mix of chemicals and spices. What kind of mad genius had created the Dorito? This was Zong Zong Boogaloo for sure. I had found it.

I ate another chip. And then another. Chip after chip was going down my throat and everything was going according to plan. But then things began to spiral out of control. All of a sudden I started shoveling Doritos into my face like coal into a furnace. Pretty soon most of them were gone and the ones that were left didn't taste as good as before. Each chip seemed worse than the last. I took a good long look at the bag and thought about things. I couldn't believe it – this dumb company had put all the good-tasting chips on top and the bad ones underneath! I was getting close to the bottom but something deep down inside told me to finish. I had to finish every meal no matter how bad it was or how full my stomach seemed to be. This was my duty. There were starving children somewhere in the world, and since I wasn't going to send them my food, I had to eat it.

It turned into a sickening quest. I kept eating Dorito after Dorito and *then* – I reached down into the bag and grabbed the final chip. I felt hungry and full at the same time. My delicious meal had not worked out at all how I had hoped. And still – there was *one more chip*. I just *had* to eat it. Reluctantly, I began to move the thing toward my mouth, and right at that moment a great unsettling feeling rose up in my stomach. It was like an earthquake or the fury of a thousand wronged slaves. I started sweating. Then my gut wrenched and I hurled the entire bag up onto the floor in front of me. I dropped the chip and decided not to eat it. My experiment had not gone well. I was sick and full and hungry and unsatisfied – all at the same time. It was the same way I felt whenever I texted too much or spent a lot of time on social media.

I got Doritoed.

Johnny Yo-Yo

Johnny Yo-Yo was the greatest actor Hollywood had ever seen. He was the star in blockbuster after blockbuster. His career had been one long string of hits – it was unlike anything anyone had ever seen. Everything Johnny touched turned to gold. And on top of this he was still young. Not only was Johnny handsome and likable, he was also a master of his craft. He had amazing range as an actor. Sometimes he played himself in a movie, but other times he got the inspiration for a part from himself, and there were even times when he based characters on his own personality.

He was the star of Revenge of the Indians. Johnny left his hair blond for the role because everyone loved his hair. In the film, Johnny played a Lenape Indian warrior who takes over New York City on horseback and returns the land to his people. Johnny sat proudly atop a horse in the trailer, wearing war paint in downtown Manhattan. A tear was rolling down his cheek. "This! Indian! Land!" he cried. "WOO BOO BOO BOO BOO BOO BOO BOO!!! You! Give! Back!" The movie ended dramatically. Johnny leaned back and let loose with a blood-curdling war cry. Then he chucked a nuclear-tipped spear across the water and hit the Statue of Liberty in the chest causing it to explode. We watched the film in media arts class one day. The professor laughed so hard when Lady Liberty blew up that his copy of Mao's Little Red Book fell out of his hemp backpack and landed on the floor.

Johnny played a robot in My Cyborg Love – a film notoriously risqué for its portrayal of inter-robot love. Androids and cyborgs were not the same and this was the first film that dared to put such a forbidden romance on the big screen. The movie showed people the sensitive side of androids. Johnny rose to the occasion and was so charismatic in the role that a pretty young refrigerator took to following him around on the set. No one was really surprised when, nine months later, she gave birth to a little dorm fridge. The thing looked just like Johnny. It was a huge scandal and the story was all over the tabloids.

Johnny also starred in Trees are People Too. And he was amazingly convincing as a tree – so much so that a bird built a nest on top of his head during filming and refused to leave. The role gave Johnny an opportunity to showcase his range as an actor. No one had ever played a tree so well. Johnny stood in one place for hours at a time and never even flinched or batted an eye. He was brilliant and people were simply stunned by his performance. The Oscar that sat on his top shelf at home was well deserved.

Lately however, Johnny had grown bored with acting. People all wanted to be something other than what they were and Johnny was no different. For some odd reason, a life of looking pretty for the camera had left him feeling hollow and empty inside. It just wasn't fulfilling. So Johnny decided to save the world by supporting

Perry the Politician. It was an easy choice. Perry was *for* good things and he was *against* bad things – and so was Johnny! Together they made a great team.

As luck would have it, Johnny was appearing at Catfish Auditorium tonight for a $35,000-a-plate fundraiser to kick off Perry's gubernatorial campaign. It was a great chance to see a legend in his prime, so a few of us snuck in through Rocco's secret exit and sat down at a table in the back. We arrived just in time. Johnny stepped on stage and flashed his trademark smile. Pearly whites gleamed. His hair was all styled up into a fauxhawk and he was wearing a leather jacket. Johnny feigned a sexy confused look and then raised an ironic eyebrow. The crowd went crazy.

"Hi!" Johnny cried. "You all paid, right! I'm against greed! So we're gonna use your money for good things! I just flew in on my private jet and I'm here to save the world!!! Perry the Politician is against climate change! And so am I! Changes in climate are bad! I don't like it when the weather is different, so every day should be just like L.A. I'm against plastic too. Check out this paper fork I made!" Johnny pulled a paper fork out of his pocket and held it up for everyone to see. The thing looked like a wilted flower but people all oohed and aahed anyway. "We gotta save plastic by using paper forks!" he shouted. "Plastic is a limited natural resource! So we gotta sustain stuff by living sustainably! And remember to put everything in the recycle bin! Even if it doesn't go there! When you put something in recycle, they *gotta* recycle it! That's the law! And it doesn't even matter if you fuck it up 'cause a guy goes into the bin later and figures out where everything should go. He puts good stuff into good places and bad stuff into bad places. Then he turns all the bad stuff into good stuff so everything is all good. I'm livin' green, baby! So I'm against *all* bad things. I'm against greed and guns too! And don't do drugs!" As Johnny said this he took a sip out of his beer, and right then a wad of hundred-dollar bills and cocaine fell out of his pocket and landed on the floor. Johnny looked around sheepishly. His private security guard surveyed the room in a cautious and deliberate manner. Then he took his hand off the gun in his holster, picked up the bag, and handed it back to Johnny.

The show went on like this for an hour or so. We watched some old clips of Johnny growing up and we ate a lot of French food. Perry the Politician even talked for a few minutes. And a few months later he was elected governor of Arizona.

Zit

It was Saturday night and I was all set to meet up with a hottie. I had somehow managed to talk her into going to a movie with me. But there was only one problem. As I was getting ready I looked in the mirror, and right in between my eyes was the most enormous zit in the entire world. It was terrible luck and I couldn't believe the timing. I leaned in and looked at it closely from every possible angle. The thing was freakishly large and there was just no way to hide it. I grabbed a ruler and held it up to my forehead. Right away my jaw dropped. The thing was nearly an inch across. It was the biggest pimple I'd ever had and the location couldn't have been any worse. I looked like a girl from India. I was standing there, cursing my bad luck when it hit me – I knew why the zit was here. It was for all the times I had pretended to have an Indian accent. This was an easy way to get a laugh. But now the chickens were coming home to roost and this zit was divine retribution for all of my mockery.

I knew I couldn't go out looking like this. I didn't know what to do and for a few minutes I just stood there, scratching my head. But then I gathered my thoughts and decided on a plan of action. Calmly and cooly I realized what I had to do – I was going to kill the zit. I would murder the thing with my bare hands.

Placing a finger on either side of the pimple, I squeezed gently. Nothing happened so I tried again. Still nothing. I figured there had to be some angle I could get it from, so I started going at the thing from all different directions. But that didn't work either. Pretty soon the zit was just plain mad, and the more I tried to pop it the madder it got. With every failed attempt the thing was growing in strength. The zit was getting madder and madder and bigger and bigger.

When you went into battle with a zit, you had to win – because if you didn't, the zit was sure to have its revenge. I was starting to feel the pressure now because I was going to hook up with a hottie tonight. There was no way I could let this zit beat me. I just had to figure out some way to win. My mind was spinning – I was racking my brain for ideas when, all of a sudden, I remembered something I had read online – butter got rid of acne! This would save me for sure! I rummaged through the refrigerator trying to find a stick. I looked and looked but all I could see was a lot of beer and hot sauce. Finally, all the way in the back, in a spot no one had ever looked before, behind some moldy old cheese, I found a stick. Right away, I grabbed the thing and started rubbing it all over my face.

I was feeling cocky now so I looked in the mirror and pointed at the pimple. "Die zit!" I cried. "I'm gonna brang the pain, bitch!" After that I went back to trying to pop the thing. But it was no use. I just couldn't kill it and the butter didn't seem to be helping either. My face was just really greasy now. I was totally confused. This butter thing *had* to be true. No one was so petty and bored that they would write lies online just to trick someone. I had to be doing something wrong, but I wiped the butter off and cleaned up my face with some soap anyway. Then I looked back at the mirror. The zit was *even bigger* now. I tried popping it some more but the thing just kept getting bigger and bigger. Finally I gave up. I stood in front of the mirror, staring at the horror in front of my eyes. The zit had won. It was perched on my brow – a second head sprouting out of the one I already had.

I called up the girl and tried to postpone the hookup, but she sounded disappointed so I decided to go ahead with it. I was kind of nervous though. What would the girl think when she saw me? Would she judge me because of the zit? I was a little worried, but the more I thought about it, the more I realized that she wasn't the superficial type. It was wrong to judge people by their looks – everyone knew that. This hottie would see me and accept me for who I was. She would know the zit was only temporary. Once I figured all of this out I felt a whole lot better. Everything was going to be just fine. I would probably end up waxing it tonight.

I slammed a couple shots of tequila to calm my nerves. Then I hopped into Bertha and drove over to the hottie's apartment to pick her up. The big moment was fast approaching. She would take one look at me and understand. I had been pretty worked up about all of this only a few minutes before, but now I was laughing. Everything was going to be just great. The hottie probably wouldn't even notice the zit. I got to her place and knocked on the door. She opened it up with a big smile and glanced at my junky old car in the parking lot. Her smile seemed to fade a little. Then she looked down at my feet. I was wearing a pair of beat up old basketball shoes. The girl did not seem pleased. After that her brain began to calculate my *score*. How much money did I have based on the car and shoes? Would I look good next to her? Did I have any potential? My score was not looking good. And then – she zoomed in on the second head in between my eyes. "Aaaaaggghhh!!!" she cried and slammed the door in my face. I just stood there for a moment, stunned. Then I slunk back to my car and started heading home. While I was driving, I took my shoes off and chucked them out the window. "Fuck you, shoes!" I yelled as they hit the curb. It was easy to ditch the shoes but I was stuck with the car and zit. I started thinking about the hottie. I couldn't believe how superficial that bitch was! All she cared about was looks! She had some nice tits and ass with blonde hair and thought she was all that! Well, that bitch wasn't nearly as hot as she thought she was! I was pissed off so I stopped at 7-11 to buy some beer.

I walked into the store and grabbed a twelve pack. Then I plopped it down on the counter.

"ID, please," the clerk said.

I fumbled through my pockets. I had money but no ID. Next to the register was a sign. "We ID under 29," it read.

"Hey," I said, "it just so happens I'm 29. Looks like you won't have to ID me after all."

"ID, please," the clerk repeated. "I don't care what that sign says, jackass. No ID. No beer." Then he looked down at my feet. It was the moment he had dreamed of for years – the chance to dis someone for two signs at once. "You wanna split hairs, dickwad?!" he continued. "You ain't even got no fuckin' shoes on! Don't you know how to read, college boy?! Here, let me help you. We got a sign in the window, too! It says, 'No shirt. No shoes. No service.' Don't they teach you assholes how to read at college?!"

My blood was boiling now. "Oh yeah!" I cried. "Well, how about YOU? Can YOU read?! I have a SHIRT on! That sign is for no shirt and shoes at the same time! Now sell me the fucking beer!"

"No it isn't, asshole!" the clerk yelled. "I get to decide what the sign means. It's for either one!"

"Well what about PANTS!" I cried. "It doesn't say anything about PANTS!" I tore off my pants and boxers, and tied one around each foot. My dong was hanging out but I didn't care. "How's that motherfucker!" I yelled. "I got shoes now!"

"Those ain't shoes!" the clerk cried. "Those is pants around feet! Now get the hell outta my store or I'm callin' the cops! And take that tiny terror with you! You just go swimmin' or what, boy! Looks like a damn worm! I'll git the security video up on YouTube later! And by the way – nice zit! Where you from? India?" Then he grabbed his cell phone and dialed a number. "Hello," he said, "police..."

I didn't want to find out if he was actually calling the cops, so I walked outside, jumped into Bertha and drove home. After that I walked into the bathroom and looked at my face in the mirror. The second head was quiet for a moment, and then it spoke. Out of nowhere I heard a voice with a ridiculous Indian accent.

"Why are you wasting time, young man? You will not be young forever. One day your brain will be full and you will not be able to learn anything. You should be like my countrymen. There are many great software engineers from my country. Americans invented this art of software engineering. But why is it that they do not want to practice it as well? I do not understand the American people. You are always saying you want to be creative. And this is the most creative field of them all. I think that when you say you 'want to be creative' what you really mean is that you want to be a special person who does not do anything that is too difficult. Perhaps you are better than this..."

Academy Awards

The Academy Awards were on and a snarky old lady was standing on stage, smirking and holding a microphone. Her job was to make fun of people and every few minutes she took a break from this to hand out an award.

"Madonna is ugly!" she cried. "And the winner for Best Actor is Johnny Yo-Yo!" Johnny stood up and walked past all the other famous actors on his way toward the stage. He had won for his performance in Revenge of the Indians. Johnny looked suave and debonaire as usual. He flashed a brilliant smile and made his way up onto the podium. His teeth were amazing. They were a shade of white that no one had ever seen before. They were *so* bright that people all put on sunglasses as he walked by.

Johnny stepped up to the microphone and started his acceptance speech. "Thank you, everyone," he said, tearfully. "I can't say how much this means to me. This is the greatest role I've ever had. I'm an evil white man and I was born an evil white man. It's genetic and there's just not a whole lot I can do about it, but somehow, deep down, I want to change. I'm tired of being evil. It felt good to throw that spear at the Statue of Liberty..." The crowd began to cheer. Just mentioning *the scene* made people feel warm and fuzzy. "Oh, thank you," Johnny continued. "But you know, I couldn't have done this alone. I want to thank my great-grandmother, and my second cousin once-removed on my father's side, and the pet fish I grew up with. And there's this ball of lint I used to keep in my pocket as a kid. I want to thank that ball of lint. But that's not all. I have one more thing I want to say, people. I'm clean and sober now, so let me tell you about this new thing I've learned about. It's called communism..."

The crowd was all ears now. Actors were the smartest people around. And no one ever got tired of hearing them talk about politics.

"I think communism can really work for America," Johnny said. "I just got an honorary degree from Berkeley and communism has gotten a bad rap. Sure, millions of people were murdered. That sucks. But I don't think anyone has done it right yet. We can make communism work here, but we should do it with a little bit of a twist. This is America after all. And we do things our own way! Right?!"

Johnny was trying to get the crowd excited. People loved Johnny and they always responded to him, so right away everyone started to cheer. "Do you know what I'm talking about?!" he cried. "Can you hear me?!"

"Yay!" people cried.

"I think I know a better way," he added. "I just took a course at Prager University. Instead of killing the rich, giving all their money to the government, and making everyone equal, we should try to build a country full of responsible people. Then everyone would be born with an equal chance to succeed. And whoever tries the hardest will succeed the most. People need an incentive. They won't try hard unless there's a reason. I just wish some kind of organization already existed – something that could teach people to be responsible and how to live. Responsible people is the key."

As Johnny was talking, his cellphone rang. One of his hos was calling. He pulled the phone out of his pocket, looked at the number, and put it back without answering.

"All we have in my neighborhood are dumb things like cafes and churches," he complained. "I guess cafes make sense. Coffee sucks unless you put in too much sugar and overpay. But what's the point of a church? They say people won't act good unless they think they're gonna burn in hell. But anyone can be good! I believe there's a unicorn behind the moon that makes people good! And my god is the best! So why do we need a bunch of judgmental assholes out there judging everyone?! We should all just do whatever we want! We need to invent a new organization to teach people values. We're Americans after all! Right?! And we can do anything!"

Johnny started nodding at the crowd to get people to respond.

"Yay!" everyone cried.

"And once we have all these responsible people, they could form strong families. And strong families would make for strong neighborhoods. And strong neighborhoods would be the foundation of strong communities. And from there we would have beautiful cities and a beautiful country. It would be the best form of communism the world has ever seen! Hey, do you guys want to hear a story? One day I watched a group of blind guys eat a pizza someone else bought. It was all sliced up evenly. But each guy figured no one else could see, so he gobbled up more than his fair share. They were all partying and having a great time. But once everyone realized the pan was empty, they all started beating each other over the head with the plates. And no one bothered to thank the guy who bought the pizza! So what do you all think? Can we do it?! Can we make communism work?!"

"Yay!" people cried. Everyone was on board.

Johnny grabbed his award and walked back to his seat. Then he sat down and texted the ho. He forgot all about the great speech he had just given. But the crowd was still abuzz. Everyone was excited about communism.

Trough

Me and Craig were bored so we decided to go live in Seattle for a while. Why the hell not I figured. We were young and could do whatever we wanted, so we drove all the way there and moved in with a couple random guys on Capitol Hill.

The first guy's name was Tim and he was infatuated with guns. Tim had a square jaw and hair that was hard-parted on the left. And he didn't talk much either. People always wanted to be something other than what they were and Tim was no different. He didn't like college and didn't care too much for majoring in business, so he wanted to be a cop. Tim had been through the police entrance exam several times, but he always managed to fail. This was bad for Tim but good for other people. A veteran policewoman had interviewed him the last time.

"Tim," she said, "you are in a store and you are confronting a shoplifter. You have told the shoplifter not to move and he has heard your command. But he has not complied. What do you do?"

Tim scratched his head for a second. "Well..." he said, "I would shoot him."

At this point the woman became exasperated. "Don't you see any other option???" she pleaded. "He isn't even armed!"

This was the moment at which Tim realized he had failed.

Tim was good for fun, though. The two of us decided to put on a skit one day when some girls were over. Tim emptied the bullets out of his gun. Then we slammed some tequila and stumbled out into the living room. All eyes turned to us.

"Hey! You! Bastard!" Tim cried. Then he smiled and aimed the gun at my head. "It was your turn! To buy! The fucking beer! How come! You didn't buy! Any fucking beer!"

I plastered a look of fake terror onto my face and dropped to my knees. "I'm sorry! Man!" I wailed. "I'll remember! Next time! Please don't kill! Me!" The girls were not impressed because Tim was just a little too convincing as a psycho. No one got laid that night.

Getting some action was complicated. You had to remember all the things girls liked and you had to try to act normal. It was a lot of trouble! So a few days later a bunch of us decided to cruise up to Canada with Raven. A guy at a party had given him the low down – "The most beautiful hookers in all the world live in Vancouver!" he claimed. "And they're cheap because of the exchange rate!" That was enough for us. We all piled into Tim's car and hit the road. I was pretty sure the night would turn out to be an interesting one. I had never nailed a hooker before but there was a first time for everything.

The Canadians stopped us at the border and asked Tim if he was carrying a weapon. Then they asked him again. And again. Tim insisted he was unarmed. His face didn't flinch and neither did his hair. Every single last strand stayed in place. But the border guards were suspicious, nonetheless, and they put on a ridiculous show of pointless questions, acting as if every American was a gun nut who was packing at all times. It was total bullshit. This lasted for a few minutes but in the end they decided to let us all through without a search. Tim started driving away. "Whew!" he sighed. "At least there is some justice in this world." He stepped on the gas but then as soon as we were out of range he pulled out his gun and started waving it around. "Ha ha ha!" he laughed. "Dumb fucking Canadians! I had it on me the whole time!" I looked around the car. Everyone was wide-eyed. Canada didn't allow guns so if the guards had searched Tim, we would have all wound up in jail for sure. Tim ranted and raved a little more, but then he put the gun down, grabbed the wheel with both hands and drove on. And right about then we all started giving him a whole lot of crap. But we got over it and before long we were all laughing along together. It was a great victory. And Tim was right. Canadians *were* a bunch of dumbasses! And we had all duped them!

Once we got to Vancouver, we drove around, looking for any kind of woman who would take money for sex. Tim was at the wheel and Raven was giving directions, but they had no idea where they were going. It was like a taxi ride to nowhere with the driver going in circles to make extra cash for himself.

Finally, we spotted a hottie walking around in a bra and tight pants. Tim saw her and right away he was excited. He stuck his head out the window like a dog trying to get some air. Then he opened up his mouth. "Hey girl!" he shouted. "We want to buy you!" We were all sure we had spotted a prostitute and just like that everyone was pointing and yelling. It was the moment we had all been waiting for – we were finally going to get some action! Tim pulled the car up next to the girl, but just as he did, she whipped out some pepper spray and nailed us with a big hit. We were all coughing and gagging and Tim almost ran over a stray cat in the road, but even that didn't stop us. We drove around haplessly for another couple of hours, looking for any kind of girl we could hire. In the end we stopped off at a bar and had a few beers. Then we gave up and went home. "Damn," Raven complained. "We should have just checked on Craigslist." We were a group that was too pathetic even to have sex with hookers.

Our second roommate's name was Kaz. He had long hair and spent most of his time stoned. Kaz was from Japan. Most Japanese were smart – it was something their culture took pride in, but Kaz was as dumb as the most brain dead American. He skipped most of his classes and was even failing the ones he somehow remembered to attend. Kaz had eyes that were small and whenever he was high, they turned into a pair of tiny buttonhole-sized slits. It was a miracle he could even see! I walked in front of him once in this condition and was amazed to watch as he tracked me all the way across the room. His head moved along slowly and robotically, like a half-broken irrigation sprinkler, adjusting for my new location every second or so. A typical day for Kaz consisted of listening to music, smoking pot, and staying up until midnight, laughing at nonsense. After that he slept until noon the next day. Kaz was out a good twelve hours – every night.

One day when Kaz was sleeping, a cat peered in at him through the window. A bewildered look spread across its face. Then the thing ran off, astounded. It could not hope to out-sleep Kaz. Not even a feline could get that much shuteye – only the dopey koala was a match. Eventually the sun began to creep overhead. And by noon it was too much for Kaz to ignore. He stumbled out of bed and staggered down the hallway, drunk from a sleep hangover as much as drugs. Kaz found himself in the kitchen, unsealing a gallon jug of milk. He grabbed the plastic throwaway part of the lid and flung it to the floor. Then he took a big swig out of the container and looked around at the landfill we called a home. "You seeing this mess," he announced. "None of it mine." And Kaz was serious when he said this. He had already forgotten about the plastic thing because the time it took to travel from his hand to the floor was longer than his short-term memory. I looked down at the plastic thing and then I glanced around the apartment. It was worse than the floor of a movie theater. Fast food bags littered the place, beer cans were strewn about all over, and somewhere underneath it all lay a carpet. The place was like an abandoned lot downtown – the only thing missing was a dead body underneath a piece of cardboard.

It was more than I could take.

"Yeah, right!" I cried. "No one created any of the mess! It just appeared out of nowhere! You guys are a bunch of fucking animals!" I ripped the leaf out of the center of the dining table and used it to push all the trash up against a wall. Then I propped the thing up to hold everything in place. My new creation looked like a trough for pigs, and it was piled up high. It was *beautiful.* A half-eaten cheeseburger sat proudly on top, daring someone to take a bite. I looked up and down the trough, admiring my work. Then I raised both arms in triumph. "Yes!" I cried. "The trough is born!"

Craig witnessed the building of the trough and he had a better idea. He challenged Tim and Kaz to a game of two-on-two basketball. Us against them. The winners would be the kings. And the losers would clean the apartment.

It was on.

The game was intense from the start. Kaz even seemed awake. His eyes were actually open, and they sparkled with a kind of life I had not seen before. I looked at Tim. The part in his hair was more severe than ever. This was serious stuff because no guy wanted to clean up after another guy. Elbows were thrown. And tempers flared. But the game wasn't even fair from the get-go because Craig was a ringer. He played pick-up ball with the brothers on the U of A basketball team, and if you could hang with them, a couple clowns from Seattle were nothing. Craig even played with Bobby Basketball. Bobby spent most of his time sneering at people who weren't at his level. He was just an awesome player and guys who weren't as good disgusted him. Bobby bounded around the court, doing the most amazing things. He took off from half court once and dunked. Another time he won a game by hitting a three-pointer with his eyes shut. Everyone knew Bobby would play in the NBA. He was pretty selfish though. Bobby had to keep his scoring average up to impress the scouts, so he wouldn't even pass the ball to his own teammates in games. But Bobby *liked* to pass to Craig. And every time he did, Craig knocked down a sweet J. Then Bobby got a smirk on his face. He couldn't believe a white guy was that good. But Craig was *that* good. And this was how we won the battle of the trough. Every time it was our turn, Craig got loose, I fed him the ball, and he floated in a rainbow jump shot that ripped the net and tore out their hearts. We won 10 to 0. And that was the end of the trough.

Perfect Girl

I was in Seattle and didn't have a girlfriend, so I started looking around for one. I decided to find myself a really cool drunk chick. Most girls didn't care too much for booze, but I wasn't about to let this small detail put a crimp in my plans. I was on a mission – to find the perfect girl. And somewhere in Seattle there was a super hot lush with a heart of gold who only had eyes for me! I hunted through every bar in town – I searched far and wide and *finally* I found my girl. I stumbled upon her in the street outside Shorty's one night. She was wearing a miniskirt and was all bent over, retching her gut out onto a fire hydrant. My heart skipped a beat. I could see most of the booty – and some boob too! Right away I was in love. I walked up and introduced myself. "Hey girl," I said. "Can I be your boyfriend?" After that we had a few drinks. Her name was Sheila.

Sheila told me all about her parents. "My dad," she said, "is insane. He lives in a mental institution. And my mom is from Micronesia. Her English sucks. She sounds like a robot."

We started hanging out all the time. One day I was over at her apartment when her mom called. Sheila smiled and put the phone up to my ear so I could hear her speak. It was a shocking moment. She *did* sound like a robot. In fact, she was so convincing as a robot that I had a hard time imagining her as human. My expression must have given it away because Sheila looked at me and started cracking up. She put the phone on mute and laughed out loud a good twenty seconds, ignoring her mom the entire time. When Sheila finally got back on the phone, her mom was still babbling on in robot language and had no idea she'd been talking to herself. Robots were usually lacking in intuition, but I had never known one to be quite so garrulous. I was standing there waiting for Sheila to finish when, all of a sudden, Grandma Inhofe's words began to ring in my ears, "Anybody who disrespects their own mom, won't hesitate to disrespect nobody else. They ain't got respect for *no one*. Nobody can make you love your parents. But if you don't show 'em a little respect, that starts a cycle teachin' the next generation not to respect you." This made me laugh. Old people were just *old*. And they didn't know anything.

Me and Sheila liked to wander around, barhopping. And it didn't take long until I had wasted all my money doing this. It was no big deal. Money was nothing. But after a few months of running around boozing it up with Sheila I was flat broke, and I had to break the news to her – we were going to have to start splitting the costs. Sheila flipped out. Girls wanted to be the same as guys when it was convenient. And they wanted special treatment when it was convenient too.

Sheila had a weak bladder. Sometimes, when we were out drinking, she would take a leak in an alley in between bars. It was the greatest thing I had ever seen. Every guy alive had pissed in public at one time or another. But I had never seen a *girl* do it. I didn't even know that was possible. One night, Sheila was all crouched down, doing her business with her skirt hiked up around her waist, when it occurred to me that she had no way to shake it off afterward like a guy.

"Hey Sheila," I said, "what are you gonna do about all that extra wetness once you're done?"

"Drip dry," she replied.

Raven had dyed black hair and loved going to raves. He also had a habit of giving people behind-the-back nicknames. A real man said stuff to someone's face, but this was just how Raven was. And I don't know if it was the alcohol or the pot or what, but Sheila could never remember the behind-the-back thing. She always managed to blurt out everyone's secret name and one day her victim was Dylan. Dylan didn't like to hang out on-the-fly. We always had to make an appointment to meet up with him, so Raven dubbed him "The Doc." Well, Sheila walked up to Dylan one time and opened up her mouth. Everyone knew this meant trouble. " Dylan..." she said, "so you're the Doc..." Her voice began to trail off at the end since Raven was making a throat-slashing gesture. But it was too late. Dylan knew what this meant – he had a behind-the-back nickname. His eyes started to get that watery, floating look and before long he was crying like a baby.

Sheila used to wobble around, defying gravity whenever she'd had too much to drink. Somehow she always managed to stay on her feet, but whenever she was in this condition she said and did stuff that other people's brains blocked them from. A bunch of us were out in the middle of the street after the bars had closed one night when Sheila backed her ass up to me and bent over. "When me and Jack get home," she announced, "we're gonna do it doggy style like this!" Everyone started laughing. Sheila was the hit of the party. It was good to know I was going to get some and all my buddies seemed jealous, but I was beginning to have second thoughts about my perfect girl. I asked Sheila to chill out but instead she lost it. She started flashing her tits at cars and then she hiked her skirt up around her waist. "Look at me, everyone!" she cried. "I'm gonna pee!" And right then she squatted and let loose with a monster stream of urine. Her piss was so loud it sounded like a broken fire hose and it flooded the sidewalk.

Sheila seemed mad for some reason the next day. "Are you alright?" I asked. "What's wrong?"

"Wow," she complained. "I can't believe you forgot my birthday."

We had been over this same issue many times. "Don't you remember?" I said. "Your birthday happened the week before we met. I couldn't possibly have known about it. We met on Friday, August 8 at Shorty's and your birthday was August 1. That was six months ago anyway. What's the big deal?"

"Big deal?!!" she cried.

This started a fight where Sheila confessed to nailing another guy. I couldn't believe it. How could my perfect girl do something like this? I was starting to wonder if being drunk all the time was such a good idea. But then I came to my senses – being drunk was good because it felt good! This *girl* was the problem! Sheila came clean just to spite me and seemed to regret it almost immediately. She started trying to walk it back. She kept talking and talking. She had a lot of excuses – but I couldn't even hear her anymore. I had tuned her out. How could I stay with a girl like this? I would never even know which baby was mine. And Sheila wouldn't know either. I glanced over at the kitchen and saw a dirty towel on the floor. Every towel was pretty the day it was born. People would hang the thing on a rack and square up the corners. It made them happy to look at it. Sometimes that towel got dirty, though. No one was perfect and that was just how life worked. You could wash the towel and make it fresh, but once the thing had been used for enough nasty stuff, it was just a dirty old rag and could never be clean again.

I pulled my waistband out away from my body with a thumb and forefinger. Then I looked down at Barney. He was peering back up at me with one sad eye. "What kind of whore is she, Barney?" I asked. Right away a tear popped out of his eye. Then he started to shrivel up. Warts shot out all over the place and he turned bright red and fell off. "Ungghh!" he grunted as he hit the ground. "Damn!"

Suddenly I realized that Sheila was still babbling. "...I think we should keep going out," she said. "But we should see other people too. Not that there's anyone I want to see or anything like that, but I just think we should be open for a while, you know. What do you think?" I thought about this. "Seeing other people" was the last stage of a dead relationship. I had been nailing Sheila for about six months, but you couldn't bang like rabbits forever. That newness always faded and then you were stuck with whoever that other person really was. All you had was personality.

"I agree with the part about seeing other people," I said. Then I stood up. "I hope things work out for you." I picked Barney up off the ground and started walking off. Sometimes you had to think more than one nut ahead.

Burrito

I was working at Dreamy Coffee Shop in Pike Place Market and it was break time. Today was a busy day. A ton of customers had come through the place and I was worn out from serving them all. I was making drink after drink, helping people get to the next level. It was a big responsibility because coffee made people *special*. When you had your hand around a fancy paper cup with a Dreamy Coffee logo, this actually made you better than other people. Bad coffee made people dumb. But good coffee made people smart. And I made good coffee. As soon as a bastard sipped one of my drinks, a glaze went over his eyes, he floated away into a dream world, and suddenly – he was at a fancy ball. It was the Renaissance in France! Girls in corsets were twirling around like tops, a lively tune was playing on the harpsichord, and people were all dancing about gayly.

It was time for my lunch and I just had to get out of there. A couple of free drink coupons were lying on the counter by the cash register, so I scooped them up and bolted out the door.

I was on a secret mission today. I didn't want anyone to know what I was doing, so I walked along as inconspicuously as possible. I kept my head down and glanced around, keeping a low profile. A guy with a Mohawk was sitting on a bench, eating a rock. Nearby, a middle-aged man was enjoying a pleasant conversation with his dog. Everything was totally normal for Seattle. I was walking past a kid with a chandelier on his head when I was rudely interrupted. The guy at the produce stand recognized me. "Yo Jack!" he yelled. "Where ya goin'?" He was standing out on the sidewalk holding a cucumber up to his crotch. "Look how big my junk is!" he cried. "It's green too! You think girls will like it?" He cracked a few more penis jokes and then started telling me about how he was going to become a world-famous rapper. I had heard his story many times before. The tone of his voice suggested it was a joke, but deep down he hoped it would come true. "Idiot..." I muttered. Most guys had a plan like this anymore. They didn't know *I* was the one who would be the rap star.

I kept walking along. A knucklehead in a clown outfit was juggling bananas for tourists and they loved it. People just couldn't get enough of this type of thing. They were all clapping their hands and jumping up and down excitedly. Behind them, not too far away, a homeless man was dead. He had just overdosed on heroin. A tourist walked past the man with a big grin on his face. He was still thinking about the clown and couldn't stop himself from laughing. Without glancing down or breaking stride, he flicked a quarter in the dead man's direction. It bounced off the man's slumped head and landed in his cup of spare change.

Finally, I made it to my destination – the burrito stand. I had an eye out for my contact, Rico. He was from Mexico. Rico was a good guy. He complained a lot – but everyone in America complained. Sometimes Rico was critical of the pale-skinned aggressors who had invaded and taken over his homeland. He was upset about the injustices that had been done to his people, but this had all happened in centuries past. Nowadays, Mexico was a great country full of vacation spots where people all went to get hammered. Mexico was so great that Rico had gone on a fly-by-night death march through a hundred-degree desert to escape. He walked on the soil of the land of the oppressor, he jumped over a rickety old fence, and now he lived here in the shadows. Millions of his compatriots had done the same. They had all voted with their feet and the results were in – America was the best.

Rico expressed some of his frustrations the last time I saw him. "I am so piss off!" he cried. "I refuse to speak this tongue of the oppressor! I hate Hernan Cortes!

The Conquistador from Espain – they burn, loot, and take over my country in 1521. Then they force all the people to speak Espanish! I swear on the grave of my madre, I will never speak Espanish again! I leave my lawless corrupt country and hope to become ecitizen of America! America must change its laws for this. What person can I pay to do it?"

Finally, I spied Rico in the back of the kitchen. He was hard at work. I kept trying to catch his eye and after a minute or so he glanced up and saw me. I gave him the secret sign and flashed the free drink coupons – just long enough for him to see that they were real. Rico nodded back and started to make my order. He knew what I wanted.

I took a seat and waited. But after a few minutes I started to feel nervous. I looked around and wondered if anyone was onto me. As far as I could tell, everything was cool. I was still worried, though, so I crouched down and did my best to seem unassuming. Next I covered my eyes with a pair of sunglasses and tried not to move. After what seemed like an eternity, Rico walked up and handed over a bag. I gave him the coupons and we did the secret handshake. Then I spun around and slunk off.

In no time I was in an alley. There were no Mexicans around, or anyone else for that matter. The area was completely free of people so I sat down. First I looked to my left and then to my right. After that I opened up the bag and pulled out a big fat gorgeous burrito. My mouth started watering just at the sight of it. I peeled back the foil covering the thing and stuffed an enormous bite into my face. It was delicious! Hot sauce began to dribble out of the corner of my mouth. The stuff ran down my chin and dripped all over my shirt, but I didn't care. I didn't even notice because I was in *ecstasy*. The beans and spices were like an angel crying on my tongue and there was nothing tastier than the forbidden fruit. I was doing something *taboo*. Life was all about taking risks and *this* was a big one. Everyone knew it was racist for a white guy to eat a burrito.

Bum Tales

Bums were everywhere in Seattle. They just loved the place and anywhere people were hanging out, you were sure to find them. I liked to sit down and chat with these guys from time to time to see what they were all about. They were often more interesting than other people – they told wild stories and did crazy things out of the blue, and they were easy to talk to, too. A bum didn't have anything so he didn't walk around with an air. It all seemed like a good way to kill time. I was bored and it beat the hell out of nothing.

One bum I talked to was a fat, happy and lovable black guy. He was in his early thirties and had medium-short dreadlocks. Real ones. Not the pretty kind from the salon. His dreads were all uneven and of different lengths. The guy had stopped taking showers and this caused the dreads to grow. One strand in particular seemed broken – it was like a mangled antenna and I found myself staring at it from time to time. The thing looked like it might break and fall off at any moment, but just like Happy it always managed to hang on.

Happy was always telling me about his life. It was hard to get a word in edgewise with him. Mostly I just listened. He said people were trying to help him. They wanted to give him a job, to get him "off the street." But it never quite worked out. He always quit the job or forgot to show up somewhere he was supposed to be, and then he was back out on the street again. The guy didn't have a care in the world and it didn't bother him a bit to lead the life he did.

One day I ran into Happy and he was really on cloud nine. It was the most cheerful I had ever seen him, so I just knew there had to be a story. Happy saw me and right away he started babbling. A pretty white girl had wanted to feel like a good person, so she bought a box full of donuts, brought them downtown, and handed them out to guys who were living on the street. She gave him one of her glamour shots, too and Happy showed me the pic. The girl was good looking. She was young and blonde – and was holding a box of donuts in the picture. Happy was so excited after telling me the story that he gave me a great big hug. He did this without warning. And it is something I will never forget as long as I live.

Happy stretched out his arms and pulled me in with a tight grasp. Time began to move in slow motion and, all of a sudden, I became aware of his odor. The smell wafted in, then it crept up and sucker punched me in the back of the head. This guy was ripe! I just stood there, dazed, as I recoiled from the blow. And before long I was gasping for air as the smell soaked into my very being. The stench was unbearable – it was like a dead body stuffed with kimchi, floating down the sewer for weeks. Like a fighter taking an eight count, I stood there with my arms at my sides, feeling like I should hug him back, but unable to move. Finally Happy released me. I stepped back and took a deep breath. Then I thanked God for all that was good in the world. I had survived the hug and *somehow* I was still alive.

A white bum with red and blue eyes used to sit out on the sidewalk with nothing to do. The first time I ran across him, he was muttering to himself about the Barbary Coast Pirates in Africa. Between 1500 and 1800 they had taken a million European slaves – and he wasn't happy about it. It seemed ridiculous to hold onto things from centuries past, but for some reason the bum was still pissed off. It was all a racial thing to him. People from Africa had mistreated whites. He kept on grumbling about it so I tried to reason with him. "They were pirates!" I cried. "What do you expect?! And it was hundreds of years ago! Who cares?!" But I was not going to win this one. Barbary was determined to live in the past.

Barbary usually had a cardboard sign on him. This was standard fare for a bum and his sign always sported the phrase of the day – anything to part a tourist and his money. "Why lie? I need a beer" was one. "Punch me $1" was another. Sometimes Barbary would whip out a harmonica and play it while he sang the blues. You wouldn't think a bum could have any talent, but Barbary wasn't half-bad in a clownish sort of way. At least everyone got their money's worth when he was around.

Barbary was always telling me he had cancer. A doctor had given him the bad news – in a few short months he would be dead. It was a sad story and everyone felt bad for him, but for some reason I had a funny feeling about it. It just seemed odd to me that a bum would go see a doctor. Most of the time Barbary didn't even seem to remember he had cancer. He spent a lot of time goofing around, blowing his harmonica, and harassing tourists. Sometimes I asked him about his prognosis, though, and whenever I did, a change swept across his face and he transformed from clown to deadly serious. Sure enough, a few months passed and Barbary's number came up. He disappeared. A couple years later, though, I was visiting Seattle and ran into him in a new location. Now some people don't believe in miracles – but I have the proof! Barbary is alive and well.

Pancho liked to sit out in the park early in the morning in the winter. It was cold and his English was terrible, but I didn't care. I talked to him anyway. You could understand most foreigners if you just put in a little effort. The guy didn't have a jacket so he spent most of his time shivering and chattering his teeth together in an attempt to warm up and stave off death. When people walked by, they practically threw money at him. He just looked *pathetic.*

An old couple took pity on him one day. The man stopped and gave him the coat off his back – he took the thing and hung it over the bum's shoulders. Well, the look on Pancho's face at that moment was just priceless. It was pure confusion and he really didn't know what to do. A few minutes passed. He was just sitting there dumbfounded, but eventually he slipped his arms into the sleeves and thanked the old couple. They smiled and walked away, but then Pancho's shivering and chattering stopped. And people quit throwing money at him too. I ran into him a few days later and was shocked – the jacket was gone. He had forgotten it somehow.

"Hey Pancho," I said. "Where'd your new jacket go? Aren't you cold?"

Pancho turned to me. "J-j-jack," he stuttered. "I no j-jacket no g-get dollar." And then, in between shivers, he flashed a smile that said "I am beating the system." This guy was smart. I was just glad the best and the brightest still wanted to come to America.

We were a bunch of drunks walking through Pioneer Square back to our car. The bars had just closed for the night and the girls had all shot us down again. We were frustrated and pissed off. Well, underneath the freeway, in an isolated corner of the parking lot, a bum had set up shop for the night. And this guy was creative. Most bums didn't have a bed, but he had managed to drag a piss-stained mattress all the way over to a secluded spot next to a freeway column. And there he was – lying on top of his bed, trying to sleep. The bum was nicely tucked in, with only his head visible, underneath an old army blanket. It all looked too perfect. The scene had a kind of perverse Norman Rockwell feel to it. I glanced around, trying to find the bum's momma. Had she just put him to bed? Where was the golden retriever? Then I surveyed the place a little more. He even had an empty milk crate as a nightstand. The poor bastard was right smack dab in the middle of the path back to our car, though. We stumbled upon him and were stunned. None of us had ever seen such an organized bum. And like anything that stood out, he became a target for ridicule. Right away we started taking out our frustrations on him.

"Don't forget to brush your teeth!" Mike cried. "You gotta do it twice a day or you'll get cavities!"

"Yeah," Craig smirked. "And don't forget to floss either! How much is the rent here anyway?"

Raven jumped in too. "Better set the alarm, dude!" he yelled. "Or you might forget to get up for work!"

We were all cracking each other up, busting on the bum. It was a sad scene. Finally the bum decided he'd had enough. He untucked himself and sat up in bed.

"Hey!" he cried. "How would YOU like it if someone came into YOUR bedroom at night and started harassing YOU?! Huh! How would YOU like it?!"

We all looked at each other and burst out laughing. How absurd it was! None of us slept in a parking lot. We all had apartments! Something like this could never happen to us.

Raven and the bum kept going at it. But then the bum started to get a seriously unhinged look on his face. Most of these guys weren't exactly on an even keel to begin with, so I decided to give it a rest. We all realized it was time to go – everyone except Raven. He was still cracking jokes but we managed to drag him away too.

A couple of bums were hanging out on The Ave in the U-District. They knew the area was good for them. It was mostly kids from UW after all. Kids were softies. It was easy to give away money you didn't make yourself. The business district downtown was much harsher. People with jobs made their own cash and they had to work every day whether they wanted to or not.

The two guys on The Ave were obviously homeless. They were sitting on their butts out on the sidewalk and trying to make eye contact with everyone who walked by. One caught my glance – and that was all it took. Everyone felt bad to see a bum so I gave him a look of sympathy. Well he latched onto that and crinkled his forehead up into the most pathetic-looking face I had ever seen. "Hello son," he said with the saddest voice in the world. "I hope you have a nice day." An empty basket was sitting next to him on the ground. I pulled a dollar out of my pocket and dropped it in. When I was half a block further down I stopped and looked back. Then I stood there and watched the two bums for a while. These guys were good. They were pulling in money hand over fist. Every time they felt a little sympathy from someone, they reached out to that person and wished them a nice day. And whenever they got money, they stuffed it into their pockets right away so the basket stayed empty.

A really old guy spent most of his time down by the football stadium. He was always pushing around a shopping cart full of junk. The thing was crazy full. It was piled up high like an ice cream cone a kid made for himself. The old guy didn't have a cardboard sign or any kind of gimmick and he never asked anyone for money. But everyone knew he was homeless. No one ever stopped to give him a few bucks, though, or to lend a helping hand. They were too busy paying all the actors. Well one day I saw the old guy collapsed next to his cart. It was the first day of the playoffs, people were all zooming around trying to find a spot to park, and Cart Guy was dead. It didn't take long for the paramedics to show up. They zipped him up in a bag and took him away. It was all very clean and went down pretty fast. This was America after all and we liked to pretend that no one ever died.

The campgrounds had signs all over the place. "Don't feed the bears!" they cried. They had a bear box at every campsite and the boxes all had latches the bears couldn't open. You were supposed to put your food inside when you went to sleep, but people ignored all the signs and the boxes. A lot of bears wound up with a taste for free food. And once that happened, they became a nuisance. The bears forgot how to hunt and spent all their time harassing campers. They didn't know how to be bears anymore, so many of them wound up having to be put down. It was best to relocate them out into the wilderness so they could relearn basic survival skills, but somehow or another that never happened.

Petty Revenge

I was confused. I had always thought that the purpose of a store was to sell things, but now I wasn't so sure. I had been waiting at the cash register for five seconds, was the only customer in the 7-11, and no one wanted to sell me anything! The register was practically abandoned. I looked around to try and figure out what was going on. Right away I located the clerk. He was holding a clipboard near the hot dog machine, his forehead was all crinkled up, and he totally focused on counting hot dogs. I had seen his act before and it reminded me of something my grandma used to say: "Happy people get their happiness by making other people happy. And unhappy people get their happiness by making other people unhappy."

The clerk tried his act out on an old man a while back. He was holding the clipboard then, too, and he was counting the cups next to the soda machine. The old man was waiting at the counter during all of this, but after a while he couldn't take it anymore, so he turned around and started to walk toward the door.

"Hey asshole!" he hollered on his way out. "Do your job!"

"I am doing my job!" the clerk yelled. "You do yours!"

It didn't make any sense. What job did an old man in a store have?

Even an idiot could seem thoughtful if he shut his mouth once in a while, but this guy just yelled whatever was in his head at the moment – and probably didn't even remember later on. Everyone remembered the bad stuff that came at them, though.

I was the only customer in the store after the old man left. The air was a little awkward so I cracked a joke.

"Hey," I said, "do you know what the friendliest school is?"

"No," he replied, "I don't."

"*Hi* school," I said. And then we both started cracking up. I was a natural-born comic. One day I would be a star.

Pretty soon the clerk was telling me about his decision to quit drinking. "Booze is bad," he said. "It caused me a lot of problems." I checked out his mug. It looked like a beat up old pumpkin. Veins stuck out here and there and he had an asymmetrical receding hairline. The guy seemed to be about fifty. I realized that he had a permanent look of anger about him, but you couldn't hold onto stuff forever. His look seemed to be fading into something more like "don't care anymore."

I was still waiting at the counter today and the clerk was still counting hot dogs. I was kind of hungover and was beginning to wonder how long his game would last. Six. Seven. Eight. Nine. Ten. After ten seconds I just couldn't take it anymore. "Hey asshole!" I yelled, "How many hot dogs are there?! Do you need any help counting them?! Why don't you go have another drink you dumb alkie!!!" Then I smashed my Big Gulp on the floor and got my ten seconds back. Now this bastard would spend more time cleaning up my mess than I had spent waiting for him.

The clerk looked shocked. "Hey!" he yelled as I stormed out. "Fuck you, kid! Clean that up!"

"No way!" I cried. "I'm not gonna! You clean it up! Clean it up with your clipboard!" Then I hopped into Bertha and drove away. I didn't go back there for a while.

Subway

I was bored so I went to Korea and taught English for a while. It was a *dream* job! Koreans were dying to learn English, I already knew it, and they were throwing money at anyone who would teach them. They didn't even care about experience. And the only thing I had to do was talk to people, so I didn't even have to teach very much! Koreans just wanted a few native speakers to hang around and chat with. It was crazy. I got random English gigs here and there and rode the subway all over Seoul giving private lessons. There weren't very many foreigners in Korea, though, so I stuck out like a sore thumb on that train. Everyone knew the 6'2" white guy spoke English, so Koreans were coming up to me all the time and trying to talk.

It got annoying.

After a while I started to understand why doctors didn't like to give out free medical advice. No one wanted to do their job for free. I was getting *paid* to have conversations with people and some of my students had studied English for over ten years, but they had never spoken a word. They needed a lot of practice and these subway riders had some gall – they wanted it all for free! I was starting to get more and more irritated with them, so I decided to pretend I was Italian.

I had learned a little Italian from a hottie I met at Wildcat House one night. This girl was straight from Italy and she taught me how to say "I'm so cool" in her language. "Vaffanculo" was how it went. I didn't get very far with the girl but that phrase sure did come in handy. It was the only thing I could say in Italian! And as far as I could tell, this was a language no Korean had ever learned. They didn't even know *one* word. It was time to turn the tables on my tormentors, so now whenever someone approached me on the train, I started gesturing around wildly like a real Italian. Then I used my word. "Vaffanculo!!!" I made sure to repeat it over and over again with a ridiculous accent, as if I were a kind of mafioso. After that I spit out some butchered Korean, explaining that I was from Italy and didn't know English. So I was boasting about how cool I was and talking to people in a different language! Who was the one practicing a foreign language for free now?! I was Jack Inhofe! And no one could stop me! I even ran into an Italian guy at the airport in Phoenix once. I told him about my routine and he thought I was hilarious! The guy laughed so hard, he actually started to cry. I was a comic genius – maybe the funniest guy in the entire world!

I had some fun on the subway but to be honest my act got old. I got bored with bragging about myself and people just continued to bother me anyway. It was tough being a minority. I wanted people to like me for who I was, but everyone just dealt with me in a stereotypical way. I even complained about this to Koreans, but after a while I realized something – no one cared. It was annoying to them even. Nobody wanted to hear about my petty little grievances because they all had problems of their own. I guess I was just looking for pity. And self-pity was the way to stay shitty.

Eventually, I put an end to my acting career and started speaking English to the people who approached me. Koreans were usually on the shy side, so I gave them a lot of credit for trying to talk to a foreigner. And practicing English seemed to make them feel good for some reason. People were weird. It was the little things in life that made them happy.

Burning Hot Coals

I started teaching English at a private institute. In one class I had a group of thirteen year olds. After a while, I realized that one of my students wasn't putting in any effort. In fact, he seemed to be purposely avoiding English. Speaking English gave you a leg up on the competition in Korea, but this kid wasn't even trying. He had a habit of causing trouble and was always distracting the other students. So in addition to not learning anything himself, he was making it harder for other kids to learn too. It was annoying.

I tried everything to get through to him. But nothing seemed to work. It was just a really frustrating experience. Finally one day I didn't know what else to do – so I kicked him out of class. On his way out he turned to me, "GET OUT!" he yelled. I was confused at first. "Get out" didn't make any sense. *He* was the one who was leaving. Why was he telling *me* to get out? I looked around to try and figure out where I should go, but then it hit me – he had said this with a perfect American accent. The kid must have learned this phrase from his old teacher! And that guy had probably been too tough on him. He had probably thrown him out a dozen times, and now the kid was filling his own head full of nothing to get him back.

I didn't know what to do with the kid. He was pissing me off and I was fresh out of ideas. I couldn't believe a kid had the chutzpah to try and irritate other people on purpose! I tossed him out a few more times and listened each time as he told me to "get out." It was kind of ridiculous. A couple months went by and not much changed. The kid wasn't learning anything. Then finally I remembered something my grandma always said, "When your enemy is thirsty, give him something to drink. And when he's hungry, bring him food. In doing this, you will dump burning hot coals on top of his head." Eventually I just adopted a tough but caring approach since I didn't know what else to do. I decided not to show any anger.

You could be too tough and you could be too easy. Life was a kind of tightrope walk. But Grandma's food idea sounded interesting to me, so I decided to give it a shot. I held a barbecue at school that week with hamburgers and soda. I was a little worried that it would backfire and lead to everyone taking advantage of my generosity, but I did it anyway. Life was a two-way street after all. I went all out and even topped the burgers off with a little kimchi to give them an extra kick. The kids all seemed to enjoy it. Then after everyone was done eating, I scooped a few burning hot charcoal briquettes out of the grill and put them into a metal pail. I walked over to the kid and lifted the thing up. I was all set to dump it over his head, but for some reason he looked up and showed me a new face. The kid decided I was alright. I wasn't like the old teacher. *Somehow* I was different. The bitterness and spite washed off his face in a moment and he broke out in a great big smile – a pure and natural child's smile. I couldn't believe it. I didn't think I was ever going to get through to him. I put the bucket down and scratched my head. Then I thought about things for a while. Maybe my grandma was wrong. Everyone liked a good meal. But the part about dumping hot coals on the head seemed a little over the top.

Triple Offer Game

I used to laugh whenever I saw Koreans in a restaurant fighting over the check. I even offered a solution once. "Hey," I said, "how about one of you guys pays the check and the other pays me? That way you can both feel good." Then I started to laugh at my awesome joke. They ignored me. It was sad but sometimes a great comic had to crack up all by himself to get everyone started.

This thing with the check was just one example of manners. Everyone knew manners were evil. They required effort and planning and were more trouble than nothing, so people all wanted to get rid of them. In the olden days, manners had been a standard of behavior that people used to make others feel better. But it was all a selfish idea! People acted politely in hopes that others would return the favor. So they were only thinking about themselves! Overcoming this type of backward thinking allowed America to make a lot of progress.

Koreans were crazy. They always fought over the check. It was a battle to the death for the thing. I even saw a taekwondo fight break out once. One man insisted on paying for dinner three times. But the other man refused. He said *he* would do it. Neither would give an inch. They kept going back and forth, each one harassing the waitress to take his card and pushing the other away. Then one threw a punch. The fight was on and it turned into a big old taekwondo brawl. The scene finally ended with a roundhouse kick to the head. The victim fell to the ground and lay there for a few moments, clutching the bill. He couldn't get up, but wouldn't let go of the check either. A minute later he began to drag his body forward with both arms in an attempt to pay. But the kicker ran up, snatched the check out of his hand, and marched ahead victoriously. He slapped down his card and paid. After that the two men bowed to each other.

Koreans also had a thing on the subway. If someone had a lot of gray hair or was pregnant, and they were standing up, you were supposed to give them your seat. And there was no such thing as a weak attempt. You had to try three times. If the person turned you down each time, then you were supposed to get up and walk away so they were forced to sit.

Koreans had a lot of triple offer games. America had one too. A coworker at Dreamy Coffee Shop introduced me to it one day.

"Can I borrow twenty-five cents?" he asked. "I'm tired of drinking coffee all the time. I wanna buy a coke."

"Sure," I said, "no problem." I gave him the money and then he went out and bought a soda. I felt good to help him out.

The next day he came by again. "Can I borrow fifty cents?" he asked. "I'm thirsty. I wanna buy a soda." He hadn't paid me back yet from the first day, but I figured this was just an oversight on his part.

"Here you go," I said, handing him the change. I didn't feel quite as good this time. The guy went out and bought another coke. Then he came back and enjoyed it.

On the third day he stopped by again. It was soda time. "Hey dude," he asked. "Can I borrow a–"

"Sorry," I said, cutting him off, "I don't have any change."

The guy seemed puzzled. He looked at me funny for a moment. "B-but..." he stuttered and then walked off.

The mayfly was a bug with a small brain that only lived for one day. The thing was a pesky critter and spent most of its time annoying humans. Its goal was to fly around aimlessly, procreate, and then die. A mayfly never thought about what it was doing at the moment, had no memory of the past, and did not see any point in planning for the future.

Hill Tribe Village

I paid a guy money to tell me where to go take a hike and now I was doing just this. I was tromping around in a pair of old boots out in Thailand with a group of random kids from around the world. It was an organized trek with a Thai guide. We had just finished riding around on an elephant and now we were on our way to see an authentic hill tribe village. My body was brimming with excitement. I couldn't wait to see these exotic new people. I wondered what they would look like. Would they look like normal Thais? Or would they look like normal Thais in funny hats? I couldn't wait.

I had planned really well for the trip. I went out and bought the most enormous backpack I could find and stuffed it full of everything I owned. By the time I was done it weighed several thousand pounds. I even brought along a copy of Beowulf I was determined to memorize. You were nothing until you could recite Beowulf! Other kids had big packs too but *mine* was the biggest. I glanced around and checked out the others. "Bitches..." I muttered. No one could top me. I was the king of the idiots. I looked like an overly ambitious suicide bomber and if my pack had been full of explosives, I could have taken out a small city, but the only bombs inside were some stinky socks and a few skidmarked underwear. It was tough to carry that pack around, but I machoed it out, lugging the thing around wherever I went.

Eventually, we arrived at the hill tribe village. I looked around. All the Thais were wearing funny hats – except for one lady. We showed up a little early and this woman had forgotten to suit up. She was still wearing a t-shirt and shorts! On her shirt was a picture of the infamous hamburger clown, Ronald McDonald. I looked at his face and a chill ran down my spine. Then all my hair stood on end. I was deathly afraid of clowns. They were *evil*. And Ronald McDonald was the most evil of them all. The clown lady ducked into a hut and a few minutes later she came out in some rags and a funny hat. After that I felt a whole lot better. We were all getting our money's worth now.

I bumbled around aimlessly for a few hours. Then I noticed that one of the girls from France was hot and wondered how many guys had nailed her. Thirty? Fifty? Who knew? The French all seemed dirty. Next I spaced out for a while. I was just standing in one spot, watching a bug fly around when I realized I had no plan for tomorrow. So I pumped a fist in the air. "YOLO!" I cried. People all knew I was cool but for some reason they ignored me. I was getting bored when, all of a sudden, the fun began. An old man with no life left in his bones pulled out a hookah and held it up. "Smoke opium five dollar," he declared. His voice was monotone and lifeless. I checked the guy out. He could no longer make an expression and didn't seem like he could even feel any kind of emotion. His body was all withered up like a dead chicken and even the muscles in his face seemed to have atrophied. All the poor bastard still had going was a set of worn out marbles for eyes, and they rolled back and forth in the sockets as he looked around.

None of the girls on the trip wanted to try opium. But every guy gave it a shot. I was so excited. Opium was some serious stuff, but I wasn't worried about it. I would never get hooked or die because I was smarter than other people.

Old frozen face gathered us all together in a circle around the hookah. Then we took turns. First he rolled his marbles this way, and then that, letting each of us know when to go. After a few minutes I was up. I took a couple good tokes and then the effect began to slowly flood over my being. I had never felt anything like this before. Nothing mattered now. My problems vanished and my worries were all swept away with the latest cloud. It seemed ridiculous that I had ever cared about anything! I was numb and happy and dumb. And then I felt it – *world peace*. The Israelis and Palestinians gathered together in front of me and held hands. Suddenly people began to pop up everywhere and they were all singing kumbaya. I realized that people were all good and they all loved each other. I was good too – I was good because I was me! A tear of joy rolled down my cheek. Then an angel floated by in front of me playing a harp. She was naked and winked at me. All of a sudden there were girls everywhere – and none of them were wearing any clothes! I looked around at everything and as I did a river of beer began to flow through the village. Next a microphone appeared in front of me. I grabbed it and started rapping about how great I was. I couldn't believe it! This opium was pure joy! I had finally found Zong Zong Boogaloo!

It was all beautiful. But then, out of nowhere, an evil crow flew across my field of vision. The scene in front of me vanished and everything returned to normal. I looked over at old frozen face. Opium hadn't worked out very well for him. He was owned. After that I glanced around the opium den. Every guy was zoned out and in his own world. We were all lost. This was one of those places where people went to find themselves. But this wasn't it. All of a sudden I realized what I had to do, so I stood up. "I'm gonna do it!" I cried. "I'm gonna find Zong Zong Boogaloo and then I'm gonna find myself!"

Old frozen face rolled his eyeballs in my direction. "It too late for me, guy," he said, "but you wanna finding self, you gotta forgetting 'bout self." That seemed weird so I just sat there and scratched my head.

Deluxe Imagizer 7.0

It was after midnight, I was drunk, and I was at a house party near campus where I didn't know anyone. And that was when I saw *it*. It was lying on a coffee table over in the corner of the room – and it was beautiful. Someone in the house was the proud owner of a Deluxe Imagizer 7.0. Everyone loved the DI7. It was the latest in a long line of hot-selling Blinkies made by Super Good Technology. This was the one that let you project an image of yourself out into the air in front of you. It came in handy. A mirror wasn't always around, so it was easy for people to forget what they looked like. And nothing made a human happier than staring at his own mug. Now, thanks to the DI7, people could do this whenever and wherever they wanted.

I glanced around the party. People were all busy talking and doing stuff. No one was looking in my direction, so I grabbed the DI and stuffed it into my pocket. Then I walked out the front door and staggered home. At home I had the time of my life playing with the thing. I was making funny faces, projecting them all around the room, and laughing for hours. It was a blast! Finally I just had too much fun and passed out.

The next morning I woke up and started playing with the DI again, but little by little a gnawing feeling of guilt began to eat away at me. I was stone-cold sober now and this thing wasn't mine. The feeling ate and ate at me. It went on like this for several hours, getting worse and worse, until *finally* I realized I had to do something about it. I had to return the DI. I decided to take the thing back to the party house and return it to its owner. This made me nervous. I didn't know how the owner would react when I brought it back. He might call the cops or try to beat me up. I had no idea. But I had made up my mind. There was only one way to get rid of the terrible gnawing feeling of guilt so I had to do it.

I drove over to the house, walked up to the front door, and knocked. A guy opened the door. I recognized him as someone who had been asleep on the couch the night before.

"Sorry," I said, and then I handed him the DI. "I was drunk and stole this from your party. Please give it back to the owner."

The guy was shocked. His mouth hung open for a second. "Wow," he said, finally. Then he grabbed the thing and looked at it. "I can't believe you brought it back."

Right about then I started to feel really embarrassed.

"Okay," I said, "I gotta go now." And then I spun around and took off.

On the way home I thought about everything. You never knew what was going to happen in your life. You could lose your car and your job. You might even lose your house. People could take it all. Someone might even swipe your DI when you weren't looking. But there was one thing you could never lose – *your integrity.* It was something people gave away all on their own.

Monkey Suit

I smoked a big fattie and started walking down the street in Bangkok. I was strolling along, minding my own business, when a shopkeeper spotted me.

"White guy!" he shouted. "You like drink beer?!"

"Sure," I said. "I like beer."

The guy cracked open a can of Budweiser and handed it to me. Then he started showing me his wares. Suits were hung up all over the place, so as far as I could tell he was some kind of tailor. His stuff looked alright, but I didn't have any interest in buying a suit.

Most suit shop workers usually struck me as kind of lazy, but this guy was on top of his game. He had a book full of pictures – and even testimonials from other white guys he had made suits for. "I making suit you," he declared. "And then sending for America. You pay first." I wasn't so sure about this. I had heard that some people in Thailand were scammers, so I wondered if I should trust him. But then I looked at a mirror on a nearby wall and saw my face. I was a white guy.

Other white guys in the book had trusted him, so I guess this meant I should trust him too.

I was drinking the beer and I was starting to get a beer buzz. The guy kept talking and talking and before long my mind began to wander. I started looking around the shop. It was nothing but monkey suits as far as the eye could see. These things seemed pointless. I wasn't even sure why they existed. I was mulling this over when, all of a sudden, I had a great epiphany – people wore suits to feel better than others! What bastards people were! Suits were making everyone judgmental, and there was nothing I hated more than judgmental people. These miserable piece of fabric were causing everyone to stereotype each other into different categories! Well, I refused to go down that road. I was better than all that. It was *always* bad to generalize or make assumptions – and I had a half a dozen car accidents under my belt to prove it! Most people slowed down when they saw the brake lights on the car in front of them, but you never really knew what that other car was going to do. Sometimes it sped up again. So you didn't *always* have to hit the brakes. It was wrong to say that something was true *all* the time. I would never judge a human. And I would never judge a car. I refused to play *that* game.

The shopkeeper kept flipping through the book of pictures. He was all business. Here was one design. Was I interested in that? Here was another. The design on this page was very popular in Italy. Another was all the rage in England. Which one did I like? They all looked pretty decent. But I wasn't about to give my money to some dodgy Thai bastard.

It didn't take long until the shopkeeper figured out that I wasn't interested in a suit. Then the book of pictures closed and a change went over the man. His demeanor switched from courteous to pure ice, and his mouth became silent. The air between us began to sizzle with a silent hatred. I realized that he would gladly kill me if given the chance, so I decided to leave the store.

I walked outside. My buzz was gone now but I was still holding the can of beer. I jiggled it. There was still a sip or two left, so I tilted the thing back and finished it off. I had stolen 12 ounces of alcohol from the shopkeeper, but worse than that, I had taken part of his life. I had wasted his time. It felt like a long time since I had been in an actual small business. America had a lot of giant corporations. And the bigger the company was, the less everyone seemed to care. I had walked into stores in America and wasted people's time before, but the air had never sizzled.

Next I started looking around for some snacks since the pot had left me with a powerful craving for orange cake. In Tucson there was a 7-11 on every corner, and you could buy orange cake at any time of day or night. But Thailand didn't have jack! No place in the entire country sold orange cake. It was just straight-up rude. I was standing there, shaking my head in disbelief, when a guy walked up and offered to sell me diamonds for half price. It was a really good deal so I was starting to get excited about it. I was so lucky that the guy had picked me! But then he dropped one of the diamonds and it cracked in half. A greasy-looking kid snatched it up off the sidewalk and took off running. This shocked the guy. "Hey!" he yelled. "You robber! Stop!" But the kid just kept going.

This country was messed up and I was getting frustrated. "Help!" I cried. "I'm stoned and I'm in Thailand! What the hell is wrong with you people! All I want to do is eat some orange cake!" A government official heard my cry and offered his services. "Hello, white guy," he said. "Do not be concern about cake. In order for complete you visit for Thailand, you must first go to Thai sex show." Then he smiled, punched me in the face, and took my wallet.

Thai Sex Show

Taxis in Thailand were called tuk tuks and they looked like little golf carts. I was walking back to my hostel when one of these things pulled up beside me. The driver leaned out of the door and waved his hand around frantically to get my attention. "White guy!" he cried. Then he whipped out a collection of postcards and started aggressively peddling them. "You liking this card?!" he said. "You liking that one?! Which one you liking? You gotta liking one!" He had seen a white guy so he was owed money. I looked at my reflection in the window across the street. I was still a white guy so I guess this meant I would have to pay. I started digging around for my wallet, but instead I found the new Deluxe Imagizer 7.0 I had bought for the trip. I whipped the thing out and started projecting my image up and down the street. This caused the tuk tuk guy's head to snap back and forth repeatedly like a robot having an epileptic seizure. White guys were everywhere! And he was owed so much money that he didn't even know what to do! After a minute or so of this, his head exploded and a puff of smoke floated out of his neck.

I kept walking and ran into a man who was sitting and smiling out on the sidewalk. "Hi America," he said. "I praying to God for all reason I grateful. I hoping be better guy." I started laughing. What a brainwashed fool! Only an idiot prayed and what was the point of reminding yourself to be grateful?! How was having a good attitude going to help you to *get* anything? I shook my head and kept going. Other people were all pretty messed up, but I was a good guy. I flexed a bicep and kissed it. Then I smirked a great big knowing smile. I was good because I was me!

Later on, I checked out a Thai sex show. I got confused about which Thai bill was which and accidentally paid too much for admission, but the cashier just pretended not to notice. She put the extra cash in her pocket and moved on to the next person as quietly as she could. A minute or so later I realized my mistake, but that money was *gone*. I would never see it again. I had a better chance of getting a refund from a boarding house ajumma.

I walked into the show and looked around. Naked Thai girls were standing on stage, swaying back and forth to the music in a lazy dance. Some were pretty and others not so much, but they all had the same expression of bored hatred on their face. These girls were ruined. They were bitter and the audience disgusted them.

The show started and girls began performing tricks with their vaginas for idiot tourists. It was great fun. One shot a banana out of her snatch and into the crowd. The thing flew through the air like a dead duck and landed on an old Japanese man's lap. "I catch!" he cried. Then he grabbed the banana and held it up for everyone to see. His face was beaming with pride – like a little boy catching a foul ball at a baseball game. The man spun around in a circle showing off the banana and then he took a big bite out of the thing and swallowed it. People all cheered. It was an exciting new way to catch a sexually-transmitted disease.

In the next segment, a girl opened up a bottle of beer with her cooter. She squatted down over the thing and managed to get the cap off somehow. The Japanese guy saw this. "I drink!" he yelled. "I beer!" He needed something to wash down the banana, but it wasn't right for one guy to have it all. After the girl got the bottle open, she picked it up – using her hand this time – and gave it to a crazy German in the front row. He downed the thing in one swig and let out a great belch. Then his tongue turned green and fell out onto the floor. "My wongue!" he cried. "Hepp! My wongue feoo off!" But no one cared about the German's tongue. The show just kept on going. People were all too busy watching the girls.

Over in one corner, a dartboard had been set up and several balloons were attached to it. Well, one of the girls was lying flat on her back with her legs spread, and she was shooting darts at the thing out of her moneymaker. This girl was good. Her aim was better than most people's hands. Every couple of tries she popped a balloon and the crowd went nuts. "Yay!" people cried. Who didn't appreciate a good display of athletic prowess?

Yet another trick had each girl pulling foot after foot of ribbon out of her beaver. I watched this go down in awe. I couldn't believe how much ribbon there was! At first I was impressed but then I became skeptical. An amount this great *had* to be produced inside. After several hundred yards had come out, I realized they were all spiders. And just then, one of the girls rappelled down from the ceiling on a ribbon and served me a drink. In a flash she grabbed all my money and zipped back up to her web. These spiders were fast and they didn't mess around. Once the performance was over I stood up. I was penniless and felt like a total loser. But still I had to applaud. What a show!

Jung

I was in Korea so I studied the Korean language for a while. It had some words that were tough to nail down in English. One was "jung." Koreans all told me that this meant "love." I knew what love was. A guy said it to a girl and then they rode the pony for a while. After that they broke up and never talked to each other again. Love was easy to figure out but jung seemed a little more *complicated*. And whenever I asked Koreans for the complete definition, they refused to tell me! I even begged one woman for an answer. "Oh, you are American," she sighed. "I not sure you can understanding meaning of word jung." After a while, I started to suspect that jung was a secret thing Koreans were purposely keeping from foreigners and that just made me want to figure it out all the more.

One day I was hiking out in the woods when I saw an old man. I came across him as I was going down a hill and right away he motioned toward me. "Be careful" was what the gesture seemed to say. It pissed me off. I was the best hiker in the world and the old jackass should have known this intuitively! So I blew him off. But a few feet later I found myself sitting on my ass, wondering how I had fallen. "Damn..." I muttered. I looked around for a moment, trying to figure out what had happened. And then I saw the slippery spot.

A few days later I told one of my grownup students about the incident. "I'm a foreigner," I said. "People don't really know how to interact with me here. And most of the time I seem to be invisible. How come some old dude on a mountain was worried about me?"

The student thought for a minute. "Well," he said finally, "old man got jung for young guy." It was the craziest thing I had ever heard! The last thing I wanted to do was bang some old man, separate, and cut all ties. I wasn't gay! I balled my hand up into a fist. I was all set to slug the guy, but then he explained himself a little more. "Jung more like interconnecting thing," he said. "If guy outranking you in Korea, he having responsibility for you. And you gotta showing respect. Korea not having free relationship like American. Peoples all having some kind responsibility. Jung is thing holding peoples together. It getting stronger after lotta time with person. Watching out for guy is type jung too."

I contemplated this for a moment. Then I scratched my head. "Poor fucking bastards..." I muttered. In America we were much better off. We were free! We had the Campaign to Make Life Better – the anti-jung! And we did whatever we felt like *all the time*. When someone was about to fall we took a picture and laughed. Looking out for other people was dumb! And so was Korea! This whole experience reminded me of something my grandma always said, "If you wanna help someone, you tell 'em the truth. But if you wanna help yourself, you tell that other person what they wanna hear." I wasn't crazy – I wanted to help myself! That was what everyone did. In America we had donut love – we stuffed a kid full of donuts and smiled. It felt good, the kid looked happy at the moment, and that was *all* that mattered. I pumped a fist in the air. Then I raised both arms above my head. "You only live once!" I cried. "I live *in* the moment and I live *for* the moment!" It was too bad other countries didn't have a system like us. They had crazy stuff like jung.

Dog Doo

My grandma was right about remembering to help yourself, so I was starting to wonder what else she was right about. She thought people should confront their fears and that they should do stuff they didn't feel like doing, too. "The time to talk to people," she said, "is when you don't wanna. And when you're too tired and lazy, that's when you gotta exercise. You gotta live a little outside your comfort zone if you wanna grow."

Well, I was walking past the park one day when I saw it – a giant dog turd. I had always had a great fear of falling face-first into one of these things, so I walked right up to the turd and stood in front of it, defiantly. "Bring it, turd!" I taunted. And I didn't stutter one bit. I was ready to confront my fears – I just *had* to get past this. Deep down I knew it was a terrible thing I was about to do, but that didn't matter because I had to do it. With some reluctance I took my hand, reached into the turd, and pulled out a big juicy handful of fresh steaming dog doo. Then I held it up to my face. My nose crinkled up from the stench. For a second I wondered if I should actually go through with my plan. I stood there waffling. But there was no turning back now. I had to do difficult things that I didn't feel like doing in order to improve. I closed my eyes and breathed in a deep breath. Then, in a moment of mad fury, I took the poo and smashed it all over my face like a piece of wedding cake. "Holy shit!" I cried. "This is awesome!" After that I chucked up my lunch and wiped the poo off with some old leaves. I looked around. Koreans were all laughing and pointing at me. This pissed me off. What did they know! Koreans were a bunch of dumbasses! And so was my grandma!

Tangerine

One day the school principal asked me to go to the store to buy some tangerines. I was trying to learn how to speak Korean and she was playing along, so she said this in Korean. The woman made eye contact with me. Then she spoke slowly and enunciated every syllable in an exaggerated manner to make sure I got it. I listened to the words that came out of her mouth and translated them back into English inside my head: "Store at, for the purpose of tangerine buy, go come back." She wanted me to go to the store, buy a tangerine, and come back. I was all over this one. Korean was easy!

I was ready to hit the store. I walked out of the school, but as soon as I stepped outside I was greeted by the most horrendous noise I had ever heard in my entire life. Four lunatics in brightly-colored clothing were marching down the street and beating on pots and pans in an attempt to create music. It was a samul nori. They were playing traditional Korean music and *it* was painful. Blood began to dribble out of both my ears and for a moment I even thought about killing myself, but instead I plugged my ears up with some gum and decided to trudge on. A few minutes later I came back with a tangerine. The principal saw me and seemed confused.

"Why only buying one?" she asked.

"Uh," I said, "because that's what you asked for."

I was still holding the plastic bag from the store, so I pulled the handles wide apart and looked down into the thing. Way down at the bottom sat one lonely tangerine. I stood there for a moment, scratching my head. Why *did* I only buy one? It was barely enough for one person to eat, much less share. What were we all going to do with one tiny tangerine? Then I took the palm of my hand and smacked myself in the forehead. I had forgotten something! The Korean language had a plural! But you didn't add it to everything – only certain things. So some words were plural but didn't actually have a plural ending. It was crazy. Koreans also had something called intuition. This concept was long dead in America. We didn't care what other people thought, so there was no point in bothering to have intuition, but somehow it worked in Korea. And for those non-plural plurals, you just had to guess when the 's' was there and when it wasn't.

Later on, the principal told all of Korea the story of the tangerine. I was afraid people might think that I was some kind of dunce for missing the 's'. But to my great surprise everyone approved. I even managed to gain a few points with the women. "We are so impress!" they said. "Being cheap is so good quality for man!"

Korean Church

"USA!!!"

"USA!!!"

"USA!!!"

That was the last thing I could remember. I had been standing out in the street in the Itaewon district of Seoul, near the American military base, and I was chanting "USA!" with a bunch of American soldiers. We were all drunk and it had seemed like a great thing to do at the time. After that I passed out and slept in the street.

I woke up with the sun and stumbled around for a while. I had no idea where I was, but then I ran across a store that was handing out free donuts and some nice old ladies invited me in to try one. It was my lucky day! I staggered into the place and picked out a tasty bastard stuffed full of chocolate goo. Then I sat down on one of the odd-looking wooden benches and started to grub it down. Other people were hanging out on the benches too. Most of them were dressed nicely and some had even brought along reading material. It all seemed like a pretty strange setup. I couldn't figure out what type of business I was in. Was this a photography studio? Maybe it was some kind of high class reading club? I just didn't know. But then, out of nowhere, music began to play and a lady stood up and sang. It sounded like a coyote had been shot, so the mystery was solved – this was a karaoke joint. I cleared my throat and cracked my knuckles. I was all set to step up to the mic and rap – but then I glanced up and saw a cross. I couldn't believe it. The old bags had tricked me with the donut! This was a church!

All of a sudden a Korean man strode up to the stage. Right away I knew he was bad. I hadn't been inside a church in a very long time and I couldn't believe what I was seeing. This was a Christian! I was in a church and it was *full of Christians!* There were judgmental assholes as far as the eye could see. The Korean man stood on stage for a moment or two and glanced around with a big fat smile. "Happy Easter!" he cried, finally. And then he started waving around a copy of the Evil Book. Next he began to belt out a sermon in broken English, but there was no point in listening to a preacher so I tuned him out. My mind began to wander. A guy at the edge of the stage was wearing a shirt that said "Heisrisen" with a picture of a hippie on it. The hippie's arms were outstretched and he was imploring everyone to drink. I was hungover and, for the life of me, I couldn't remember where Heisrisen was brewed. I wasn't sure if it was Munich or somewhere in America. But then I realized something – it didn't matter where Heisrisen came from, it was just *wrong* to wear a beer shirt to church. I started to chuckle a little under my breath. "Hypocrites..." I muttered. These Christians would let just about any clueless dumbass walk through the door! They were beginning to bore me, so I started drifting back to my own childhood memories of Easter...

The Easter Bunny was the savior of all children everywhere. He had been sent here by God and he was the perfect bunny. The Easter Bunny could perform miracles – like laying eggs, hiding eggs, and making unlimited amounts of eggs. This confused me. I didn't even know rabbits could lay eggs and I was worried that some of them were brown. Tommy the Troublemaker in Sunday school was all over this. "Those eggs are rabbit turds!" he cried. "They came out of the Easter Bunny's booty!" Tommy tricked the other kids into throwing away their eggs. Then he dug them out of the trash and scarfed them all down when no one was looking. Whenever the Easter Bunny wasn't performing miracles to prove he was the real deal, he tried to help people by teaching them the right way to live. But one day some bad guys got a hold of him. People had predicted this would happen. The bad guys were jealous of all the attention he was getting, and they weren't too keen on the lifestyle tips either. They took the Easter Bunny and crucified him. He died. But three days later he came back – just to show everyone he could. People had predicted this too. And since it all went down just like everyone had said, this meant the Easter Bunny was legit. He took one for the team and we were all good after that.

All of a sudden I started hearing some of the sermon. The preacher was still speaking and he was really excited about something. "What important thing?" he asked. "You guy not know. Important thing love. Like Beatle band singing 'bout. All you need love. But I not talking 'bout same love they talking 'bout. That one causing lotta trip to doctor for treat STD. I talking 'bout different kind love. Okay?"

The church was packed. It was mostly Koreans. But there were a lot of Americans too.

"How you get love?" the preacher continued. "People all disappoint with other guy, right? But no can see self. They not know how use mirror. This biggest problem! Greatest battle in life is fix self! Human just like Italy race car. You not doing maintenance for car, it not gonna running good. Okay? I got dream. We making people *all* like Italy race car zooming around. Then world is good one. You got it? You guy gotta using mirror. Making reflection good for other guy. I not talking 'bout stomach muscle looking good. I talking 'bout inside one. You gotta fixing self. Okay?"

The preacher was on a roll now and everyone was nodding. I flexed my stomach muscles underneath my shirt and felt them with my hand.

"This whole point of Christian I talking 'bout. Life like hourglass. Christian not only thinking 'bout what happening when sand gone. We making sand good while still going to bottom from top. We making good every grain! Okay? We teaching good one. I talking 'bout *value*. If you guy not get value from church, then you getting value from TV and movie. Them guy not caring 'bout value. Them guy wanna making money! Them pandering for base instinct. That why Jesus coming down first time. He telling all guy not do base instinct. When people having self-control, then they not gonna doing bad thing every time. This winding up good for all peoples. This making civilization."

There were a few cries of "hallelujah" and "amen" in the crowd. Then the preacher continued.

"I visiting America. American not go church anymore. This not because American no believing God. American no wanna be accountable. Not for God! Not for spouse! Not for parent! Not for anyone! American wanting all everything stuff free without any obligate for other peoples! I seeing lotta lonely peoples. Good Christian guy like wine. Him getting old, getting better. If guy not going church, him like old milk – getting rotten. I seeing lotta rotten milk. It better if guy think he gonna get judge by God when die. Then him living better life while still alive. American making up lotta new idea nowaday. You guy wanna be *own* God! People only worshipping self! Now Korean like this too! Storm hitting Korea! What happen America?! America I knowing is great place, saving Korea in war one time. But now God is devil and devil is God. You guy changing into Opposite World! Rejecting all thing that was take you to top!"

"Aw crap..." I muttered under my breath. I was awake now and the preacher seemed really pissed off. *I* was mad too – all the donuts were gone! And no one had even offered me a chocolate bunny. This place was super dumb. There was a speck of something stuck in my eye. I tried to pick the thing out but I couldn't get it. Then I looked over at the guy in the Heisrisen shirt. He was nodding at everything the preacher said. What a hypocrite! I couldn't believe how ridiculous this guy was. He would probably go home and have sex with his dog too.

Racist Baby

English class had just finished. I was hanging out with one of my adult students and we were walking up the stairs to his apartment. I couldn't help but wonder what his place would look like inside. From the outside, it seemed like your typical Korean apartment. It was small and unspectacular – kind of like Korean people themselves. But the people always fooled you. The small peppers were usually spicier so when Koreans wanted something they went for it. And if you were standing in the way you were likely to get bowled over. I wondered what surprise the apartment would bring.

As we neared the front door I heard a baby crying. "That daughter," my student explained. "She becoming one year old." He opened the door and we walked into the apartment. After that I glanced around. The place was small and unassuming for the most part. His wife was standing in the kitchen holding the baby, and it was bawling at the top of its lungs. I had never heard such a cacophony in all my life – it was like an airplane crash-landing on top of a fire engine. I took a good look at the baby. The thing's eyes were closed and its mouth was covered in a kind of shiny goo. All babies had this same goo on their mouths. What was it? I was puzzled but didn't have any time to figure it out because the kid just kept crying and crying.

All at once it occurred to the baby that some new people had entered the apartment. And it wanted to see who we were. The creature rotated its head in our direction. Then, suddenly, in mid-cry, it opened its eyes and saw me. A look of complete and utter shock swept over its face. The crying came to an abrupt halt – but the eyes stayed *wide* open. The baby was truly dumbfounded. A crazy-looking white creature was standing in front of it. There weren't very many foreigners in

Korea. And in all its time on earth, this baby had never seen anything quite as odd as me. I was clearly being treated differently for no other reason than my appearance! I wasn't Korean. And this baby was not about to let me forget it! She even bit me later. The baby was obviously a racist.

Donnie the Rock Star

Donnie was a mentally challenged kid who lived down the street from Grandma Inhofe. He was twenty-five but still went to high school. Donnie spent most of the day walking around, hitting himself in the head. It seemed like an odd thing for someone to do, but Donnie's brain was just different than other people's. He didn't really seem to be on the road to success, but he had a goal. Donnie wanted to graduate from high school one day and become a politician.

Other kids picked on Donnie and they had no shortage of barbs. One of the great things about mentally challenged kids was that people were always coming up with new words to make fun of them. And every few years someone invented another. It all started with "special." Then came "mentally challenged" and "handicapable." But nowadays everyone just said "rock star." Things had changed and we were supposed to call retards "rock stars." It was all great fun and kids always managed to adopt each new word as the latest barb.

The neighborhood bully saw Donnie on his porch one day. Donnie was holding a copy of the medieval classic, Canterbury Tales, and he was drooling on the book. Well, right away the bully lit into him. "Hey Donnie!" he yelled. "You're not retarded. You're a special, mentally-challenged rock star!" Then he laughed at his own joke. "Ha ha ha ha!" And pretty soon everyone in the neighborhood was laughing along.

Donnie thought about this for a moment. Then he looked up at the bully. "I got something for you, guy," he said. "I sitting on present."

Everyone loved a gift so all of a sudden the bully seemed interested. He walked over to where Donnie was sitting. "What is it, Donnie?" he asked. "What do you have for me?" Out of nowhere, Donnie ripped the most outrageous fart anyone had ever heard. It was like an atomic bomb. People in the neighborhood were all terrified, small animals began to scurry about, and a rabbit even played dead thinking it was an earthquake. The bully ran away crying and tearing his hair out. For a few frantic seconds everyone was just stunned. But then we all realized what had happened and started busting up. The laughter reverberated throughout the neighborhood and echoed across all of Tucson. Donnie became a hero and no one ever forgot the day of the outrageous fart. His popularity soared. Donnie was elected to the Arizona assembly and later on even went on to become governor. He was the smartest governor Arizona ever had. Donnie truly was a rock star.

Rice Plant

Koreans always tended to the rice. They spent a lot of time caring for and doting after the stuff. It didn't make much sense and, for the life of me, I couldn't figure out why they bothered. Why didn't they just buy rice at the store like everyone else? I was totally baffled.

Well, I was walking by a rice field one day and I was curious, so I decided to check the place out. There were plants everywhere. When one of these plants was young, it was cute and everyone liked it. The plant had potential and people all wanted to see what it would become. But if no one ever took care of the thing, it would wind up stunted in its development. The plant wouldn't ever grow and become ripe. A mature plant wasn't quite as nice to look at, and that hope-for-the-future thing was gone, but it was useful. People could stuff it into their face and get nourishment. That was a plus. And the healthier a mature plant became, the more it bent over from the weight of all it had soaked up in life. The thing sort of looked like it was bowing and showing respect. But at a certain point in life, if a rice plant was not healthy, no amount of care could help it. An immature plant stood straight up, arrested in its development, and incapable of bending over for others. It was of no use to anyone but itself. And it didn't have much to offer anyway so who cared? Everyone liked to help a plant along while it could still grow, but once the thing was full-sized, all bets were off. There wasn't much you could do at that point. When people saw an old rice plant, and it was still standing up straight, that just meant the thing wasn't any good.

Mexican Train

It was spring break, we were on the train to Mazatlan, and I was all lit up. I looked around. Everyone on this thing was partying like crazy. The overhead lights were flickering on and off and drunk kids were staggering around all over the place. Every once in a while, an old Mexican worker shuffled down the aisle and swept all the loose trash off the train in between cars. It was a beautiful scene. I was just standing there taking it all in when, out of nowhere, a blonde girl walked up to me and smiled a crooked smile. A few minutes later I had her underneath a blanket, feeling her up. Her tits were big! And I was really excited about this. I was trying to figure out some private place to take her – but we were on a train! And there just wasn't anywhere to go. I was beginning to feel frustrated because of this – and right about then a bullet whizzed past my head. It was another drug cartel shoot out.

The cartels were going crazy, fighting for the right to sell drugs to Americans. They were killing people left and right and smuggling all kinds of crap into the U.S.

It was enough to piss a guy off. I just sat there for a moment and thought about things – there *had* to be some way to stop them. I was trying to figure out how to eliminate the source of the problem, but thinking about this made my head hurt so I whipped out a bong and fired it up. The blonde joined in.

I took a big hit and held it in as long as I could to maximize my high. "B-bastards..." I coughed. "Fuck 'em." I tried to keep the smoke in as I spoke, but a few wisps floated out of my mouth anyway.

The blonde couldn't hear me. "Whaaat?" she asked.

"The. Drug. Car. Tels..." I choked out. Then I blew smoke all over the place. "They're killing people left and right, chopping people's heads off. What the hell is wrong with them?!"

The blonde agreed. "Yeah!" she cried. "Who the hell do they think they are!" Then she took a hit, held her breath for a few seconds, and exhaled.

I was impressed with this girl. She was smart. I was sitting there drunk and half-stoned, thinking about how cool it was to hook up with a smart chick. But then I remembered something – she had let me touch her boobs! This meant she would probably let me do it again. I completely lost my train of thought and pulled the blanket back up over our heads. Then I grabbed another handful of those juicy melons and suddenly my brain felt a whole lot better better.

The train pulled into a small village a few minutes later. I stumbled out of the car and walked around a little to check everything out. Mexico didn't look anything like the U.S. It was a beautiful uncomplicated place and Mexicans were the sweetest people in the world. They were simple. These people didn't have anything more than huts to live in, but *somehow* they were happy. No one here had a care or even knew the time of day.

A woman with a big old pot on her head made her way slowly down to the train station. She put the pot on the ground, took off the lid, and started selling tamales. I bought a few and scarfed them down as fast as I could. I was starving and they were the best things I had ever eaten in my entire life. The woman smiled as she watched me. "Comida es amor," she said. And all of a sudden I realized something – I knew what this meant! "Food is love." It was the name of a restaurant just off campus. I couldn't believe I had just figured something out in a foreign language. I stood there, stunned. The weed had somehow given me an amazing ability to understand foreign languages! I needed to put this skill to use. I looked around the village. The women all seemed normal here. They were out on the streets gossiping and the men all looked like family guys. They had on cowboy hats and boots and were standing around looking macho. The pace of this town was *slow*. No one seemed to be doing much of anything. I was standing in one spot soaking it all up when I started to wonder if everyone else was stoned too. I was the fastest-moving guy in town – and I was baked!

I decided to try and score some of the local stuff, so I turned to a guy on the street. "Hey dude," I said. "Hook a brother up. Who's got the Acapulco Gold?"

The guy got a puzzled look on his face. "¿Qué?" he asked.

I was confused too. He was telling me about letters of the alphabet, but 'K' didn't make any sense. It was totally random. It was also funny as hell, so I started busting up. "L," I laughed, reciting the next letter. "Ha ha ha ha. L."

The guy was cracking up now too. "Él," he said. "Él está *loco*."

Now he was telling me about words in Mexican that *started* with L, but hell if I knew what he was saying. We both just kept laughing for a few minutes and then another bullet whizzed past my head. That seemed to be my cue to go, so I forgot all about scoring pot and decided to get back on the train.

I walked back and hopped up onto the thing. A minute later a couple of little kids ran up right as the train was starting to pull away. They were waving and smiling at all the drunk college students. Seeing foreigners was an exciting thing for a couple kids from a small village. It was about then that one of the Americans decided to practice his Spanish. "Hey kids!" he yelled as the train chugged off. "¡Chinga tu madre!" And then he fell off the car and got his leg severed under one of the wheels. It was pretty bad. The guy got up after that. He was holding the leg and hopping along after the train as fast as he could, trying to catch up, but he wasn't fast enough. And pretty soon he was just a speck on the horizon. Life wasn't fair. All the poor guy wanted to do was practice his Spanish with two little kids. And now he only had one leg. Some things just didn't seem right.

Haircut

I walked into the lobby at Supercuts and checked in at the counter. It was your typical chain haircut place. There were lots of TVs, style books were strewn about, and people were all waiting patiently for their chance to receive a great haircut. I sat down and started looking through one of the style books. It was nice but I wasn't sure which purple Mohawk was for me. I just *had* to get one to show everyone how special I was, but there were too many choices. I couldn't make up my mind between a super spiky Mohawk, a fauxhawk, or one that was short and fuzzy. I was sitting there scratching my head, considering my options, when a guy with no ear walked out. I looked up and saw him but didn't think much of it.

All of a sudden the girl at the counter perked up. "Next!" she yelled. "Jack! You're up!"

A stylist came up to greet me but something didn't seem quite right. The girl couldn't make eye contact. And her face was expressionless – like a condemned man in the electric chair. I sized her up. She was a chunky white chick with a layer of makeup caked on to hide the zits. The no-eye-contact thing wasn't a defensive move because she was too hot. She just straight up didn't care. And even seemed proud of it.

The chunky girl led me back to her station. I was glad to be getting a haircut, but as we walked I began to feel a vague sense of unease. Something was wrong and I couldn't quite place my finger on it. All of a sudden a bloodcurdling scream rang out in one of the back rooms, but I figured it was nothing. Someone had probably just stubbed their toe. Next I caught a glimpse of the chair I would sit in to receive my haircut. It was cold and black. I sat down and right away the girl slapped a clamp over each wrist, immobilizing me. After that she whipped out a clipper and stood there, brandishing it. Her eyes were alive now. The girl flashed a devilish smile. Then she glanced down at the clipper and stroked the blade softly with her free hand.

"Hi," she said, "I'm Lisa. How would you like your hair done?"

"Uh..." I said. And then I wimped out on the Mohawk. "Not too short. And keep the bangs."

But the girl wasn't listening. She lurched forward all at once and jabbed at my ear with the clipper. Then she ran it all around the side and back of my skull, shearing me like a sheep. Loose hair fell to the ground in clumps and suddenly I was in pain. I checked out my reflection in the mirror. My ear was bleeding! Then I looked down at the floor. A good-sized chunk of my ear was lying on the ground – and there were other ears too!

"Damn!" I cried. "Are you gonna sew that back on or what?!"

"Oops," she said, putting her hand up to her mouth in an attempt to act coy. "Looks like I cut it a little too high up on the sides. We'll have to do a combover to keep the bangs."

I looked all around Supercuts. People were pale and scared and there were bloodstains all over the floor. How had I missed all of this?! I was kicking myself for being too spaced out when the girl leaned back and let loose with a ferocious Indian war cry.

"WOO BOO BOO BOO BOO BOO BOO BOO!!!"

I was just stunned. I couldn't believe what was happening to me. Everyone knew it was racist for a white person to make an Indian war cry. All of a sudden I started to worry that she might kill me. This was annoying, but what really bothered me was that I was about to be scalped by a politically incorrect bigot! It was outrageous! I struggled in the chair, trying to free myself, but it was no use. My arms were locked down tight and there was nothing I could do. I was totally helpless and before long I began to feel faint. I had lost a lot of blood. The last thing I remember was the girl swiveling me around in the chair and pointing at the mirror. It was all kind of fuzzy. I saw her standing behind me. She was holding my scalp up above my head and motioning as she described the style of the cut. I handed her some money. And I don't remember anything after that.

When I came to, I was standing in front of the mirror in the bathroom at home. I took a look at my hair. First I checked out the front. And then I looked at each side. After that I grabbed a mirror and examined the back. It wasn't blended in very well. And the bangs were all zigzaggy. It was a pretty bad haircut – maybe the worst one I had ever had. But there were more important things in life than hair. Sometimes it was good just to be alive.

Bidov's War

"Oil companies are evil!" Bidov cried. "They make too much money! And money is the root of all evil! As soon as I get a little more I'm gonna give all of mine away."

Bidov wasn't happy about oil companies or corporations in general. He often lumped them all together into one group and derided them. But saying that all corporations were bad was the same as saying that all black people ate celery. Stereotypes were always wrong! Sometimes corporations *did* do bad things, though, and we had to fight against that – it was our duty as Americans! So one of Bidov's proudest moments was the day he typed out a scathing email to the CEO of Walmart on his brand new MacBook Pro. Bidov told the man to give his workers a raise. And he even received a response!

> Dear Toedl Bidov,
>
> We thank you for your feedback and apologize for any inconvenience.
>
> Sincerely,
>
> Elmer Smith, CEO of Walmart

Bidov was making a difference! He was so happy to get a response that he sent another email to the CEO. In this one he expressed gratitude for all the cheap products he had purchased at Walmart over the years. And he received another response!

> Dear Toedl Bidov,
>
> We thank you for your feedback and apologize for any inconvenience.
>
> Sincerely,

Elmer Smith, CEO of Walmart

But Bidov forgot about all the times Walmart had thanked him and went back to ranting and complaining. "Corporations are evil!" he cried. "They're only trying to make money! Why can't the world run on love?! I don't care about money – really I don't! But some people sure do have a lot of it! And that's not fair! We should make all the rich people give their money to the government! And then they could give it to people like me! This would allow me to take care of all my basic needs like food, cell phones and Internet. After that we could give the leftover cash to the homeless. Once we do all of this, the world will run on love!"

Some time passed. Bidov went to college and became a climate scientist. Then he defaulted on all his student loans. After that he decided to get a job. There were a lot of job openings for people who could demonstrate that the earth was warming, so Bidov was hired right away.

Bidov discovered that man-made CO2 emissions were causing climate change. And most of this was being done by corporations! Climate change was a big problem. And it was more than just global warming. It meant the earth was getting hotter – except when it was getting colder. It was getting wetter and drier and calmer and windier too. Ice in Antarctica was even increasing. Whenever Bidov noticed any of these things, he alerted everyone in the world using his Twitter account. His words swept across the planet like wildfire. The Internet was amazing – you could get a message out so easily! And as long as you repeated it often enough, it was sure to sink in. Without the Internet, many people would have remained ignorant of the effects of climate change. But now everyone knew it was an extremely dangerous situation. Humans had no other choice. We had to stop what the corporations were doing. We had to put an end to climate change.

Bidov was invited to the White House one day to celebrate his accomplishments and the story was all over the news: "President to meet climate scientist, Bidov!" blared the media. He received a Purple Heart for all of his hard work and got to see the Commander-in-Chief. Bidov ran into him as he was coming out of the bathroom. The president was busy zipping up his pants, but he stopped and gestured to Bidov with his hand.

"Climate change is a big problem!" the president declared. "But this guy is like me. This man Toedl E. Bidov and his fellow scientists are gonna lick it!" People all cheered when they heard this because they were against climate change too. "Now who's up for lunch?" the president continued. "Anyone like Vietnamese food? How about some pho? You know – the soup that rhymes with 'duh'? It was great to see that guy Bidov. But I'm ready for action. What about Pho King? It's pretty good! You guys all like Pho King, don't you?"

One of the reporters decided to speak up. "Mr. President," he said, "with all due respect, sir, there are too many people in D.C. hanging around Pho King with their thumbs up their butts. It's too crowded."

"You mean we're in for a big line?" the president asked.

"Yeah," the reporter said. "I bet you're used to pho queues, but why don't we head over to Kudd Wharf? You can bring your mom."

"Sounds like a great idea," the president said. "Let's check it out."

"Great!" the reporter shouted. "Once we get there, we can go to Pho Kudd Wharf."

"That's perfect!" the president cried. "I was getting a little bored with plain old Pho King anyway, but I'm excited now. I'm ready to go to Pho Kudd Wharf with my mom!"

Pizza Face

We were at a house party and we were all drinking a lot of beer. It was a decent time. Everyone was hanging around, laughing and joking, but I was disappointed in one thing. The party didn't have very many girls, and the ones I did see weren't very pretty. One in particular was a hideous beast. The girl was as wide as she was tall and had a face like a pizza – with makeup caked on to try and hide the pimples. And the makeup wasn't helping much either because I could see all the zits through the coating. Her face looked like a ceiling from the 1970s – the kind with that sprayed-on snow look.

I kept looking around for a hottie. Then I started grumbling about it. "This party sucks," I moaned. "Where are all the girls? How come they don't wanna hang out with a buncha drunk dudes?" After that I looked up and saw a clock. Now I was worried. It was almost 11 and if you waited until late to hook up, the pickings were slim. Time was running out and I was starting to feel bored. Before long I was downing beer after beer. Whatever was in my hand I drank, and then I went and grabbed another. But after about a dozen or so beers, I started to notice something – the zit girl was actually pretty! I had been too harsh in my assessment of her earlier. I wasn't sure exactly what had changed but she was a totally different person now. Her short, badly bleached perm had morphed into the lovely blonde flowing locks of a goddess. Her beauty was *mesmerizing*. The girl even seemed a few inches taller. I moved in closer just to be near and looked into her eyes – they were the deep blue of the ocean in paradise. She was the most amazing creature I had ever seen in my entire life.

Somehow, I wound up in a room alone with her. I couldn't believe how lucky I was! The two of us started making out and before long we were rolling around on a bed. Our tongues danced together in the hazy alcohol-induced fog. A bra came off.

Then I grabbed a big handful of boob and sucked on it. After that I caressed her cheek, but when I did I received a rude shock. It was coarse like the bark of a tree. This confused me. Where was the goddess? Was this the beast I had seen earlier??? What was happening? Lost and not knowing what to do, I staggered out of the room and collapsed outside the door. My buddy Dan was waiting out in the hallway. "Haw! Haw! Haw!" he taunted. "Did you get some? I guess you're in love with the pizza face! When are you two gonna get married? Haw! Haw! Haw!"

Dan didn't know when to quit. Years later he was still razzing me about the night I wore the beer goggles. Maybe I deserved it. I was a big dumbass. The girl looked like a pizza but she had feelings too. And I had probably gotten her hopes up. For a few minutes that night she thought she was going to hook up with a really awesome guy. I felt bad now and regretted what I had done.

Life was kind of funny. Every guy wanted to find the hottest girl he could get. It was part of our DNA. But a goddess usually had the heart of a beast and a beast usually had the heart of a goddess. The sex was all the same once you made it past the six-month itch, so it wasn't always good to get what you wished for.

It's the Thought that Counts

It was Christmas over at Uncle Sal's house and I was ready to collect some presents! I made sure to get some stuff for their family too. I went out and bought a few things. Sal always liked to smell good so I got him a bottle of aftershave. Aunt Betsy collected chicken art so I bought her a decorative chicken to hang on the wall. And Nathan liked toy cars so I got him one. I had a happy feeling inside as I watched them open up all of their presents. They were all smiling from ear to ear.

A lot of other gifts flew back and forth that morning. They were all opened up and most were quickly forgotten. I thought everything had been handed out and that no one had remembered me, but then I took a deeper dive and looked under the tree one last time. There was still *one present left.* And as luck would have it, this one was for me! I glanced at it. The thing seemed to be a kind of last minute job. It wasn't in a box like all the others. It was sort of oval-shaped and had been wrapped directly. The paper was all wrinkly and held together by a last minute scotch tape job full of fingerprints. I bent down and took a closer look. Something round and yellow was itching to get out from underneath. Now I was curious. What kind of cool present was this? I couldn't wait to find out, so I picked the thing up and grabbed the card.

"To Jack," it read. "From Uncle Sal."

"Oh Sal," I said. "You shouldn't have."

I just knew something awesome was inside. Pausing dramatically, I looked at Sal with a feeling of adoration. What a great guy he was! Then I tore off the paper and held the gift up in front of my face. It was a bottle of French's yellow mustard – and it was still cold. "Wow..." I mumbled. I just didn't know what to say. I was completely speechless.

Sal had been busy patting aftershave on his cheeks, but he seemed to sense that something was off. "Uhhh..." he stuttered, "we thought you were a little short on food at the apartment. Right Betsy?" Betsy nodded frantically. "So we got you some mustard. This is the yellow stuff. Tastes good. Goes with everything!"

"Yeah!" Betsy cried. "It's the thought that counts!"

Just then Nathan piped up. "You're easygoing, right Jack?" he said. "So you won't mind if we give you some cheap mustard. It's the thought that counts!"

I popped the seal and took a few swigs of mustard. "Mmm..." I said. "Tastes good." Then I walked over to the couch and sat down. I looked at all the presents I had bought and suddenly I felt a sick feeling in my gut. I realized something that day. I had been totally missing the point of Christmas. It wasn't only about *getting* stuff. It was really much much more than that. Christmas was a great opportunity to regift or unload stuff on suckers.

Ho Hike

"Women who dress like hos are hos!" declared Perry the Politician. He didn't know a microphone was recording him. Perry the Politician had gotten himself into trouble again. He was on the national news that evening and pretty soon he was backpedalling, trying to dig himself out of the mess. "I'm sorry," he said, a tear rolling down his cheek. "Women who dress like hos are not hos. I'm a politician. When I said that I was lying. Sometimes I lie. And sometimes I lie about lying. But I can promise you one thing – as long as there is still breath in these lungs – I will never lie about lying about lies!" Then he pulled out a comb and started fixing his hair.

Perry had made a valiant effort to right the wrong of his words. But the damage was already done. Before long, a nation-wide movement took root. Women everywhere started taking part in "Ho Hikes." They put on slutty clothing and hiked around town. This proved that they were not hos. The women dressed in revealing clothing to feel good about themselves, and the reason they felt good was because guys with boners were chasing them around, showering them with attention. The guys wanted to get the rest of the clothes off, too, so they could bang them like hos.

Perry the Politician had just come back from a chic $50,000-a-plate fundraiser where he had railed against greed. He showed up at one of the hikes. Perry was a politician so, according to the law, he was required to speak at any gathering of more than a hundred people.

"Being a ho is all in your mind!" he cried, taking off his hat and hanging it on the bulge in his pants. "You can be with one person and be a ho if you think you are, or you can be with a thousand and be a virgin if that is what you believe! Promiscuous sex does not water down a woman any more than melamine dilutes milk! It's a good thing! Everyone should do whatever they want!"

A huge roar went up from the crowd. Guys started winking and giving each other fist bumps while women shook their booties and danced. Everyone agreed with Perry. People should do whatever they wanted! And whatever they imagined they were, that was what they were!

Next a dog jumped up and grabbed the microphone. "I'm not a dog!" it barked. "I'm a bird."

"Yay!" people cried.

Everyone felt a visceral connection to the dog. The canine soaked up the love for a few moments. Then it ate a piece of cake and tried to convince people it was still there. After that the dog spread its paws wide apart and jumped off the stage, flapping furiously. It hit the ground pretty hard and lay there for a few minutes. Then it limped off.

About that time, Perry saw a black guy in the crowd. "Hello black man!" he cried. "Thank you for coming to my hike! Let me tell you one thing! People are all racist against you! So there is no reason for you to try! You have no hope! But never fear, I am here to protect you! I will provide you with a small pittance every month – just enough to keep you alive! And for this you will owe me a great debt!"

The black guy just stood there for a moment with a puzzled look on his face. Then he pumped a fist in the air. "Haaaoooohhhh!!!" he yelled.

The crowd was really excited now. "Yay!" people cried.

"We must hold together the coalition of the oppressed!" Perry cried. "Women, African-Americans, Latinos, Muslims, gays, Jews and transgenderoos. Well wait...not Jews. They are out. But the rest of us will all bond together and strike back against the Man! We will fight the oppressors!"

A few weeks later, Perry the Politician was impeached and thrown in jail. Then he was hanged and shot by a firing squad. People all loved Perry. But a crime was a crime and justice had to be served. Perry had violated the ordinance of one bad word.

Philosophy Class

Phil the Philosopher taught philosophy at U of A. Philosophy was a very useful subject. It was also a requirement for all medieval poetry majors. I *had* to take philosophy, but that didn't mean it wasn't my favorite class anyway. I loved it. Everyone loved philosophy.

One day Phil walked into class with a prop. "Look at what I brought!" he cried. "I am holding an empty box! Does everyone believe this box is empty?" As Phil spoke, he looked around the room wide-eyed like a magician performing for small children.

I gave the box a once-over. The top was closed so there was no way to know if the thing was empty, but then I started to put my gray matter to work. Phil wasn't just asking rhetorical questions. He liked to challenge his students. We all loved Phil's style. He didn't give tests or assign homework and grades were based solely on in-class participation, so whoever came up with the most *philosophical* answers to Phil's questions got an 'A'.

A kid in the back row didn't believe what Phil was saying about the box. "No way!" he cried. "That box ain't empty! There's somethin' in it!"

"You're right!" Phil cried as he opened up the box. "This box is not empty! Inside of it is – another box!"

The kid was amazed. "Wow," he said. "A box inside a box. That's kinda like holdin' two mirrors together and seein' an infinite number of reflections!"

"That's nothing!" Phil cried as he opened the second box. "This second box is empty! If a box contains nothing more than an empty box, does that mean the first box is empty too?!" When the kid heard this, his head blew up. Brains splattered all over the wall and he collapsed onto the floor in a heap. Philosophy class was tough and not everyone could handle it.

"What if a forest grew inside the second box?!" Phil cried. "What if a tree fell in that forest?! Would anyone hear it?!"

"No!" yelled a white kid with dreadlocks. "The first box is empty! So no one can hear the second one!"

"Right!" Phil cried. And then he grinned. He was always happy when people *got it.*

"I'm a bird!" shrieked a girl in the front. "I live in a tree in that forest. Does anyone know I'm alive?!"

"Uh...okay..." Phil said. He didn't know what the girl was talking about, but she had big tits so he gave her an 'A'.

I was starting to get really excited at this point. I loved philosophy and I wanted to be just like Phil when I grew up. I was racking my brain, trying to figure out some way to add to the conversation. My mind was spinning and spinning. Finally something popped into my head, so I decided to chime in. "I like beer!" I cried. "It comes in a box!"

I was pretty proud of myself and I was smiling at first, but then the room started to get real quiet. My smile began to fade a little. I looked around. Phil was standing up at the front of the class and he was shaking his head. That was when I remembered that beer was for dumb guys. Sophisticated people took drugs or anything some guy in a trailer cooked up. I was shaking my head now too. It was bad that I had forgotten this. After a while Phil stopped shaking his head and then, to my great surprise, he decided to call on *me*. Suddenly I was excited again. Interacting with Phil meant an opportunity to gain knowledge.

"What about the question of self flatulation, Jack?" he asked. "If our own farts smell good to us, but other people's don't, then tell me – what would happen if our own gas was bottled and secretly exposed to us? Would we like it or not? What do you think? I am expanding your mind here, Jack. This is one of the great questions of our time!"

I stood up. "It would smell good!" I cried. "Our own farts always smell good! We would know it was ours!"

"Wrong!" Phil said. And then he frowned. "I actually did this experiment back when I had free room and board at the mental institution. People only like their own farts when they are sure they belong to them. The only exception is that everyone seems to like the smell of my own personal fart. I used to give exams before I realized how useless they were, and a few years back I cut the cheese before I passed out the final. Then I asked each student if they liked it – and to my surprise they all responded that they did!"

I hung my head in shame. Philosophy class was tough. Maybe I wasn't meant to be a great philosopher like Phil. Not everyone could be a deep thinker. I was disappointed about this for a few minutes, but then I forgot about it. I was going to become a world-famous rapper anyhow.

Best Way to Cheat

I have been cheating on tests for a long time. I'm an expert! It's always a tempting thing to do whenever I've forgotten to study. My old technique was usually good enough to get me a 'C' or a 'D'. That was enough to pass. And I have to admit – I felt pretty smart getting a 'D' without even trying. It was awesome. But there's one thing about cheating that pisses me off – sometimes the teachers trick me. They take questions I never learned from old tests and put them on new ones. And then I end up missing stuff I got right the first time. It's not fair!

Cheating can be embarrassing too. I got an 'A' for a report I did on the Canterbury Tales. I copied the entire thing from some website. And nobody was the wiser! But sometimes I'm too smart for my own good. The professor was so impressed with my report that she asked me to give a speech about it on-the-fly. I stood up in front of the class. "Uhhh…" I stammered. "There was a guy from Canterbury and he had a really long tail." Everyone was laughing at my great humor, but the teacher was not impressed. She couldn't believe I had already forgotten the material.

Cheating can be complicated too. Making a really intricate cheat sheet often takes more time than it does to study – but nothing will ever stop me from doing my very best! I have to find the right place to sit during tests, too, so I always look for a spot next to the Asian kid with the thickest glasses.

Cheating was working out great for me, but ultimately my old style was a pain in the ass. One day I found a better way. I was drunk in the library, scrawling out punch lines for my comedy routine when it hit me – I could just *secretly memorize* everything that might be on the next exam. And that is exactly what I did. Once all that information was inside my head, there was no way for anyone to find it or prove how it got there. After I figured this out I was able to answer all the questions correctly. My plan worked like a charm. I aced the test and ever since then I have been secretly memorizing lots of stuff. I've been getting all A's! And best of all I never have to worry about getting caught.

Meatball

It was New Year's Eve and I was all set to be the designated driver for two of my drunk homies. I hopped into Bertha and picked them up around 10 PM. As soon as they saw me they were both really excited.

"Dude!" Dan cried. "We're smashed and we're gonna get laid tonight!"

"Yeah!" Craig yelled. "Thanks for driving!"

I was stone cold sober but the two of them had already downed a night's worth of booze. Right away everything seemed weird because this was a position I had never been in before. I was always drunk too. Something about Dan and Craig didn't seem quite right. I couldn't put my finger on it at first, so I just sat there scratching my head. Normally they were both hilarious – a laugh a minute – but they weren't even funny now. And neither one knew it. They kept repeating the same jokes over and over again, and they couldn't remember what they had just said or even hold the same train of thought. They were like a couple of over-the-hill comedians who weren't funny anymore, but no one had told them. And after a while they just seemed obnoxious. I had to look each one in the eye and speak loudly to have any hope of getting a response.

We started driving around. My tabs and insurance were expired, so I kept checking the rear view mirror for cops. Mirrors were funny. Some were simple and others were fancy, but they all had one thing in common – they let you see yourself. And sometimes you were even looking into one and didn't know it.

We drove from bar to bar looking for excitement. At one point, we passed a big group of Mexicans hanging out on the corner. Dan stuck his head out the window. "Hey beeeaners!" he yelled. "Fuck yooooooo!!!" We were in a car and they were on foot, so Dan didn't have to worry about getting beat to a pulp. I slowed down and pulled off the road to make him sweat a little. "H-hey," he stuttered. "What are you doing, man? Don't be crazy. When you mess with one bean, you mess with the whole burrito!" Drunk people didn't make much sense. Dan's girlfriend was Mexican and he was always nice to her – he just liked to irritate people whenever he was bored or smashed. I waited for a few seconds and then decided to pull back onto the road to avoid a brawl. We kept cruising around and for some reason Dan stopped yelling out the window. He was boasting now instead.

"I'm so cool!" he cried. "I can slam more beer than both of you guys combined!"

Craig didn't agree. "Oh yeah?" he said. "Well I bet you can't do this!" And at that moment he picked a dirty smelly meatball up off the floor of the car. No one knew how long it had been there. There was lint all over the thing and some fuzzy green stuff too. I looked closely – a short curly hair was even stuck to it. "I'm gonna eat this bad boy," Craig declared. Then he stuffed the meatball into his mouth and gulped it down greedily. "Mmmm," he added. "This bitch tastes good!" Dan and I couldn't believe what we were seeing. It was a horrible shameful thing we had witnessed, and from that day on Craig was no longer called Craig. He was known as "Meatball."

Cow

I met Amy at a party one night and it didn't take long until I was seeing a whole lot of her. She was fun. The two of us liked to eat spicy hamburgers together, so we always ate at a place called Whataburger. It was our favorite restaurant. Whataburger was a low-class fast-food joint near U of A. It was like McDonald's but worse. There was no evil clown or gimmicky dude in a styrofoam head – the place didn't even *have* a mascot. And it looked like a hideous red-and-white-colored jail. But the burgers were good. Whataburger burgers even had *real* jalapeños. Most places just spiced stuff up with the same version of lame hot vinegar sauce. But Whataburger was the real deal. It tasted good to a drunk!

Amy had a big rack and blonde hair and she still lived with her mom. I was over at her house one day when her mom asked her for a favor.

"Amy?" she said. "Can you clean up your room?"

"Not with this hair and these," she said, motioning to her breasts. "I ain't doin' nuthin'!"

"Hey Amy," I said later. "How come you still live with your mom? Aren't you gonna get a job or something? You could get your own place."

"Hell no," she replied. "I got big tits. I ain't gettin' no job."

All my buddies were giving me fist bumps for scoring Amy. But after a while I started to wonder if I should look for a girl with a little more substance. The rack was nice but you could only grab a boob for so many minutes a day. I decided to break up before it was too late.

A few months later I ran into Amy at the mall. We stood out on the sidewalk and talked for a while. Knowing I had a hit, I brought up Whataburger.

"Remember those spicy burgers?" I asked. "We used to munch on them whenever we were smashed."

Amy winced. "God, those greasy things???" she said. "I can't believe I used to eat them."

I was completely shocked. Back when we were eating the burgers, Amy was totally into it. She was always nodding and chewing away excitedly whenever I raved about the great jalapeños. But now the truth was out – she had been acting the entire time and everything was all a lie! I just stood there scratching my skull. There was no reason to buy the cow as long as the milk was free and you never knew what you were going to get until you actually bought the thing. Who knew what was true with a girl! I felt like a big dumbass now that I knew Amy was faking. This pissed me off for a while but I got over it. At least Amy had always supported me. She thought medieval poetry was a great major and was constantly telling me I'd be a famous comic one day. I was just glad she had never faked it when we did the dirty deed. She was always moaning and yelling out crazy stuff so I knew it had to be real.

Comic

I was sitting around watching stand-up comedy on TV and I was pissed off. Anyone could do what these clowns were doing! They weren't even funny. The entertainment industry was in desperate need of a comic who was actually humorous. They needed *me*. So right then and there I decided to go all in – I was ready to become a world-famous comedian. And this time it was for real. I had a crinkled up scrap of paper with some jokes I had scrawled out in the library. It had six or seven jokes on it. I was a natural so I figured this would be enough to launch my career. I grabbed the scrap, hopped into Bertha, and drove down to open-mic at Laffs Comedy Club. Then I scoped out the place. It was all losers! Guys got up on stage and cracked jokes – some were funny and some bombed, but even the funny ones weren't as good as me. I couldn't wait to show everyone how great I was, so I signed up to perform. The big moment was fast approaching – a star was about to be born.

The closer it got to my turn, the faster my heart began to beat. I could barely stand it. The anticipation was just killing me, and then – the emcee called my name. "No joke, folks. The next comic is a medieval poetry major. Let's give him a big hand. This guy could use it. He just drove down here in his car – Jack Inhofe all the way from the University of Arizona!" Right away people started to chuckle.

Instinctively, the crowd could sense I was a great comic and they simply couldn't contain themselves. I leaped out of my seat, jumped up onto the stage, and grabbed the mic. I was nervous. But I had high hopes. I was about to bring down the house.

"Hi everyone."

"My name is Jack..."

"I'm a comic!"

I was expecting more laughs but instead I was greeted by crickets. People were all just glaring at me. They seemed to be daring me to make them laugh. It was a tough crowd so I opened up with my best stuff.

"How come my socks never match?!" I cried. Then I pulled up both pant legs to make my point. "Look! I lost one at the laundromat! I just put it in the dryer! And then – it was gone! Is there a monster in there that eats socks or what?!"

I looked around the room. No one was laughing. The crowd seemed stunned. People were not moving or even breathing. But that didn't matter. I wasn't about to give up.

"Knock, knock!" I cried.

A kid in the front row looked confused. "Who's there?" he asked.

"Les," I said.

"Les, *who*?"

"Les rock everyone!"

People just continued to stare at me with blank expressions on their faces. No one was smiling. And the kid in the front actually looked mad. It was like I was wasting his time or something. In desperation I pulled out five bucks and handed it to him.

"Please!" I begged him. "Please laugh at me!"

"Fuck you!" he answered. "And keep your money, jack ass!"

I continued on with the act for another minute or so, but things only got worse. I had never been in a library as quiet as this. The room kept getting quieter and quieter and then, suddenly, I became aware of a burning hot light. A spotlight was shining down on me. The thing was blinding and before long it was all I could see. The light just kept getting brighter and brighter and hotter and hotter. It was the sun. And I was stranded in the middle of the Sahara Desert. Sweat started to bead up on my forehead. One of the beads grew too big and then gravity got the better of it. The thing broke free and began to trickle down the side of my face. I was melting! Next my left ear turned into goo and slid off my head. After that the room began to take on an eerie calm. It was the moment of deathly quiet just before an execution. I watched a piece of dust slip off one of the ceiling fans. It drifted slowly down to the floor and hit the ground with a loud BOOOOOM!!!

The only laughs I got were after I stepped off stage. The other comics snickered long and hard. This was the only time they ever laughed – in between sets! They refused to crack so much as a smile at each other's acts. One guy even seemed disgusted. His mouth was all pulled up into a smirk and he was making a crinkly eye. I took a good look at him. This guy was the only genius in the room. We all were. We were all going to make it big. There wasn't much room at the top, though, so that meant other people were not geniuses and were not going to make it big. A heart like this didn't have room for anything else. It belonged to someone who was small. We all wanted to be big stars. But we were living small.

A crazy girl got on stage after me. She had a glass eye and kept making jokes about it. And every time she did, people laughed. Now I was really salty. How come this chick was funny and I wasn't? It was total bullshit. I was just too damn good looking and didn't have any obvious defects to fall back on for laughs. That's what it was! Well I would fix that! I glanced around the table – a butter knife was lying in front of me. "I'm funny too!" I cried. Then I grabbed the knife and started to hack away at a finger. "Look! I'm missing a finger!" But it was no use. The knife barely left a mark. It didn't even break the skin. But the girl on stage noticed me. "I got my eye on you!" she said and people all started rolling in the aisles. I decided not to become a comedian after all. So now I had no other choice. My future was etched in stone. I folded my arms real dope-like across my chest and stood up. "Word!" I cried. "I'm going to become a world-famous rapper!"

Farley

I was standing in the dairy aisle at Walmart holding an egg and I was confused. "Damn..." I muttered. I had always thought that eggs came from a chicken – or maybe a rabbit. But at every supermarket, no matter wherever I went, they were always sitting there right smack dab in the middle of the dairy section. Dairy meant cows. I knew that much. So this meant eggs came from a cow. I just stood there for a moment scratching my head. How did it all work?

I glanced down the aisle. A large overweight man was examining a container of Yoplait light yogurt. The regular yogurts all had names like Cherry or Lemon, but the light ones were different. This one was called "Triple Sick and Ridiculous Chocolate Fudge Cheesecake Death!" I looked at the guy's shopping cart. It was stacked to the hilt with dozens and dozens of frozen microwaveable dinners. The packages all looked inviting and the ingredients were long exciting paragraphs full of words no one could pronounce. I was standing there, admiring all of his food when I saw...*it*. Walmart had been trying to get into the high-end food market, and sitting proudly on top of all the frozen dinners was a great big mouthwatering hunk of golden choco cheese. A little piece of this stuff cost a hundred bucks. And it was worth every penny. GCC was super old cheese that had been salvaged from an ancient shipwreck off the coast of France. It was pulled from the ocean by skilled underwater divers and deep fat fried by a famous French chef. After that it was dunked in expensive chocolate and sprinkled with ultra-thin flakes of real gold. GCC was the best thing ever.

I was about to walk past the cart when I realized something – I knew this guy! This was Farley, the Cat Blogger's brother. The two of them lived in a trashed old house down the street. Farley was older than most students. But he was cool. He didn't care what people did. The Cat Blogger was a little off, though. He spent all his time online, writing about cats he had seen and cats he liked. It was hard to get committed anymore.

I hadn't seen either one of the brothers since the night of the dead comedian at Wildcat House. A big group of kids were hanging out. Farley was there too and he was all lit up. The guy was tossing down drinks with both hands – faster than a movie star popping pills. And it didn't take long until he was doing an impression of his namesake, the late comic, Chris Farley. His act was dead on. At first everyone was laughing – even people at nearby tables were cracking up. Who didn't love to hear a maniac screaming things in a bar? But stuff got out of control pretty fast. The dead comic only had one line. Farley was feeling it at first but then the well started to run dry. The laughs weren't coming as fast as they had before. And then – they were nothing but awkward chuckles. He was dying. But an aging fighter never quite knew when to quit, so he ripped off his shirt to try to bring the act back to life. Then he ran around the bar, yelling the line at the top of his lungs.

"I LIVE IN A VAN DOWN BY THE RIVER!!!"

"I LIVE IN A VAN DOWN BY THE RIVER!!!"

"I LIVE IN A VAN DOWN BY THE RIVER!!!"

It was crazy. Rolls of fat were flying everywhere. Farley was just one giant blob of discombobulated goo. And he wouldn't stop screaming the line. It was the greatest thing I had ever seen in my entire life. Kids were shocked. Girls clung to their boyfriends, or any guy who was near, and everyone did their best to pretend he wasn't there. People just wanted him to go away. A minute or so later Farley tripped over a chair, hit the floor like a ton of bricks, and passed out. He was down for the count. And right about then, the bouncer started to make his way over to the spot. He had a big smirk on his face. The guy was striding along, flexing his muscles in gleeful anticipation of the beating he would give. Farley was about to get pummeled. It was looking bad but me and the Cat Blogger acted fast. We lifted his carcass up off the floor and dragged him out of there. A guy who put on a show like that didn't deserve to get beat. The bouncer looked on with great disappointment. He would have to find someone else to hurt now.

Farley was still staring at the yogurt in the dairy aisle today, though. He seemed mesmerized by it.

"What's up, Farley?" I asked.

He looked at me and smiled. "Hey Jack," he said. "Wanna try some GCC?"

Lucky Beaver

We had a cat when I was little. It was there to make everyone happy. The thing purred a lot and did its job for the most part, but whenever it was on my lap for too long, I would start to feel bad. I wanted to move but didn't want to disturb the cat. The thing just had a way of looking comfortable. After a while, choosing not to move could even become a sort of torture. First my legs would feel sore and then they would cramp up. Before long I was in pain. Eventually I just had to deal with the situation.

Me and Rocco decided to go to the Lucky Beaver Strip Club one night. Rocco raised his arms into the air. "Woohoo!" he yelled. "I can't wait to see some t-and-a!"

"Yeah!" I cried and gave him a fist bump. "Lucky Beaver rules! This is gonna be awesome!"

We drove to the Lucky Beaver and arrived just in time for happy hour. We were both really excited. A dance beat was pumping and there were disco lights flashing all around. The music grabbed us and pulled us in. A fog machine up by the stage was pumping out smoke, but all I could see were boobs – they were popping out at me from every angle. Rocco spied a couple of seats near the front and we sat down. Topless girls were everywhere! They were smiling the fake smiles of beauty pageant contestants and trying to make eye contact with every guy, but it was the opposite of the real world in here. Guys all ignored them. Eye contact meant paying for lap dances, and it didn't make sense to pay for something you could already see for free.

After a while, two girls approached us. "Can we join you?" they asked. Even without clothes on neither one was pretty, but it seemed rude to say no.

"Okay," Rocco said.

"Sure," I agreed. "Why not?"

The girls sat down – one on each of our laps. And then we all started talking. These girls were different. They weren't like the ones on stage. The girl on my lap was overweight with the bright pink complexion of a pig. She had stretch marks too. And Rocco's girl was an emaciated Hispanic with dark circles under her eyes and a vibe of doom. The conversation seemed to be on life support so we bought them a couple drinks to try and liven things up.

The pig was sitting on my lap. And it only took a few minutes of this until the weight was killing me. My legs started to cramp up and before long I was in pain. I was just sitting there, racking my brain, trying to come up with some reason to move, when suddenly a great idea popped into my head – I would go to the bathroom! So I got up and walked over to the spot.

The restroom at the Lucky Beaver was an amazing place. It was covered wall-to-floor with shiny black tile and bright lights. A dude was in there. And he was sitting on a chair, doling out paper towels to the masses. I was impressed. This joint was first class! Any place with a guy in the bathroom was high end for sure. I was starting to feel pretty special, but then I looked a little closer. The attendant was a sad old black man. His hair was all white and I could tell his life had not gone well. The man oozed regret. He moved slowly and the expression on his face did not change. But at least he still had his dignity. Here he was, working at whatever kind of job he could still do.

I didn't actually have to piss, so I just stood at the urinal for a few seconds, pretending to take a leak. I washed my hands for real after the fake piss and the attendant handed me a towel. I dried off my hands. Then I pulled out my wallet and gave him forty bucks. It was all the money I had left. After that I went back to the table and sat down.

The Pig got back up on my lap and started crushing my legs all over again. It was a horrible, intense pain – like childbirth or being burned alive, and finally I just couldn't take it anymore. I picked up a bottle of beer. I was going to break the thing and use the jagged edge to amputate my leg, but suddenly I was distracted. Two new girls were on stage and they were coked out of their minds, pretending to be lesbians. Guys saw this and started jumping up all over the joint. They were throwing money at them like it was the end of the world. Bills were flying around like ticker tape in a parade! It was amazing. Even the government couldn't print money this fast. The club was alive and pumping with an unbridled female sexual energy. But the dance ended and the atmosphere sucked out of the room like air from a balloon. After that a terrible thing happened – I lost my buzz.

I looked around the club. Everyone in this place was a loser. There were dopes wearing sunglasses indoors and clowns in full-length leather jackets. A muscle-bound Cro-Mag was standing at the door cracking his knuckles. Everywhere I turned there were naked girls, but what was the point? This was like dying of thirst on a raft in the middle of the ocean – I couldn't touch any of them! Only a moron hung out in a place like this. I was starting to feel pretty dumb about it all, so I figured it was time to go.

Me and Rocco got up and left. On the way out I glanced back at the two lap girls. They were not happy. They had sat with us for over an hour and all they got were a couple of drinks. These girls wanted *money.* But no one wanted to buy what they were selling. There were a lot of different jobs in this world but everyone needed to be useful in some way. You either figured out how to do your job or you did something else. No one liked a lucky beaver.

Purple Day

I was drunk. I had downed a bunch of tequila trying to figure out what was at the end of the universe and I was at a loss. I just didn't know. If there was a wall then what was after the wall? And if there was no wall then how did *that* work? Thinking about all of this made my head hurt, so I wound up drinking the entire bottle.

I was in the bathroom standing in front of the mirror. And that was when the realization hit me – I was awesome! And I was me! I was awesome because I was me! And life was all about me. People did not understand me. And how could they?! I was me. And they were not me. It was *impossible* for them to know what it was like to be me. They did not have the faintest fucking clue. And this was why I hated them. I was special. I was one special motherfucker. And I was about to show all these other motherfuckers just how special I was. I thought about getting a tattoo, but that meant being special without having to accomplish anything. Anyone could get a tattoo. I wasn't just some run-of-the-mill bastard drunk with the self. I was drunk for real! And I was my own kind of special. I was super special!

Suddenly, I realized what I had to do with my life. I saw it all unfold in front of me. A crowd of lunatics was chasing me down the street. They were stalking me wherever I went. "Sign this paper!" they cried. "Sign that one! Touch us!" I was going to be *amazing*. Just like Yagalooga, I was going to become a world-famous rapper.

A gallon of purple paint was sitting next to me on the counter. In a moment of mad fury, I grabbed the thing and dumped it over my head. Paint ran all down my face and body. It splattered all over the counter and floor, making a huge mess, but I didn't care. Nothing mattered. I was a purpler now! And I didn't give a damn about anything! I looked at my face in the mirror. "Aaaaaaaaaaaaaggghh!!!" I cried. "I'm bad!" Then I flexed my muscles and scowled at my own reflection. People hated me because I was purple. It made me feel good to know this.

According to scientists, humans were most racist against the color purple. Every year, the government spent billions of dollars studying this. It was important work and most of it was done at UC Berkeley. Researchers at Berkeley had dyed millions of laboratory mice purple to prove their theories, and the results were in – the purple mice all died. Then the normal mice shunned them. They were racist! And since mice acted like this, that meant humans were racist too.

Every year, the group People Eating Tasty Animals (PETA) protested the experiments. It was always a big controversy. "How can we eat these mice?" they complained. According to PETA, the dye contaminated the mice and made them unsafe for human consumption. But scientists at Berkeley rejected the charges.

"People should trust us!" they insisted. "It's perfectly natural to ingest random purple chemicals. Look at all the Gatorade people drink!" But PETA held their ground and ultimately a compromise was reached. Both parties agreed to bury the dead purple mice in a mausoleum near the school entrance. This would honor their deaths and commemorate the sacrifice they had made in the name of science. Berkeley also changed its mascot to a purpler.

There was nothing greater than being a purpler. And now I was one too! I jumped on my bike and headed for Walmart. I was covered head to toe in purple paint. It was *everywhere* – on my seat, all over the handlebars, even inside my nostrils. I was a crazy purple bastard and I was cruising down Speedway Blvd at rush hour. People were driving by and they were all yelling at me out their windows, but I ignored them. They were idiots and had no idea what it was like to be me.

I made it to the parking lot, jumped off my bike, and ran into Walmart. People were all staring at me. I knew they hated me but I didn't care. I glanced around the store. Every cashier had a microphone in case they needed to do a price check. The mics were shiny and pretty – and I had my eye on the one at cashier number seven. It was time for my big break. A star was about to be born! I grabbed the mic like I owned it and started busting rhymes.

"Oh when I get up in the morning
He's already awake
I gotta bend the motherfucker
Just to go drain the snake
He got a 'fro down below
And a helmet on top
Oh he's a one-eyed monster
But he can't see at all
Oh no he ain't got no clothes
Just a raincoat alright
And only wears the sucker
When he wants to go inside
Hates the pool, hates the cold
And don't like it outside
He wanna hide in a hole
And to go for a–"

I was just like Yagalooga! My voice was echoing throughout the entire store. Shoppers were all looking around and trying to figure out who the dope rapper was. They were amazed by my skills! I was drunk. But never before had I rhymed so well! I had never been this smooth! I was the world's greatest rapper! And I was on a roll!

But it was all about to come to a screeching halt.

"Freeze scumbag!" a man yelled.

I dropped the mic and spun around. A policeman was holding a gun and he had it pointed right at me.

"Step away from the mic!" he screamed. "No one uses that except the cashier!"

I couldn't believe the cop was interrupting me. Sure, I was drunk in public and using the important microphone without permission. But I was in the zone! This guy was a hater! I took a few steps back and then accidentally knocked over a big display of cans. The can at the top of the display fell straight down and landed on my head. "Ouch!" I cried. "Bitch." But the cop didn't even care if I was hurt. He just grabbed me and threw me in the back of his squad car.

"Okay purpler," he said, gruffly, "what's your story? You know it's illegal to use the mics here. We got a law against that. Who the hell do you think you are?"

"I-I'm special," I stammered. "Super special. And I just had to show everyone. If I don't show people I'm special, how are they supposed to know?"

The cop wasn't buying it. "Right," he said, sarcastically. "Everyone's special. That's why you all got different IDs. Now let's see yours, purpler."

I whipped out my ID and gave it to the cop. He ran the thing and got a shocked look on his face.

"You ain't even got a record, kid," he said. "What are you doin' out here? And what's this stuff you got all over you? Paint? You ain't even a real purpler! Let's get you washed up. I hate to see a good kid go bad. You got a life ahead of you. Don't ruin it by purplin'. Anyone can be special pretendin' people hate 'em. How hard is that? That's failin' without even tryin'. Hell, it's a built-in excuse for failure! Why don't you try to be special by makin' somethin' of yourself? You ever think of that, kid?"

I glanced down at my shoe and scuffed it on the floorboard nervously. Then I looked back up at the cop. "Yeah," I said, "I guess you're right, officer. I better get my act together."

The cop let me go so I hopped back on my bike and started pedaling home. While I was riding I thought about what he had said. The guy could've hauled me off to jail, but he was giving me a second chance. I decided not to blow it. My head hurt from getting hit by that can, but it felt different too. Something had changed inside of my brain. I was smarter now or something. Right then and there, I made up my mind – I was going to change my major. Medieval poetry was no good. There wasn't even *one* job for that in the real world. I decided to switch to computer science. A guy could get a job in computers! That was about all there was anymore.

And at that moment an odd new feeling began to sweep over my body. It was something I had never felt before. I just sat there confused for a while. And then I realized what this new feeling was. I felt proud. I was going to do this! I was going to show everyone I was special by making something of myself!

The Catalina Project

All of a sudden I was motivated, so I started looking for a new job on Craigslist. One ad in particular looked really good. A guy was paying people a hundred bucks an hour to wash computer monitors! The only problem was the thousand dollar application fee. I kicked myself for not having that much money in the bank. If only I had a thousand bucks, I could make millions! Life just wasn't fair. The rich got richer in this country.

I kept scanning the site and pretty soon I found another good job. The government was hiring. They needed help on something called the Catalina Project, and it was just my luck – I was the first person to answer the ad so they hired me. My buddies all gave me fist bumps when I told them about it. Government jobs were awesome! You got lots of money, didn't have to do any work, and could never be fired! I had never been so excited in my entire life. I was going to work for the government of the United States of America! And I would be working at a secret lab hidden away in the Catalina foothills.

One of the guys in HR gave me the low down on how everything worked. "Hahahahahahaha!!!" he cackled. And then he punched himself in the side of the head. "We don't actually need any new employees here at the Catalina Project! And this is exactly why we are hiring! Welcome to the team, Jack. You're gonna love it!" I scratched my noggin. I was a little confused by this guy, but I was still excited about landing such a great job.

I showed up for my first day of work the following Monday and I was raring to go. The Catalina Project was located inside of a beat up old warehouse at the base of Mt. Lemon. I stood outside the building, admiring it as I prepared to walk in. The thing was *awesome*. And it was big too. One pathetic scrawny-looking tree was lounging around all by itself near the entrance. A guy with a leaf blower was hanging out on the sidewalk and he was harassing the tree. Every time a leaf fell off of it, he powered up his tool and blew the thing out into the street. A second guy was standing on the sidewalk across the way. He had a leaf blower too. And whenever the first guy blew a leaf in his direction, he sent the thing right back at him. The two leaf blowers were busy doing battle. They spent their day driving each newly fallen leaf back and forth across the street for hours until it disintegrated, and thanks to them no one had to suffer through the indignity of stepping onto any leaves. I was just standing there admiring how clean everything was when a stray dog sauntered up to the tree, crouched down, and busted a grumpy. I stepped over the dog doo, yanked open the front door, and walked into the building.

I was a technology worker now and this was an important job. The government needed people to type URLs into browser windows all day long because if no one did this, their computers would suffer from electronic atrophy. I looked all around the building. The Catalina Project was in full force. There were thousands of workers. Millions maybe. And there were too many cubicles to count. Each cube had a guy in it and he was busy testing all the websites in the world to make sure they worked.

Everyone was in their cube working hard. The Catalina Project was humming with energy and activity, but every place had its bad apples, and one sat in the cube next to me. This guy never bothered to check any websites. He was confused about his assignment and people had all begun to grumble about it. "Fuck Prairie Dog," they complained. "All he does is convert oxygen into carbon dioxide." Making CO2 was bad for climate change. Everyone knew that. But this guy didn't even care! Every day he sat in his cube destroying the planet and rarely ever did anything else. Occasionally he scheduled a meeting to hear the sound of his own voice, but that was about it. Prairie Dog was starting to go gray and didn't have any children, so his main concern in life was the problem of extraneous noise. It drove him nuts. And from time to time, his head would pop up above the cubicle wall and he would yap in the direction of the sound.

Prairie Dog had a PhD, so the common sense had been purged from his body like the contents of my gut after too much tequila. People with no common sense were annoying! This guy couldn't even use Google. Typing things into a browser was too routine for him. Instead, he ran a program that combined the results of every search engine, took two minutes to finish, and came back with stuff worse than Google.

Next to Prairie Dog sat the Puzzler. He spent his day filling out crossword puzzles in a notebook. The Puzzler's computer had broken years ago but he had never bothered to have it fixed. Instead, he spent his day kicked back in a chair, drinking booze secretly out of a coffee cup as he learned new words. But being drunk on the job was against the rules, so he always toted around a broken breathalyzer. He stumbled into the break room one day clutching the thing. "Hellooo evyone!" he cried. "Pleashe excuuush my loquaciousneth! I haf blown anosher 0.0! Whad osher shober pershon would like to yoosh my breashalyzer to prove id workshe?"

No one took him up on the offer.

After a while I got tired of testing web addresses. It was beginning to baffle me – how could people just do this all day long?! I was bored out of my mind and was beginning to think of suicide as an escape, so I scrawled out a suicide letter on a

Post-it note. Then I jumped out of my seat and started marching around the building. This place was pure hell! It was a kind of Chinese milk torture to endure this daily nothing and I just couldn't take it anymore. Tears began to well up in my eyes and my brain started spinning out of control. Life wasn't fair! I was better than this! I was special! Where was a gun or some pills when you needed them?! I was looking everywhere, desperately trying to find some high place to jump from. And then I saw *it* – some workers were repainting the hallway, and a gallon of purple paint was lying on the floor! I grabbed the thing and lifted it up to my mouth. I was all set to guzzle it but, right at that moment, a man walked by and wanted to talk. "Hi," he said. "Do you have the time?" The guy was wearing a pair of thick glasses. They were *so* thick he could barely see, and it was just my luck – he was bored too! He wanted someone to talk to. I was really happy, but then I realized that something was wrong with him. This guy wasn't normal like me. He was the *Whisperer.* His voice was barely audible and his eyes kept darting back and forth as he spoke. He had several long antennas sprouting out of what appeared to be eyebrows and each one seemed alive. This guy was old! I couldn't make heads or tails out of anything he was trying to say. He droned on and on and on. All I managed to catch was that he planned to "work another ten years" to get the "maximum possible pension."

I decided not to kill myself that day. I wound up walking back to my desk, and on the way there I thought about things. The leaf blowers, Prairie Dog, Puzzler, and Whisperer all seemed to like it here. People all wanted to do the easiest thing and then they hated themselves and wanted to die. Being a government employee was awesome. It was so great that I walked into the boss's office and quit. "Please stay!" he begged me. "If you leave we'll lose money for next year's budget. And then I won't be as important. I'll give you a raise! Two hundred grand a year! I can't pay an intern any more than that!" It was a lot of money. But there was no price for torture. I turned in my badge, grabbed my backpack, and took off running as fast as I could. It was easy to be lazy but I'd had enough. Stuff that seemed good at the moment had a way of turning out bad. And stuff that seemed bad at the moment had a way of turning out good in the long run. A piece of broccoli was lying on the ground. I picked the thing up and looked it over. "Mmm..." I grimaced. And then I popped it into my mouth.

Coasting

People had all kinds of different ideas for coasting. In high school Psycho Steve liked to ride his skateboard down Saint Hill. It was steep and had a stop sign at the bottom, but Psycho Steve liked to coast right on through. There wasn't usually much traffic, but one day a car was coming and it didn't have time to stop.

Psycho Steve missed the car, but he had to jump off his board to avoid being killed. He hit the ground and tore himself up pretty good. The next time I saw him, his body was one big scab – with two holes for his eyes. Some guys liked to coast by rolling blind.

I was overconfident in second semester calculus last year and the first test was a review of the first semester. I had already secretly memorized the material once, so I figured I knew it all and didn't bother to study. I was just planning to coast right on through. Well, I bombed that test and wound up playing catch up the rest of the semester. Being too cocky was no way to coast either.

Coasting reminded me of my Uncle Joe Bob. One time when I was little, Joe Bob was standing in Grandma Inhofe's living room – he was going commando in a pair of overalls and holding a forty-ouncer of beer.

"Boys," he said, "there's three things that's important in life."

"Really, Joe Bob?" we asked. "What are they?"

"Well boys," he said, "I'm glad you asked. The three important things is eatin', shittin' and sleepin'. You gotta coast along to git along. Don't do nuthin' too hard."

After that Grandma gave Joe Bob some money to go gambling and buy a hooker. Then she picked up where he had left off.

"Your Uncle Joe Bob is right, boys," she said. "There *is* three important things in life – three things you need to do when you is young if you wanna coast. And you gotta get you some speed up. Coastin' at zero miles per hour is called stalled."

We all looked at each other. "What are they, Grandma?" we asked. "What are the three things?"

"Boys," she said, "the first important thing is studyin'. If you don't study hard when you is young, you'll wind up old and stupid. And that'll prob'ly make you depressed. It's also a little known fact that once you turn thirty, your brain is what scientists call *full*. You can still learn things. But when you do, it pushes out other stuff that's already inside your head. Sometimes that old information is somethin' important like your name or one of the twenty gazillion passwords we all gotta memorize. It might even be somethin' you just learned the day before! And then you gotta learn it all over again! You gotta get a good education before your brain is full."

"Wow," we said.

"If you do important thing number one and get a good education, then you're on track for important thing number two. You gotta get you a good job so you can get some self-respect. And makin' a little money don't hurt none neither. When you're young, bosses are willin' to give you a chance. They know you got the capability to learn. But once them gray hairs start poppin' out, people get a little more reluctant. They know all about the *full* thing."

"Tell us more!" we cried.

"Boys, one reason makin' money's important is because a snowball picks up more snow when you roll it from the top of a hill. It gets bigger and bigger and can be pretty nice by the time it hits the bottom. But once you're over-the-hill like me, things is different. If you start a snowball too close to the bottom, it won't ever pick up alotta speed, and you ain't never gonna get alotta snow. It's sad to say, but snow will get you some respect when you're old. It can ruin you, too, if that's all you care about."

"What's important thing number three, Grandma?" we asked. "Tell us!"

"Well, if you do important things one and two, you got a good chance at number three. You gotta find you a permanent hookup. In the olden days we called this *marriage*. Men and women balance each other out and kids keep everyone from gettin' selfish and bein' bored. Chasin' skirts in a casino ain't no kinda life. You don't wanna have no regrets. Time marches on and before long you'll be cuttin' your toenails with a saw. It's tough to find a girl when you're old and penniless and stupid. Hair even starts to grow out your ears at some point. That's a sign to the world that you're no longer available for procreation."

"Wow Grandma," we said. "Are you available for procreation?"

Grandma burst out laughing. "Hell no!" she cried. "I done procreated all y'all! I finished up a long time ago!"

Golden Corn

Great-grandpa Inhofe lived to be 136 years old. He died when I was little. Great-grandpa was a pretty normal guy except for one thing – he had a robot arm. His real arm had been severed in a horrible accident and for a long time he just walked around with one arm. But technology kept advancing and Great-grandpa kept saving up money, so eventually he was able to buy the new arm.

When Great-grandpa was young he used to work in a cornfield every day. That was all they had back then – corn. It was just about the only thing that existed on earth. Since there was nothing but corn, people didn't have much to do. They spent all their time shucking corn and everyone used to fight over which row in the cornfield was the best to work in. Great-grandpa lost a lot of teeth in corn fights. And this was how he lost his arm too. A guy sawed it off with a corn saw during a big brawl. This happened when he was trying to grab the *golden* corn. People said that every cornfield had one ear made of pure gold and there was always a big battle to find it. A lot of men lost limbs in this quest and some even lost their lives. Families were ruined. And sometimes a guy burned down an entire field when he couldn't find the golden ear. The funny thing, though, is that this all ended up being a myth. It turned out that there was no such thing as golden corn – it didn't even exist! People finally figured this out one day and then they all felt really dumb.

Big Game

It was the biggest game Arizona football had ever had. We were 14-0 and were facing Arizona State in the national championship game. ASU was having a great year too. They were 13-1. Whoever won today would be crowned champion. Everyone was super excited. All Arizona had to do was win *one more game*.

The last time Arizona won it all was in the year 13 BC. We *always* lost the important games. But today was the big day. Everyone was pumped up and things were going to be different this time. No way would Arizona blow it. The atmosphere in the stadium was electric and people were all yelling and screaming as we jumped out to a huge lead. Our quarterback was throwing touchdown after touchdown and we were up 57-3 at halftime! People in the crowd were all jumping up and down, high-fiving each other, and spilling beer in gleefully anticipation of victory. Everyone knew we were going to win. We were the best team ever.

But then the second half began.

I looked at the ASU mascot down on the field. It was a devil holding a pitchfork. Arizona State was the most evil university in the entire country. All of a sudden an ominous feeling came over me. Evil always triumphed when you let down your guard. I looked around. People were celebrating too soon. A sick feeling deep in my gut told me that Arizona was going to lose again.

I looked at our defense down on the field. The players were all spread out. Arizona had begun to play the dreaded "prevent defense." This was the strategy a team adopted when they stopped playing to win and instead decided to play not to lose. The goal of the prevent defense was to let the other team get fifteen yards on every play until they scored a touchdown. Then you punted the ball back to them and let them do it again. Everything had been great in the first half. The team was aggressive and we were playing to win. Since that had worked so well, the coach decided to switch things up. Now Arizona was playing not to lose!

The second half was a complete reversal of the first. Arizona State reeled off eight straight touchdowns and won the game 58-57. Their quarterback dived into the end zone for the final score as time ran out. Then he spiked the ball and started dancing around. After that ASU fans poured out onto the field and began to celebrate. It was the greatest comeback in college football history. Even the devil mascot got into the act. A kitten was walking innocently on the sidelines. He stabbed the thing with his pitchfork and started roasting it over a fire.

All told, it was the most crushing defeat in Arizona history. I was standing there, stunned, with my mouth hanging open. But then everything started to make sense – this was just how life worked. You never knew what was coming next. The momentum could change at any moment so you had to stay focused. And you couldn't ever let your foot off the gas. One extra-long blink was all it took to invite a good punch. In this world you could either play to win, or you could play not to lose. Sometimes things didn't go your way, but the next day was a new day and the next year was a new year. Arizona had a lot of good players coming back and we were ranked number one in the super extra early preseason poll. I thought about it. Next year was Arizona's year! No one could stop us. We were the best team in the country. And we were going to win it all!

Interview

I was majoring in computer science now and wanted to get an internship at a software company, so I went on another job hunt. I decided to be a little more discerning this time around. I looked and looked and after a while I found a company that was hiring. It was the place that made all the cool stuff – Super Good Technology. I applied for a position as a software engineer and a few days later they called me in for an interview. I couldn't believe how lucky I was!

On the day of the interview, I went to the HR department and checked in. Then I glanced around the building. The place was really high tech with a lot of bright lights and shiny things. There were screens everywhere. The same video was on every screen and it was playing over and over again. I didn't have anything else to do so I sat down and started watching it. A confident man was talking in the video. "We are Super Good Technology!" he boasted. "We make people happy! We do stuff! We make people's lives better!" Then a pretty girl held up a blinking object and caressed it in front of the camera. It was not clear what the thing did but it sure was shiny. "No one can make Blinkies like we do," she cooed. After that it cut to a scene of people beating each other over the head at a store. They were all trying to be the first one to buy a Blinkie.

Eventually a lady came out and greeted me. She took me on a long walk down to the interview room. On the way there we passed a giant wall-sized screen, and on that screen a message was flashing repeatedly. "Don't settle for good!" it cried. "Be super good!!!"

After the giant screen, we passed through an area where everyone was talking on a headset. This was the customer service department, and it was a good thing customers couldn't see who they were talking to. Every manner of freak had been given a job! There were people who could barely even dress themselves. And everyone's backbone seemed to have gone out. Guys were all slouching around and doing their best to look like gangsters. Some wore jeans that were way too tight – my balls hurt at the sight of it – and others had on ridiculously saggy pants. Plus none of them were sporting a belt! Instead, each sagger had one hand dedicated to his waist to keep his pants from falling off. Girls were dressed as scantily as possible, so boobs kept popping out at me from every direction. It was a crazy scene. One girl was practically naked. She dropped a pen on purpose, then bent over to pick it up and checked to make sure I was watching. Some people were a hundred pounds overweight, and some a hundred underweight. Others were so big they looked like balloons. Soda and empty pizza boxes littered the hallway and every person was inked up to their neck in bad unoriginal tattoos. Tats seemed to be a sort of unspoken requirement for the job. A kid in the back had the Superman symbol stamped on his forehead. I glanced at him. His head was tilted back and he was glaring at me with the look of death.

We made it past the circus and arrived at the interview room. Then the lady had me sit down and took off. A few minutes later an important-looking man walked in. He was the manager. And he had a set of shifty eyes on him.

"Where did you tell your boss you were going today?" he asked, hoping to catch me in a lie.

I looked at him, puzzled. "I don't actually have a job right now," I said. "I'm here for the internship."

This seemed to fluster him. He looked down at my resume for a moment and tried to recover. Then he stood up. "Okay!" he cried. "We'll have someone in here to interview you in a minute." After that he walked out.

Next a woman with messy hair entered the room. She looked about forty and didn't seem to know where she was. Her palms were facing up and she was shrugging, but I knew she was in the right place. With one glance I could tell she was a software engineer. She just had that *look*. Things were inside of her brain but she didn't know how to express them to others. All she knew about was techie world. Suddenly I was interested. What was this strange and mysterious world that techies lived in? I was curious and wanted to find out more. The woman located a chair and sat down. "I don't know why they're having me interview you!" she blurted out. "I've only been here two weeks!" She didn't have any questions for me either. Instead we just talked about life at college.

After the unprepared woman left, a guy walked in. He was younger than her but with a few gray hairs and an intense air. The guy sat down and asked me some coding questions. I bombed the answers badly, not even getting one right. After a few of these he took pity on me. "You know," he said matter-of-factly, "you don't want to work here. This place sucks green donkey dicks."

It was the funniest thing I had ever heard!

The guy started slapping his knee and hooting like an owl. And I was just dying. I fell off my chair and landed on the floor, clutching my gut. A tear was rolling down my cheek. "Hahahahahahaha!" I cried. "A donkey! With a green dick!

And someone sucks it!" The thought of a donkey with a green shlong was funny enough. But someone blowing it was more than I could take. Neither one of us could stop cracking up, but a few minutes later I managed to get it together and climb back up onto the chair. We had stopped laughing but were both still smiling from ear to ear. Next we started talking about football. We were both excited about how good Arizona was supposed to be next year and spent the rest of the interview talking about it. Once we were finally done, the guy took me down the hall to see the most important person of all – the director.

I walked in and met the guy. Right away I could tell that something was very wrong. The man's spirit had died a long time ago, but his body was still alive. His eyes were like a dead dog I had seen once on the road in Mexico. And it barely seemed to register that someone new was nearby. Even a mannequin had more life than this guy! He shook my hand with a lifeless grip and then I gave him my resume. The man held it in his palm as if it were a type of strange and rare artifact from a museum. He just didn't know what to do with it. Finally he brought me into a room and decided to read through it line by line as he proceeded to verify each and every word. What was my title at this job? What did I do at that one? My first thought was that *he too* was trying to catch me in a lie. But that wasn't it. This was all the poor bastard had left.

After meeting the director, I was taken into yet another room and asked to wait. A few minutes later a man walked in. "Hey kid," he said. "I'm from HR. We gonna hiah youz. Waddayou say, kid? You wan' da fuckin' jawb or wot?"

I wasn't expecting the guy to swear so I was a little surprised. "Uh, y-yeah," I stuttered. "I wanna be a software engineer."

"You gonna be like de uddaz, kid?" he asked, looking me over. "Lemme tell youz about sumpin'. Life? It's like washin' youz hands. Some guys use soap. Dat woiks. But udda guys don' use no soap. Dey only wash wit' wodda. Well, dat don' kill no goims. It ain't nuttin' bud a show! And some guys – dey don' wash nuttin'! Dey don' give a rat's ass! Well, we gad alodda fuckin' schmucks wawkin' aroun' heah. Dey wawk real fast...all tryin' a look good...but dey don' do no woik. You know wad I'm tawkin' about? We don' need no soap."

"What's *woik*?" I asked. I couldn't understand the guy.

"You know, kid," he said. "Woik! When youz doin' stuff."

"Oh," I said. "*Work*. Yeah, I wanna work."

"Dats good, kid," he said. "But I'll believe dat when I fuckin' sees it, a'ight? Hey, I gad some pichaz fah youz tah loog at too." Then he pointed at a screen full of workplace mugshots. "You see deze sons of bitches?"

"Yeah," I said. "I see 'em. Who are they?"

"You don' know deze sons of bitches," he said. "But youz gonna know 'em. Deze is da sons of bitches youz gadda tawk to *every* fuckin' day you woik. Deze is youz cowoikaz. You don' tawk to 'em, dey gonna hate you. Dats how dey think. You gad it?

"Yeah," I said. "Okay. What else?"

"I'm glad you asked, kid," he said. And then he brought up another set of mugshots. "You see *d*eze sons of bitches?"

"Yeah sure," I said. "I see 'em."

"*Deze*," he said, "is da sons of bitches you gadda know if youz wanna ged anywheah."

"You mean I'm supposed to suck up to 'em?" I asked.

"Nah kid," he said. "Don' think like dat. It' like dis – you like goils, right?"

"You mean, girls?" I said. "Yeah sure. I like girls."

"Goils got da goods, right?" he said. "And dey like tah heah a guy tawkin', don' dey? Dey don' wanna be aroun' nobody too quiet. Da bosses is like dat too. Dey got da goods *too*. So dey don' approach nobody neithah – unless dey gadda problem. You gadda come at dem if you wanna ged anywheah. You gad it?"

"Okay," I said. "I think I got it. Thanks for all the tips."

"No fuckin' problem, kid," he said. "We'll see youz on Monday."

Sneeze War

I started working part-time at Super Good Technology. I sat in a cubicle inside a maze of cubicles. And the walls of each cube were just high enough that no one could see over the top. Everyone got used to the privacy and as a result people did not want anyone to see them. So if you walked by a cube and glanced inside, the person got mad and barked at you with their eyes. Every dog defended a slightly different radius, though. Some only barked if you were near their property. Others guarded everything within their field of vision.

A few days later I found out about the sneeze war. There were two rival camps on the team, and they had all pretended to get along on the day of the interview, but I quickly realized they hated each other. It was just my luck. I had been thrown into the middle of a passive-aggressive battle between the Hatfields and the McCoys, and I had been preselected as a McCoy. I found out who was on which side by listening to who blessed who whenever anyone sneezed. There were several reciprocal blessing arrangements going on and no one ever blessed anyone from the opposing camp.

I decided to become a peacekeeper. Like the guy who showed up at the party carrying the keg – I would bring everyone together! I had made up my mind. I was going to break down the walls. Whenever the Hatfield Passive-Aggressive King sneezed, I tried to broker the peace. "Bless you," I told him. I blessed the other rivals, too, whenever I had a chance. I tried and tried. But it was no use. The walls of this conflict were just too high and the Hatfields all pretended not to hear me. I never got a "thanks" or even an unintelligible mumble in return. These people were unbreakable. And whenever *I* sneezed, only my own camp ever blessed me. This went on for quite a while, but then one day I sneezed and didn't hear anything at all. I was stuck in a cubicle, of course, and I couldn't see anyone, so right away my mind began to race. Had the other McCoys heard me? Or were they all wearing headphones? I got up and walked around to check it out. Secretly I peered into each cube. No one was listening to music. This seemed a bit odd. The other McCoys had all heard me sneeze but none of them had blessed me. And later on I started to feel some funny looks. The McCoy leader even eyeballed me for a half second longer than normal. His head was cocked to the side and the hamster was running on the wheel. And his eyes were barking. *I* was a sneeze traitor.

A few months later the economy cratered and the CEO was all over it. It was a golden opportunity. He had a lot of company stock and whenever he cut costs, the price of that stock went up. So he fired people in America. Then he brought in new workers from China and India. When a guy was on a visa, and you could boot him out of the country at a moment's notice, he worked pretty hard. Plus these guys liked America better than where they were from anyway, so they all worked hard. Other companies did the same thing. I still had a job but a lot of Hatfields and McCoys got laid off.

One Hatfield was Goth Girl. She had transformed her cube into a really cool looking fort. Upgrades included a tarp for a roof, black fluorescent lighting, and plastic bats hanging from strings. Sometimes people did stuff like this for Halloween. Decorating was fun. But her cube was a fort all year long and every day was Halloween. Goth Girl had a medical condition – extreme light sensitivity (ELS). Most of her kind were afflicted with this. ELS also caused her to wear black clothing and scowl. And every year she spent the month of October covering her home with giant red-eyed spiders, zombies, and bloody decapitated skulls. Then, on Halloween, she entertained children as they danced through the streets, gorging on sugar and pretending to be things they could never be.

Another victim was the Passive-Aggressive King. He liked to fight with people – but never to their face. One of his targets was the Hundred-Year-Old Lady. She was a McCoy. The Hundred-Year-Old Lady liked to sit out in the sun and never drank anything but vodka, so as a result her face looked like cracked mud. The old lady had the inside scoop on an affair the King was having. She had seen him kissing Goth Girl and he was worried about what she might do with this information. So, in a preemptive strike, he went to HR and made up a story about her not doing her job. People in HR were smart. They were experts at working with other humans, so to resolve the conflict they put the two people who hated each other into a room together and tossed in a mediator. This would allow them to work out their differences. The sessions went on for several weeks and, for some reason, they weren't making any progress. No one could convince the old lady she wasn't working. One day, however, there was a big breakthrough. The Hundred-Year-Old Lady found herself alone in the parking lot with the King after a session, so she got up in his face. "If you make up one more story about me," she said, "I'm going to kill you. And then I'm going to pour vodka all over your body, set it on fire, and bury it with the others."

She never had any problems after that. HR noticed that the two of them were getting along better, so they canceled the rest of the sessions. Super Good Technology was quick to recognize excellence, so the mediator was promoted to VP. But the King never knew when to quit. He kept causing trouble so eventually he wound up holding a box.

Some McCoys lost their jobs too. The Juggler bit the dust. He was a congenial fellow and most of the time his face was stretched from ear to ear in a ridiculous grin. But the poor bastard just hated to do work. It crushed his spirit. So he spent his time hanging out in the hall, tossing objects into the air and catching them. But according to rumor, a juggling employee was an embarrassment to the boss, and some things were a little too obvious to have to explain. People got butt hurt when they heard the truth anyway, so it was easier just to pretend that everyone was perfect until layoff day. Sure enough, that day came and the Juggler got yanked off stage. A lot of people wound up holding boxes.

There seemed to be a weird two step process for keeping your job. The first step was to not act crazy. You had to figure out how to get along with your coworkers. This was America and lots of people were crazy, so the bosses liked to keep as many normals around as possible to balance everything out. It made their life easier. Step one was complicated but step two was even worse. You had to figure out how to do your job. And when you were supposed to get something done, you had to find some way to do it. Sometimes people even figured this out before the boss had to tell them! It was some kind of odd requirement to get promoted. All of this stuff was a big eye-opener for me. I had always thought I would get money just for being special and that everyone would recognize this. But that wasn't how the real world worked. Other people didn't get it – they all thought that *they* were special too! And companies didn't have infinite money to pay people for doing nothing. Everything I used to think was wrong. The world was a crazy place and somehow I still had a job. I wound up getting transferred to a new team.

Coffee Table

I was knocking on the front door at Uncle Sal's house when I realized something was wrong. Sal had a dog and normally the thing barked its head off at the slightest sound. But today I was standing at the door and there was nothing. I stood there waiting. A few more seconds passed and then Sal finally opened up the door.

"Hey Jack!" he cried. "It's great to see you! Come on in!"

"Good to see you too, Sal," I said. "Where's Fido? He usually greets me at the door."

"Oh," Sal replied. He seemed down all of a sudden. "Fido's seeing his shrink today. He has a bad case of Seasonal Affective Disorder, so we decided to take him in."

"Damn," I said. "That sounds serious."

We talked for a while and then the two of us walked over to the den and sat down. Sal called this his "pimp room." It had all the latest technology and before long my eyes were wandering around, checking out his gear. Sal owned every Blinkie that Super Good Technology had ever made. I had never *seen* such an array of shiny gadgets. The room was was all lit up like the Vegas Strip. I couldn't believe it – Sal even had a TV wall. This was Super Good Technology's latest invention and people were all dying to buy one. It was a revolutionary high-tech device unlike anything anyone had ever seen. It was like a normal TV – but bigger! I couldn't take my eyes off of the thing. Lots of people were getting TV walls and now I wanted one too.

It had been a few months since the TV wall was invented. Uncle Sal was always on the cutting edge of technology, so he was one of the first people to buy one. I looked the thing over. It was *beautiful.* And it covered every inch of the wall. My mind began to drift back to the day when the TV wall was first invented. People had all run out into the street to celebrate. "This is great progress!" they cried. And now everyone was getting one. A new tax break was even created so some of the more needy people could pick one up for free. Life was better with a TV wall, and now, no matter what people were doing, they never had to miss a show.

Rich people typically had every wall in their home converted into a TV wall. This was to keep their necks from getting tired. Walking from room to room meant having to turn your neck to stay focused on the screen. It was a lot of trouble! And no one wanted to use their neck any more than they had to. Multiple TV walls were still a luxury, though, and "going multi" had resulted in some unfortunate side effects. Many wealthy people were beginning to develop Lazy Neck Syndrome (LNS) due to a lack of neck exercise. Some even had to wear neck braces and, as a result, it became a sort of status symbol to wear a brace. The supermodel Fanny Fantastico wore one. And she was on TV all the time. "Look at my br-r-r-race!" she cried, rolling her r's. "And look at my fanny too. Eet eez fantasteek!" Fanny Fantastico had been hand picked for fame by the world-renowned fashion designer Gary Gaye. She looked like a boy. Her butt was bony like a skeleton and she had two mosquito bites for boobs. This was the sexy new look. Neck braces were all the rage on the runways of Paris and Milan, but the neck brace phenomenon led to resentment among the commoners. Not everyone could afford an extra TV wall. So people with LNS were sometimes derisively referred to as "linsers."

We were still in the pimp room today and all of a sudden Uncle Sal jumped up. "Jack!" he cried. "I gotta show you something!" Then he pointed at his coffee table.

The thing was unimpressive. I looked at it and then I turned back to him. "What's so special about it?" I asked. "It's a coffee table."

And that was when Sal started that playful little game of his. He wrinkled up his brow, pretending to be confused. Then a sly grin spread across his face. "C'mon, man!" he cried. "You don't know why it's so great?! Sit down. I'll show you." I took a seat. Then Sal clicked on a button and the top of the table popped up into eating position. His sly grin was now a great big self-satisfied smile. He was very pleased with himself.

"Wow," I said. "Awesome! I usually have to wear earbuds when I'm eating to tell everyone to buzz off. But this is even better!"

Sal didn't say anything. He just stood there beaming with pride. And then all of a sudden the microwave went off.

"Hey Jack!" he yelled. "My Hot Pockets are ready. You wanna try one?"

"Sure," I said. "Hot Pockets rule!"

"They're pretty tasty alright," he said. "Only one problem..."

"What's that, Sal?" I asked. I couldn't guess what was bad about Hot Pockets.

"Well," he said, as the brow wrinkled, "I was thinking about cutting out the middleman."

I scratched my noggin. "Huh?" I said. "What do you mean?" Now I was doubly confused.

Sal pulled the Hot Pocket out of the microwave. "Damn," he griped. "It isn't even five minutes after I eat one of these things that I'm sittin' on the toilet droppin' a load. Maybe I oughta just heat 'em up and flush 'em straight down the bowl!"

"Hahahahahahahah!!!" we both laughed.

The two of us were just standing there busting up. Sal was funny. *Dumb* but funny. What kind of idiot flushed a Hot Pocket? Those things were gold. I grabbed one and sat down in front of the coffee table. Then I put my earbuds in and took a great big bite. Sal turned on the TV wall and stuffed one into his face too. I couldn't quite place my finger on it – but somehow, something seemed wrong with all of this. It reminded me of my old apartment for some reason, so I turned to Sal. "Be careful," I warned. "We used to eat on the coffee table at my old place. When we moved out, there was a huge stain in between the table and couch from all the food we spilled. We didn't even know it was there until we started dragging everything out. You never know what the side effects of eating here all by yourself might be."

Sal heard this, chuckled, and slapped me on the back. "Haw, haw, haw!" he laughed. Then he got up and went to the toilet.

Smitty's Pub

I was going to happy hour with these crazy bastards for a while. We were all coworkers at Super Good Technology and we liked to hang out at a place called Smitty's Pub.

A married couple used to show up from time to time. Their names were Dan and Jill. Dan's head was always moving back and forth like an oscillating fan, tracking every girl in the bar. He liked t-and-a so much that Jill bought him a membership at the Lucky Beaver Strip Club. This seemed like a really good idea to me. Guys all wanted to jump anything that looked good and at least Jill was smart enough to admit this. There was no way that anything could go wrong with her plan. Dan and Jill both had weight problems. Dan was alright with himself – he was your basic jolly fat guy and people liked him, but Jill wasn't handling her size very well. She tried to poke fun at herself one day. "Maternity clothes fit me," she joked. "Ha ha. It's just easier to wear them." Everyone started cracking up, but it wasn't always good to laugh at things that were funny. Jill paused for a moment in mid-laugh and shot me the look of death. I had laughed *a little too loud.*

Every once in a while you could catch a window into someone's soul with a random glance. Some people could hide what they were thinking, but others were obvious and everyone knew. Jill was sitting in the lobby at Super Good Technology one day and the green-eyed monster was out. She was looking around at skinny women with envy. It didn't make any sense! Being fat wasn't her fault. Obesity was just a great big mystery and no one really knew what caused it. A lot of scientists were trying to figure it out and there was a lot of debate. Even Donnie the Rock Star had an opinion. "Bein' fat," he said, "is caused by eatin' too much food."

A gay guy named Jordan was always at the bar. He was about thirty and for some reason had never read the manual about gay dudes being well-dressed. The guy was one sloppy-looking bastard and even had hair sticking out of his nose, but none of this seemed to matter since he never had trouble getting any action. This was just how the world worked. When a guy and a girl went out, the guy always wanted to do it. And when two guys went out, the guy always wanted to do it.

Jordan liked to brag about his adventures. He told us all about his lust for teenage boys. The guy had fling after fling and in his stories the boys had all just turned eighteen. Jordan was training the next generation and nobody seemed too worried about this or the age gap. He got a pass and everyone just accepted him as normal. America had made a lot of progress.

We were both picking up beers at the bar one day when Jordan gave me the sales pitch. "Hey Jack," he said. "You like to ride the pony, right?"

"Of course," I said, "I'm a guy."

"Well..." he said, pausing for a moment. "I know a way you can have lots of sex and less responsibilities. And you don't have to deal with women unless you feel like it."

"Wow!" I said. This sounded great. "What do I have to do?"

"Just be gay!" he cried. "Being gay is awesome! I never have to grow up!"

"Yeah..." I said. "I don't know about that." I was starting to wonder where he was going with this.

"I figured you were gay anyhow," he added. "You used to work in a coffee shop, right?"

"Huh?" I said. "So what? I like goat's milk cappuccinos. Who cares? What's so great about being gay anyway?"

Jordan gave me a serious look. "Dude," he said, "women are annoying. They have zay zay."

I was confused now. "Zay zay?" I asked. "What's that?"

"*You* know," Jordan said. "That clingy thing. It gets activated once you do them. After you nail one, they start hangin' around. It's like you owe 'em or somethin'. You gotta stay overnight after gettin' some or they cry about it. And pretty soon they want you to remember stuff like keepin' the toilet seat down and when their birthday is. Guys don't come with that same sort of emotional price tag. You know? Guys don't have zay zay. And they can't get pregnant either," he laughed. "Babies are evil!"

"I don't know about all that," I said. "I'm not into hairy asses. Maybe I'll just be a straight player. I'll sleep with one girl after another and not grow up that way."

Jordan shrugged. And just then his friend Halie walked up. She overheard my last comments.

"Jack!" she cried. "That's a terrible thing to say. You should grow up and be responsible! And who cares if Jordan likes hairy butts! It's only natural! He can't help who he is! Who are you to judge?!"

I looked at Halie. I shrugged too. Then I went back to the table. I started thinking about what Jordan had said. It was true! After you slept with a girl you had to be there for her. Girls needed that. They wanted a protector. They needed a calm rational influence in their lives and they were all looking for one guy to fill this role. But guys didn't have zay zay and we just wanted to be free. The more I thought about it all the more I realized that Jordan was right! Girls were always raining on my parade! They were always telling me I was too drunk or getting mad when I threw bottles at cars. They ruined all the fun! Being gay was awesome!

A drunk guy was sitting all by himself at a table. He had a lot of problems and was drinking himself stupid to forget. All of a sudden the booze got the best of him and he passed out – his head dropped out of the air like a brick and smacked down hard on the table top. This caused his beer to tip over. The table wasn't level, so I watched as the beer dribbled slowly off the thing and onto the floor. The path of least resistance was amazing! It was great for any kind of liquid. Anything that was super squishy and formless would always follow the easiest path and was bound to end up somewhere low.

Jordan was usually hanging around with Halie. She was always drinking, smoking, and wearing a cynical face. When I first met her she was a hot twenty-five-year-old blonde with a giant rack. And she always had it on display in some sort of tight top. Her tits were huge! They were so big it was like a couple of midgets were hiding out under there. Guys were always drooling all over her, but by the time she was twenty-seven she looked beat up. She started complaining about getting used and, to make things worse, Jordan would break in mid-story and razz her about the "expiration date" on her eggs.

A guy named Randy was the manager when I first started. He had jack-o'-lantern teeth and a ponytail with a bald spot in the middle. He also had a habit of complaining about the job and talking smack about his own employees. According to Jordan, Randy was from the Mickey Mouse School of Leadership. I didn't even know Disney *had* a leadership school. But I doubt it's very good because Randy wound up having to step down.

Randy was giving another guy a bad time about being from Alabama one day. I considered this for a moment. It didn't make any sense! Randy was from West Virginia and this was the number one place to harass people about being from. So I started busting on him for the West Virginia thing. Randy didn't like it. And pretty soon he had a big old constipated look on his face. Randy could dish it out but he couldn't take it. No one liked a guy like that. One of the most important things about being a guy was knowing when to dish it out and when to take it.

A younger kid used to hang out with us. His name was Justin and he was barely old enough to walk through the door. This kid wasn't pretty so Jordan didn't like him. He had bright red hair, was pale as a ghost, and sported eyes smaller than any Asian. But he was an absolute genius and could operate a computer without even touching it, just by using his mind. The kid was only good with gadgets, though. He was just too nice. Girls didn't like him and he didn't seem to have a masculine bone in his entire body. Despite all of this, he managed to find a girlfriend. Justin lost his virginity almost a decade later than some kids. There was snickering behind his back, but I guess whoever laughs last, laughs the loudest. He showed us pics of the girl. She was cute and at first glance seemed normal, so I looked closer, trying to figure out what was wrong. But I just couldn't put my finger on it. The young ones didn't like guys who were too easy. They liked bastards. And the bigger the bastard, the better. So I was just totally confused. I never did figure that one out.

Me and Justin worked with a middle-aged guy called Fabian. He was the team lead. Fabian was forty-two but still acted like a kid. The guy was pretty kooky and was always telling us that growing up was bad. "I like bein' young," he said one day. "It's awesome. Bein' responsible sucks!" This confused me because Fabian's hair started at the top of his head and he had wrinkles around his ears to show where his face used to be. I didn't know who he was talking about.

Fabian helped me move one day. He found out I needed a hand and offered his services out of the blue. "Dude!" he cried. "I'm there! I'll see you tomorrow!" But the next day came and Fabian was nowhere to be found. He had seemed really gung ho, so I gave him a call. It went straight to voicemail. He never called back or showed up, so the next time I saw him I had to ask what had happened. "Oh dude," he moaned, "I was just too tired to lift my body out of bed that day. I was lying there promising myself I would answer the phone – if only you called one more time." Fabian liked to commit to things and then decide later on if he would actually do them. He wanted to keep his options open.

Me and Fabian were hired the same day. He started off at work like a house on fire. But after a while things got tough and he gave up. Before long he was coming in stoned and spending all his time trading stocks online. Fabian was like most potheads – he didn't think anyone noticed the red eyes or delayed reaction time. He thought he had us all fooled. The guy was pushing his luck, but even this level of slacking wasn't enough for him. Fabian couldn't finish any of his work but was relentless in pushing the limits of what others would tolerate. I was thinking about this when, all of a sudden, I realized something – Fabian's bad boy chip had never been deactivated! And the U of A library was still trying to hire a porn surfer! I told Fabian about the job but for some reason he didn't seem interested. He just kept pushing his luck at work, doing his best to get fired. A few months passed and then he wasn't even at his desk most of the time. No one knew where he was, and for a long time nobody even seemed to care. But after Randy stepped down, a new manager took over the team, and he couldn't understand why one of his employees was stoned all the time, didn't do any work, and was nowhere to be found. He took Fabian into his office and put him on a performance improvement plan, but Fabian quit on the spot. A few months later his wife gave him the boot too.

Mel was a guy who showed up from time to time. He was about forty, too, and always came across like a punching bag. But as soon as you took one hit without defending yourself, more were sure to come. Even guys who weren't naturally sharks would lay into him. Mel also wasn't very familiar with the female anatomy. We found out about this one day when Randy posed a question to the group.

"How many orifices does a woman have below the waist?"

Mel was quick to answer. "Two!" he cried. After that an awkward silence filled the room. He was the father of three children.

Even Jordan knew this one. "Five!" he shouted. And then we all started busting up.

Word got out that Randy was getting married, and everyone was excited because this meant a chance to go to a strip club. Except for the Internet and other strip clubs, this was the last time Randy would ever see random naked women. So it was a special day. We all grabbed him, piled into Mel's SUV, and hit the Lucky Beaver. Once we were inside a group of strippers set Randy up on a chair at center stage and started dancing around him in a circle. The girls were really excited, but one was a little *too* pumped up. She was standing in front of Randy, dancing and shaking her boobs as fast as she could when one of them exploded. The breast implant fell out and plopped down onto the floor at the edge of the stage. The thing was just lying there and for a moment no one knew what to do, but as luck would have it one of the girls was a quick thinker. She picked the thing up, dusted it off, and handed it to Randy as a souvenir. Then the crowd cheered and the show went on. We stayed at the Lucky Beaver for a couple of hours. Mel was sitting way up front and he was having the time of his life. He kept paying for dance after dance, and before long he had dropped a few hundred bucks. Shortly after this his wife left him and became a lesbian.

Cato was an old guy who made an appearance every once in a while. He had a pot belly and liked to wear tight t-shirts. It was not a good look. But Cato did not seem to know this. He liked to tell everyone that he had been a surfer back in the day and he still had a habit of throwing around the "hang loose" sign. To do this, he stuck his pinky and thumb out and wiggled them back and forth in rapid motion. And whenever he did the sign, he got a look on his face that said "I am cool." Cato was married but spent most of his time hitting on old ladies. His favorite trick was to send a drink over to a woman he had his eye on. The cocktail waitress would point him out as the admirer and then he would wink in her direction. And Cato liked to be as obvious as possible when he did all of this. He opened the eye as wide as it could possibly go and then squeezed it shut with pure brute force. Crow's feet spread out across his temple and the head usually wobbled a bit. It was all pretty comical and he appeared to be in pain more than anything else. Worse yet – this was the only move Cato had. He was always lounging around at Smitty's, buying drinks for older women and working his crow wink.

Scientists liked to perform experiments on rats. One involved hooking a rat up to electrodes and stimulating the pleasure center of its brain when it pushed a button. This sounded like fun, but the button only dished out pleasure hits at random. And the random thing wound up being the key. The rats turned hedonistic. They just couldn't control themselves. Rats were always looking for a new hit of pleasure and would keep on pushing the button over and over again, hoping to get more.

Options

I was sitting in a chair at a fancy chain restaurant with Bobbie Sue and Sarah. This place was top of the line. I could tell by all the random stuff that was nailed to the walls. Random stuff meant quality and the more stuff a restaurant had, the better the food tasted. I looked all around – there were street signs, lots of old pictures, and even an anvil. The anvil was dangling from the ceiling above some unknowing guests in the lobby.

I checked out the special of the day – processed chicken sautéed in MSG. Right away I started licking my lips. I was ready to order and so was Sarah, but Bobbie Sue was having trouble deciding. He just couldn't make up his mind, and who could blame him? The menu was fourteen pages long! It was dripping with adjectives and chock full of exciting pictures. Having too many options was kind of like jumping off a third floor balcony. You would probably live but the experience was likely to paralyze you. The waitress kept coming back to our table, trying to get us to order, and finally after her third attempt, Bobbie Sue picked out a dish.

While we were waiting for our food, Bobbie Sue told us the story of how he and Sarah had met. Bobbie Sue was born a man but deep down had always felt he was a woman. So he had an operation. The surgeon got rid of the hotdog, carved in a clam, and tacked on a couple of headlights. That made Bobbie Sue a woman. But after a while she got tired of being a woman. Bobbie Sue was fed up with feeling crampy and complaining all the time, so she had another operation. The surgeon took back the headlights and plugged up the clam, but no one had remembered to save the hotdog, so he attached a utilitarian apparatus in its place. A team of medical technicians from the University of California at Berkeley designed the apparatus. Then the surgeon stapled it on to where the clam had been. After that Bobbie Sue was a man again.

Sarah was one of the nurses at the hospital where Bobbie Sue had the operation. Her job was to make sure the utilitarian apparatus worked correctly. She kept on with her assignment after Bobbie Sue was discharged and shortly after that they were married.

Bobbie Sue and Sarah were a normal couple – they didn't see eye to eye on anything. The only thing they could agree on was that they both wanted to split up, and today was the big day. The divorce was final. Bobby Sue was so excited – he was free! After one last dinner together, he and Sarah were each planning to head off to separate divorce parties to celebrate their newfound freedom.

Our food arrived. We wolfed it down since the waitress was giving us a hurry-up look, and then we all prepared to go our separate ways. Bobbie Sue gave Sarah one final kiss goodbye. After that he turned and started to stroll towards the lobby. A tear began to roll down my cheek. People thought divorce was easy – but they were wrong! Quitting took guts! And Bobby Sue was just ballsy enough to pull this off. I stood there with joy in my heart, watching him as he took the first few steps of an exciting new life. One day he would find the *perfect* person. Every American was destined to find their soulmate – a lackey who did everything for them. I imagined the beautiful future Bobbie Sue had ahead of him and I couldn't contain my enthusiasm. "Go get 'em, Bobby Sue!" I cried. "Break a leg!" And at that very moment, the anvil broke loose from where it was hung in the lobby. I looked up in horror. It was falling fast. The thing was headed straight for Bobbie Sue! Sarah saw it too and her face was gripped with terror. "Bobbie Sue!" she cried. "Watch out!!!" He stopped in his tracks and looked up. And just as he did, the anvil smashed into his face and brought him down. The impact caused a cotton gin to fall off of a nearby wall. The thing crashed to the floor and crushed Bobby Sue's leg. Everyone in the restaurant was shocked. People all wanted to do something to help, but it was already too late – blood was beginning to gurgle out of Bobby Sue's skull. He was dead. And his leg was broken too.

Several days later, the funeral was held. But in the interim, Bobbie Sue's secret diaries were discovered. And in the latest entries, he had changed his mind again and decided that he wanted to be a woman. So the surgeon was called back. He chopped off the utilitarian apparatus, remade the clam, and inserted the headlights back into where they rightfully belonged. Bobbie Sue was a woman again. And that is how she was laid to rest. All was right with the world.

The Man Who Hated People

I decided to help Jay and Lisa move. Jay was a really smart guy and Lisa was pregnant. The two of them had recently made the decision to start a life together, so they were moving from an apartment into a house. Jay didn't want to get married just yet, though. He was keeping his options open since it was always possible to meet a hotter girl, and being married made this more complicated.

Old school dudes always did stuff in a certain order. They found a good job, got married, bought a house, and had a baby – but no one knew why! Nobody knew why the order mattered. It was just dumb. Keeping your options open made the holidays a lot more exciting. You got to visit all the half-cousins and the step-grandpa. And every year a new relative popped out of the woodwork.

Lisa was really organized about the move. She was emailing people for weeks in advance to see who would lend a hand. They seemed to really need the help so I signed up.

The day came and about half the people showed up. We made a few trips back and forth in a U-Haul and then stopped off at a storage unit. I went along with Jay for this. Somehow he managed to forget the key, though, so the two of us wound up sitting outside the unit as we waited for Lisa to bring it back. And this was when Jay told me about his philosophy for life. "Man," he complained, "I hate people." Right away I started scratching my head. *People* were helping Jay move. Because of this, I figured he would like people, but then I realized something – Jay was talking in opposite language! He didn't actually mean that he hated people. What he really meant to say was "people hate me." He had done many things in his life to irritate others, and because of this they did not like him. Next Jay let me know about his plan to stay at home with the baby while Lisa worked. "I got my own company!" he bragged. "I'm sellin' shades and blinds. I buy stuff wholesale, jack up the price, and pay Mexicans to install it. Once I start rakin' in the dough I'm gonna put the baby in daycare and watch football all day." I wasn't so sure about his business plan or the idea for the baby. A baby was a crazy, screaming blob that needed attention 24/7. And if you didn't give the thing love, it would grow up and eat you.

I tried to help Jay get his business started. "Hey," I said, "you want my grandma's number? She's thinking about getting some new blinds."

"Great," he replied. "I'm on the Internet. She can send me her info online. Just google Jay's Blinds."

I got online later and found the site, but it didn't look very professional and there was even a typo on the homepage. Instead of "Jay's Blinds," it said "Jay's Blind." I entered Grandma's contact info and hit the submit button. Then the page exploded. It puked up a whole bunch of random characters all over the screen.

We moved a lot of stuff for Jay and Lisa that day and by sundown everyone was beat. So we all headed home. Jay promised to have us over for beer and pizza later on as a thank you, but that was the last I ever heard of it. He washed out as a stay-at-home dad. The guy was more of a stay-at-home nothing. The baby spent most of its time in daycare and Jay never made any money. Then one day he found himself in a suit standing in front of a judge. Lisa was raking him over the coals for child support, so now he was forced to find some kind of job. It was a little rough but at least he will always have an exciting time over the holidays.

Boss

Joey was standing on top of the Gould-Simpson building at the University of Arizona. He had been kidnapped and blindfolded by the terrorist group

GWASHASOD. Their leader was a masked man who went by the name of Antonio. He had jet black hair and a big mole on the side of his face, and he always dressed in black. Most people hated GWASHASOD, but not everyone was against them. Some people actually supported their cause.

Antonio was standing behind Joey. He was holding a dagger with one hand and twirling his mustache with the other. "Will you kill yourself, Joey?" he asked calmly. "Or do I have to do it for you?"

"Wha-what?!" Joey cried. "Why me?! What did I do?"

"Joey," Antonio said, "you were at the company party just now, weren't you?"

"Y-yeah," Joey replied. "What about it? Wh-why does that matter?"

"And," Antonio continued, "you said your wife was your boss, right?" As Antonio said this he poked Joey softly with the dagger to show he meant business.

"Ow!" Joey cried. "I d-did. People always laugh when I do that. So what?"

"Well, Joey," Antonio said, "I am from the group called Guys Who All Still Have A Shred Of Dignity. It's a long name. I know. But you can just call us GWASHASOD."

"Wh-what?!" Joey cried. "What are you saying?"

"Joey," Antonio said, "every time we find a guy who says his wife is his boss, we kidnap him and make him kill himself."

"Oh no!" Joey cried. "I've heard of you guys! Please don't gwash me! I want to live!"

"So," Antonio continued, "how do you want to die? Will you commit hari-kiri with this dagger? Do you want to jump off the building? Or do I have to push you? Are you even a man?"

Joey was stunned. He just stood there for a moment considering his options. Joey was like everyone else. He didn't want to die. But after thinking things over he realized that his shame was just too great. The only way to make up for all the emasculating jokes was by dying some kind of honorable death. Joey took the dagger from Antonio. Then he steeled his gaze and plunged the thing into his own mid-section. "Aaaaaaaagghh!!!" he cried. Blood began to stain his shirt and he crumpled to the ground in a heap. Joey moaned and twitched around for a few minutes and then he was dead. Hari-kiri was one of the most painful ways to die. But enduring this type of death allowed Joey to restore his good name. Gould-Simpson was even renamed the Joey building in his honor.

After Joey was finally dead, Antonio smiled. He looked like a father doling out tough love. And just then his cell phone rang. "Antonio!" cried the voice on the other end. "We have another one! His name is Jeff. He was drinking a frappuccino at Starbucks..."

Crosswalk Syndrome

Me and Zozo lived in an apartment near U of A and to get to class we had to cross a busy street, so we always used the crosswalk. Whenever we were walking in the thing, Zozo took his sweet time, and while we were strolling along he liked to bitch and moan. "Those bastard cars better stop!" he complained. "'Cause we're in the crosswalk and we're special!"

Sometimes we drove down that same street in Zozo's car. And whenever we got near the crosswalk Zozo started to whine if people were in it. "Those suckers better move!" he griped. "I don't have all day!" It was amazing how long some people took to cross the street.

Cool Old Queefer

Fabian gave me a call. "It's my 43rd birthday!" he cried. "Let's meet for lunch! I'm over at Queef's!" He was at Queefer's Hot Wings – a place right across the street from Super Good Technology. I cruised over. Fabian was wearing a t-shirt with the word "Fuck" stamped in giant letters across the chest. He jumped up as soon as he saw me. "Dude!" he cried. "Fuckin' good to see you!" I sat down and joined him. Fabian ordered the spiciest thing on the menu – the *nuclear* wings. They were dunked in something called ghost pepper sauce. This was the same pepper that North Korea used to torture political prisoners.

After we ordered our food, we just sat there and texted each other for a while. It was awesome. A few minutes later the waitress tossed our food onto a tray and started to make her way over to our table. She was still ten feet away when the smell of radiation began to waft through the air. First I started sniffling and then my eyes began to tear up. A fly was buzzing happily above the table. All of a sudden the thing died – it dropped out of the air and hit the ground like a brick.

Fabian picked up the first hot wing. "I love these fuckin' things," he said, trying to convince himself it was true. He put the wing into his mouth and I heard a sizzling sound. The smell of burning flesh started to fill the air. Sweat began to bead up on his forehead and his face turned bright red. A wisp of smoke even floated out of one nostril. His eyes were crazy now – they were all bugged out and he had a vacant look about him. I was afraid the bastard was going to keel over on the spot, but he just kept on eating. Fabian wasn't about to stop. "N-n-nuclear wings are the b-b-best," he stammered. And then he started flailing around for a glass of water. He found one and dumped it down his throat as fast as he could. "These wings aren't as hot as I like 'em," he claimed. "I'm just kinda thirsty. I haven't drank anything all day."

Some stuff you could get back. But other stuff was gone forever. And it was only then that people missed it. Fabian managed to choke down the entire plate of wings and it only took him three glasses of water to do it. Then once he was done he looked at me and winked. "Fuck me!" he cried. "These suckers are gonna burn twice!" After that he nudged me to make sure I got the joke. "Hey," he added, "I'm gonna run a marathon tomorrow! I haven't even trained or nuthin'. It's gonna be awesome! How about skydivin' on Saturday? You in?"

Star

She had the body of a porn star and a head the size of a raisin. I swear to God it was that small. Or maybe it just looked extra tiny in comparison. Well, in any case, no one was looking at her head. Her name was Star and Super Good Technology hired her to work in one of the test labs.

Star liked to dress in revealing outfits. Above the waist she wore nothing – a band aid covered each nipple. And down below she had pants that were painted on. There weren't a lot of girls at Super Good Technology so Star wanted everyone to know she was female. Star did this because she was a strong woman – she had the power and the confidence to do it.

As soon as Star joined the group we all looked around and noticed that our members were rising. It was embarrassing. Our secret plot to keep girls out of the software industry had failed. Star was really flexible and was able to perform a lot of different positions for the team, but she wasn't the only one who was so versatile. Guys liked to work late and try out new stuff with her in the lab whenever we could. Then we got off and went home.

A lot of girls were desperate for male attention. None of them seemed to have a dad and Star didn't have one either. This was one of the great advantages of no one having a dad! I remember the first time I ran into Star. It was over at the water cooler. I had just kneeled down to fill up a cup of water, I was turning around, and I guess I was moving a little too quickly – because before I even knew what happened, my head was stuck in her cleavage! I was shocked. And right away I lost the ability to think. I had never been lodged so tightly in between a set of knockers before. Not knowing what to do, I pulled out a dollar to tip – it was just a natural reaction. I tried to tuck the thing into Star's waistline, but it was no use. Her pants were too tight and I wound up dropping it. The bill fluttered helplessly through the air and landed on the floor below. At that point I wasn't sure about what to do next.

"Star," I said, finally, "you look zeb zeb."

Star picked up the dollar. "Oh thanks, Jack," she replied. "You look zeb zeb too."

Zeb zeb was the only thing people were allowed to say anymore since it was illegal to compliment another person on their appearance. The Supreme Court had ruled on this in a landmark case, but so that people weren't awkward all the time, the court gave an exception for zeb zeb. Zeb zeb did not mean anything. It was the same as telling someone they looked like nothing, and this was why the phrase had been approved.

The court's ruling created a lot of new jobs. Before it, many lawyers were in danger of starvation. Times were tough and all they could do was pray for more slip and falls, but there just weren't enough ambulances to chase anymore. Now, thanks to zeb zeb, America had hope. At Super Good Technology, lawyers were hiding in closets and underneath tables – they were all hoping to overhear a man complimenting a woman on her appearance so they could sue.

I grabbed my cup of water and started to walk along. All of a sudden, a leg popped out of a cabinet in the break room. I tripped over the thing and fell to the floor, cursing. Then a lawyer jumped out of the cabinet.

"You're hurt!" she cried. "So you better sue the company! This floor is unsafe! And it just so happens I'm a lawyer! I can help!"

I got up and brushed myself off. "I'm okay," I said. "But you look..."

"What?" she asked. "What?!"

The woman was dying for a payday, but I was no dummy. I made eye contact and then I raised an eyebrow. "You look," I said, "very zeb zeb."

"Aaaggghhh!" she shrieked. After that she started tearing her hair out in clumps and ran off. I stepped over a big chunk of hair and walked into the test lab. Zabo was inside.

"Oh my God, Jack!" he cried. "Did you see what Star is wearing today! Those band aids are smaller than ever! They just keep getting smaller and smaller! And her tits just keep getting bigger and bigger! I can't believe it! They're like a couple of giant marshmallow pillow-balloons!"

"Yeah," I said, "I know what you mean. I just got stuck in between them. I was–"

"Are you serious?!" he cried. "That's awesome! Star is so hot! I wanna bend her over and give her my zeb zeb!" After that Zabo started making pelvic thrusts to get his point across. Then he reached an arm out. "First I'm gonna grab her left zeb! And then I'm gonna grab the right one! I bust a zeb zeb every time I think of her! Holy shit! I couldn't even sleep last night! And when I woke up this morning I was all covered in my own zeb!"

Zabo was too much. "That's great, dude." I said. "Thanks for the visual."

A year or so later Star got pregnant and Zabo started running a betting pool on who the dad was. It was a big mystery. No one seemed to know so people were all walking around, asking each other, and whispering things. The whole office was pregnant with rumors. Star was married but for some reason no one was betting on the husband. Well time marched on, Star's belly kept getting bigger and bigger, and then a baby girl popped out. The baby didn't look anything like the husband, so he found a new zip code. I guess that makes one more girl without a dad.

Wine Bar

Some guys at Super Good Technology drank beer and other guys drank wine. The wine guys always hung out at a local wine bar since they were connoisseurs. These guys liked to sit on fancy wooden stools and memorize the adjectives people used to describe each bottle. It seemed like a lot of fun so I decided to join in. We all got off work one day and cruised over to the place. And that was when the show started.

I walked up to the bartender. "Hi," I said. "Can I get a glass of Pinot Zinfandel?"

"But of course!" he cried. And then he pulled out a bottle. "Here is our best Pinot Zin! It's a blend! Half of it is from the Bordeaux region of Burgundy. And the other half is from the Burgundy region of Bordeaux! It's the most magmorific thing in our collection! And it was bottled in the year 12 B.C. Look at the label!" Then he spun the bottle around and pointed at the date. Sure enough it was from 12 B.C. "This wine would go very well with our house specialty – chocolate snails from France! Would you like to try some?"

"No snails," I said. "I'll just stick with the wine."

The bartender glared at me. "Pfftt!" he snorted. For some reason he seemed disgusted.

I looked around the bar. Everyone had their pinkie sticking out and was busy looking up adjectives in a dictionary. A guy behind me was doing his best to memorize the description for the Pinot Zin. "Magmorific..." he muttered. "Did I hear that right? Did he call that one magmorific...?" The guy started asking everyone around him to make sure he had it right.

A second guy at the bar couldn't believe what he was hearing. "Yeah," he laughed, "it's magmorific alright. All Pinot Zins are. Don't you fucking know anything? Where are you from anyhow? West Virginia?"

"Fuck you!" the first guy countered. "Pinot Zins aren't all magmorific. Some are soft and flavacious – just like you! You want some of me, bitch?!"

It was on. The two wine experts stood up, got all up in each other's mugs, and started huffing and puffing. They were all set to throw down to prove who was more sophisticated, but then a rich old guy jumped in. "Come on, dudes," he said. "Life's too short to waste fighting when we have all this wine to drink. Why don't you both sit down and join me?" The two wine experts decided to overlook their differences and join the old guy, and pretty soon the entire bar was over at his table, freeloading off of his generosity. Everyone from Super Good Technology joined in.

"Hey, check it out," the old guy announced. "I got a special carafe so my wine can breathe. Wine needs to breathe so it can taste good."

The bartender walked by and nodded. "Yeah," he said, "wine's gotta breathe. If you put it in a container with the wrong shape, it will die. And then *you* might die from drinking it." Combatant number one whipped out a pen and started taking notes.

I tried some of the old guy's wine. The bottle cost two hundred bucks so I figured it would be pretty tasty, but his stuff was the worst crap I had ever tried. It was like turpentine and dirt mixed with ass – like piss in a bottle! And I couldn't believe everyone was just drinking it and pretending to like it. I was confused for a moment, but then all the fog lifted from my brain and I had a great epiphany – the Holocaust made sense to me. People would go along with just about anything as long as they figured everyone else was on board too. This place was crazy. I just sat there swirling the piss-wine around in my mouth for a minute or two – I was afraid to swallow it, but finally I managed to choke the stuff down. Right away I felt nauseous. And then – I threw up inside my own mouth. I wasn't quite sure about what to do at that point. I was about to stand up and go to the bathroom, but then a guy from work started asking me questions.

"Hey Jack," he said. "How's school going? When are you supposed to graduate anyhow?"

I just shrugged and made an I-don't-know noise. If I opened my mouth the puke would spill out, and I didn't want that to happen.

"Well, you should graduate already," he said. "Super Good Technology needs people. Computers are about all there is anymore. Don't you want a full-time job? Don't you want to have some kind of life when you're older?"

More questions. I shrugged and made the noise again. Then I got up and went to the bathroom.

"Damn," he complained as I was walking away. "What a dumb fuck! These kids today don't even care. They all think they're gonna be young forever. He doesn't even have anything to say about his future."

Later on the old guy started ordering lots of rotten cheese. We were all sitting around gorging ourselves on moldy snacks and guzzling piss. It was a great time. And then the old guy ordered one single glass of wine and passed it around. "What is it?" he asked. "Who knows what kind of wine this is?"

"It's Pinot Zin!" yelled the first combatant. "From Antarctica!"

"No way!" cried the second guy. "This is Noir Blanc! From 12 B.C.!!!"

I just couldn't take it anymore. "What?!" I cried. "You guys are nuts! This is Welch's grape juice mixed with cheap vodka. I saw the bartender stirring it up in the back!"

Everyone stopped what they were doing. They all stared at me. And then they turned and looked at the bartender. He dropped the can of Welch's he was holding. The thing fell to the floor and clanked around for what seemed like an eternity. After that the room got really quiet and the bartender began to look a little sheepish. He glanced down at the can and let out a great big sigh. Then he looked up again. "Sorry," he said. "My bad."

Leprechaun

A leprechaun worked at Super Good Technology. This struck me as odd and to my amazement no one else even seemed to care. As far as I could tell people were all oblivious to him. They were all just walking around in a casual manner and acting as if everything was normal. It was crazy. But I had my eye on the bastard. I knew it wasn't right for a leprechaun to be in an office.

The guy spent his day walking around the place and rarely ever got a second look. People just let him go about his business. And his business seemed to be about the same as everyone else's – he was collecting paychecks in exchange for pretending to work. Now most people would have probably let all of this go. But I was wary. I couldn't believe that no one was *onto* the Leprechaun. He was just so *obvious*. And it wasn't just his height that gave it away. He had a bushy head of hair and it was just long enough to cover up a set of ears that were no doubt pointy. Plus he had that evil look they all possess. He was old too. The Leprechaun's eyelids sagged badly and to look up at me, he had to tilt his head backwards. Then, using all his strength, he raised two droopy eyelids and created a tiny slit to peer through.

I came across the Leprechaun one time in the bathroom – he was dying on the toilet. All kinds of horrendous noises were coming out of the stall and the Leprechaun made no attempt at all to mute the sound. Once he was finally done, he pushed the stall door open and flung it to one side – like a gunfighter entering a saloon. Then he tilted his head back and glanced around. His eyes spoke his words: Who dares to make a joke about my ass? No one did. It was a bathroom and guys were terrified to talk to each other already. Plus we were all a little jealous anyway. The Leprechaun had reached a certain age and he no longer cared what anyone thought.

Whenever the Leprechaun wasn't ambling around or dying on the toilet, he was on the phone in his cube discussing his pot of gold with financial advisors. Other than that, he hung out in the break room and grumbled about layoffs. Some people had been laid off – but not the Leprechaun. He still had a job. And he wasn't happy about it. The Leprechaun was hoping to receive a lucrative severance package, and this was what he talked about all day, every day. The only time he wasn't bellyaching about it was when he moaned about having too much money left for the amount of time he was likely to live. Everyone got tired of listening to him, but the squeaky wheel always got the grease. I heard the news one morning – the Leprechaun had finally been laid off. I was sad at first. I had grown used to him and he had helped me to overcome my fear of his kind. But I felt happy too. I was glad he had finally gotten his wish – he was given a lucrative severance package. The Leprechaun would be satisfied for a short time, but I knew it wouldn't last long. He would either die or he would find some new people to complain to.

Billy worked with us and he kept in touch with the Leprechaun after he was let go – just to make sure he was doing alright. Every once in a while we got an update. Somehow the Leprechaun was managing to make ends meet. He had a pot of gold worth five million dollars, but he had kept himself busy collecting unemployment benefits. And every day he drove down a street full of potholes, past a library that was only open from 11 to 2 on Tuesday, and picked up a pint of Ben and Jerry's ice cream with his EBT card. A man had to eat. But to keep getting the free money, he had to apply for a certain number of jobs every week, and one of these was at the Department of Motor Vehicles. It was a government operation so that meant they would hire just about anyone. The DMV didn't care about race, color, creed, conscience or anything. The Leprechaun was worried about this so he asked Billy to be a reference for him. And there was only *one* condition – the reference had to be bad to make sure he didn't get the job. It had to be so bad that he couldn't meet the lowest bar in the free world. This pissed Billy off. He became judgmental and took offense to hearing that a millionaire was milking the system. "It's bad enough when a regular Joe does this!" he cried. "But a millionaire! That's crazy!"

Well, the DMV called Billy up asking for a reference on the Leprechaun. And they got one. Billy gave him the most amazing glowing recommendation a man had ever received and after that the Leprechaun got a call. It was possibly the most disappointing day of his entire life. He had a job offer. If he turned it down the free money would end. And if he accepted he would be forced to work. As long as the cash was coming in, the Leprechaun wasn't about to retire. It just wasn't in his blood, but I guess he was a little ticked off about it all. A few weeks later the DMV website crashed. We all had a good laugh when we heard about that.

Anti-Depressant

I was lying on my bed looking around and all I could see was quicksand. One wrong move and I was sure to get stuck. Quicksand was a terrible thing. It could trap you for long periods of time and sometimes people even died in the stuff. I didn't want either one of those things to happen.

No matter what I did or how hard I tried, I had come to a certain realization – I was never going to be perfect. I had always figured I would be perfect one day, but now a huge cloud was hanging over my head. It just wasn't ever going to happen. I was never going to find Zong Zong Boogaloo and because of this I was depressed. Depressed was no fun without crazy, though, so I decided to start taking an anti-depressant. Going crazy seemed exciting. It was a good way to get attention, and it was also a requirement for anyone who wanted to become a great artist. First you went nuts and then amazing art just poured out of you like water from a broken toilet. This was just how life worked. It didn't even matter if you weren't an artist before you lost it. Crazy made art. And since I was going to become a world-famous rapper, it was very important for me to be crazy. I was ready for *action*.

I was all set to pop my first anti-depressant, so I went to the store and bought a pack of Bing Bings. I opened the thing up and pulled one out – but I never got a chance to swallow it. I was just standing there, holding the pill when all the lights began to flicker. Then the power went out. Next a mysterious gas was released into the air. This caused my arm to straighten out and jut back behind my body as far as it would go. After that a boot grew out of the pill. The boot reached full size and started kicking me in the ass – over and over again, repeatedly. And every time it kicked, I moved one step closer to the front door. Finally, there just wasn't any further I could go. I was standing in front of the doorknob, so I turned the thing and walked outside. And once I was out in the great outdoors, the kicking stopped. I just stood there for a moment taking it all in. It was so refreshing! I felt relaxed and I was beginning to forget about all of my problems, but the boot wasn't done yet. All of a sudden the thing opened up its mouth.

"You are now a greeter and a phone-answerer, bitch!" it yelled. "When you see someone you greet them. And when your phone rings, you answer or call back! Got it?!"

"Uh...yeah," I stammered. I was a little surprised that a boot was kicking me around and yelling at me. I didn't know what the thing would do next.

"Let's turn that frown upside down!" it cried. The boot gave me a quick uppercut to the chin. It kicked me so hard that I wound up upside down, standing on my hands. "Perfect!" it yelled. "Looks like a smile from here. Now keep it up. You gotta fake it till you make it!"

The thing kept kicking me around and started making me talk to people. And that was when I began to feel better. For a moment I even forgot about how much I hated going outdoors and talking to people. But then I remembered and was pissed off. I was not at all happy about being happy.

"Goddamn boot..." I muttered. "Makin' me go outside and talk to people..."

"What!" it cried. "What did you say?!"

"Oh nothing..." I mumbled. I didn't want to piss the thing off.

"Bitch!" it screamed. "Love is a well-placed kick in the ass! Depression is caused by navel-gazing! And you gotta lose yourself to find yourself! There is quicksand all over this world and no one is happy all the time! But staying down is your own choice! Being depressed isn't an emotion or a feeling! It doesn't happen because of the weather or where you live! And it isn't caused by life events! It's a decision some people make. They want to be depressed!!!"

Sonic Fart Chair

Gadzookistan was on the cutting edge of social progress. The country had implemented the Campaign to Make Life Better thousands of years ago. And because of this, people did whatever felt good. In Gadzookistan, it was rude not to do whatever you felt like doing. If you were mad you yelled at people, when you were horny you took off your clothes and jumped the nearest warm body, and if you had gas you stuck out your booty and let one rip. Gadzookistan was a model for America.

Gadzookie people had a lot of experience in farting. The World Fartmaster was even from Gadzookistan. The Fartmaster had once passed gas continuously for 793 seconds. It was an amazing athletic accomplishment, and most experts agreed – this was a record that would never be broken. Breaking wind was the only thing Gadzookies were good at, so the Fartmaster's record was celebrated every year on National Fart Day. This was a day of great joy for Gadzookies everywhere as they revelled in the pride of their one national accomplishment.

The Fartmaster had many fartistic skills. He could change the pitch and tone of his flatulence in mid-rip. And he was said to be able to float an air biscuit on cue. The man truly had a gift. He could create noxious odors at a moment's notice. And once, he had even killed a bird in mid-flight. Pointing his ass skyward, he had cut the cheese at the unsuspecting creature – and his foul fart foiled the ill-fated fowl. The bird turned green, fell out of the air, and hit the ground with a thud. "Fart smell bad," it groaned. "Me die now." To honor the Fartmaster's achievement, a statue was erected and the bird's last words were etched onto a commemorative plaque.

America was not as far along as Gadzookistan in the Campaign to Make Life Better. This was something that took time. In America it was still considered rude to fart out loud in public, but the government was working hard to solve the problem. Congress had allocated billions of dollars in fartological research, and as luck would have it, Super Good Technology won the contract. Everyone in the company was excited – we were going to change life as we knew it. We were going to make America better! Super Good Technology was taking the lead in developing the world's first Sonic Fart Chair. It was a dream that would soon become a reality. Before long Americans would be able to sit in their own special chair and pass gas freely without the fear of reproach from others. This was the first step in breaking down America's repressive social culture of restrained gas.

The idea of the Sonic Fart Chair was simple. When someone sat down and ripped one, the chair sucked up the gas using a stealth vacuum located underneath the seat. And it muffled the sound with sophisticated noise-cancelling software. This made the fart undetectable to the human ear. The chair also deployed a high-end Queefinator to analyze the contents of the surrounding air and emit a neutralizing scent. The Queefinator was self-configuring. It adjusted to the odor of the user and eliminated the smell regardless of the person or type of gas it detected. The thing was truly a miracle of modern science. It could even overcome the dreaded Guinness and nachos fart.

The Sonic Fart Chair was still just a dream, though. The design was complete and some of the individual components were ready, but development on the final product had only just begun. Super Good Technology had placed Hugh Jasso in charge of the project. Hugh was the smartest engineer in the entire world. He was a genius and didn't mix well with others, so the company decided it was best for him to work from home. For months Hugh slaved away. He was making great progress but he hated talking to people or using a phone, so whenever someone contacted him he always responded by text or instant message. And Hugh was fast. He got back to people right away, addressed their concerns, and made sure to explain how the project was going.

One day Hugh's boss had a hookup scheduled with one of his girlfriends. Now this guy really knew how to impress women, so he took the girl out for Mexican food, and then drove her over to Hugh's to demo the Queefinator. But to his great surprise – Hugh wasn't even there! The front door was unlocked and no one was home. And when he walked inside, all he found was a fridge full of rotten cottage cheese.

It didn't take long for Hugh's web of lies to unravel. He had spent several weeks coding up an instant messaging auto-responder to send fake replies based on keywords in the messages he received. This made it look like he was always online and working. Hugh had fooled everyone! And then he had outsourced his own job to China at a fraction of his salary and pocketed the difference. Hugh was in Hawaii when they found him. He was guzzling vodka at a luau with some hookers when the cops showed up. "Get him!" they cried. "Throw that Hugh Jasso in the squad car!" His scheme was foiled but Hugh still had *one* last trick up his sleeve. He grabbed his phone. Then he activated the Kingdome virus and imploded the Internet across the world. It was a terrible day for humanity. The Internet was down and people were all forced to talk to each other again, and the Sonic Fart Chair was back to the drawing board. Super Good Technology took all the engineers they had diverted to the project and put them back to work trying to create the world's first poopless dog. "We can do it!" cried the CEO. "This is what the people want! They don't like to clean up poop! We are Super Good Technology! And we are more than just Blinkies! We can do anything!!!"

Double A

I was jogging down the street shirtless and people were all staring at me. It was irritating so I furled up my brow and opened my mouth. "I took my shirt off!" I cried. "Because I'm hot!" A guy was walking over on the other side of the street. And he had ditched the shirt too. But he was a big hairy bastard. He was so hairy it looked like he was wearing a sweater. That asshole needed to put a shirt on! I started shaking my head but then all of a sudden I did a double take. *Was* he actually wearing a sweater? I was confused for a moment since I was hung over and couldn't focus very well. Kids wore knit hats when it was 130 degrees out, so maybe summer sweaters were a new thing? I started looking closer to see if there was a logo or something. Finally I just decided I was right the first time.

Girls in Arizona didn't wear a whole lot of clothing either and guys were really excited about this. We loved to see a scantily-clad chick strutting around if she was hot. We lived for this! It was how all the humans on Earth were created! And when guys were looking at hotties, there wasn't much else that ever got done. But if a girl wasn't pretty, and she was showing it off, this was annoying. Me and Rocco saw an ugly chick parading around on the mall once. She had a muffin top, tramp stamp, and boobs that were popping out all over. "How come that girl doesn't know she's fugly?" Rocco complained. He was pissed off. A group of sorority girls saw her too and started going off.

"Tramp!"

"Oh my God! Did you see that whore!"

"What a bitch! I can't believe it!"

"Was that Medusa?! Someone help me. I can't move!"

"I think I caught a disease through the air!"

"Girl, you already had that disease!"

"Bitch, what did you say?! The first thing you do every morning is walk home!"

"Oh yeah! Well whose room smells like rotten tuna! We had to put in a fan!"

The sorority girls started fighting each other while guys all stood around laughing and taking videos. Everyone loved a good cat fight – but nothing good ever lasted. In the end campus security rolled in on their Segways and broke the whole thing up.

I kept jogging today and passed the hairy dude. Then I went by an old couple. The lady smiled at me – I was a fine upstanding young man to her, but her husband had a different reaction. His face turned down into a frown. He even seemed a little intimidated. I guess a shirtless guy could seem threatening to other males. It occurred to me that wearing a shirt was a kind of manners, so right away I was disgusted. "Hmmpph!" I snorted. Manners were an old-school idea! They weren't for the person who had manners. They were for everybody else. They made other people feel better. But secretly, the person with manners hoped to trick others into responding to him in the same way. Then he too could receive good treatment. So it was all a selfish idea! This was why manners were evil.

I thought about the clothing thing some more. So people all had different reactions to the human body depending upon their gender, the gender of the other person, and the attractiveness of the other person. It was crazy!

I finished jogging and found myself standing in front of a convenience store. A sign was in the window. "No shirt, no shoes, no service," it said. I couldn't believe it. Even 7-11 knew about this! I laughed for a second and then walked inside.

An old redneck with one tooth was working behind the counter. "Damn, boy!" he cried. "Git you a shirt on! We cain't have folk walkin' all over the store without no clothes on! We don't need no Double A goin' on in here – people gittin' all appalled or aroused 'coz of the skin in front of 'em. That ain't no good! Ain't you never wondered how come evr'body kept the clothes on in the olden days. Covrin' stuff up is what sep'rates us from the animals. It keeps all the emotions in check. Takes away Double A! Some people think seein' skin don't affect 'em. They say we all oughta just run around naked an' git used to it. Well ain't that a load of horseshit! Only a goddamn idiot'd try somethin' like that! We gotta take away Double A not promote it!"

"Alright," I said. "Alright! I'll put the damn shirt on. Why don't I just cover myself up head to toe like some Muslim woman?" Old school dudes were some dumb fucking bastards.

"That ain't no good neither, boy!" he cried. "You cain't take away nobody's face like that! That's like sayin' they ain't even a person! An' people gotta know what they ain't s'posed to do. You cain't just run around forcin' 'em. What's wrong wit' you?"

I went to the fridge and grabbed a Rockstar energy drink. Then I held it up with one fist, triumphantly. "I'll tell you what's wrong with me!" I cried. "I'm a rock star!"

The old redneck just shook his head. "This ain't the animal kingdom!" he shouted. "We don't need no bright-colored males up in here gittin' evr'body all riled up so they can git some! That ain't right! A man's s'posed to *be* sumbody so he can git some! Don't you know nuthin'!!!"

This guy didn't make any sense. I was standing there victoriously, holding my Rockstar, when a car zipped into the parking lot. The driver was blasting techno as loud as he could and had his hair spiked up all over the place. Tattoos were everywhere. He stumbled out of the car and adjusted his shorts to expose a pair of bright orange boxers. Then he thumped his chest a few times and cried out for joy, "Haaaoooohhhh!!!"

Drunn Kanhigh

Drunn Kanhigh is my bitch. I own her. I've known her ever since my first week freshman year when we hooked up at Wildcat House. She always gives me a big boost. I'm super smooth around her! It's been a few years since then and we've gotten together so many times I can't even remember. Guys love her and girls do too. She's fun and makes a great first impression. That's just how she rolls. Everyone wants to be Drunn Kanhigh. She's the fuel that keeps the party going!

Drunn Kanhigh is a great translator. She helps me meet other people. She's the ultimate sentence-finisher so I don't even have to think around her. I just start blabbering along a mile a minute and my thoughts turn into words instantly. Sometimes I say stuff I regret later, but that doesn't matter too much since I usually don't remember anyway. It's great to be social and make friends, but sometimes my buddies don't like to do stuff together without Drunn Kanhigh. I have to bring her along whenever we hang out. I wonder if I'm really friends with these people. Maybe we're only friends with Drunn Kanhigh?

I do her whenever I get the urge but sometimes she turns all clingy on me. And that gets kind of old. Whenever that happens she seems like an old computer game, one I've already mastered and don't like anymore, but for some reason I'm still playing. I wonder if it's bad to hook up with Drunn Kanhigh too much.

Drunn Kanhigh makes me feel good. A couple drinks is no big deal. It's good to connect with people and have fun, and you've got to let off a little steam every once in a while. But I always seem to want *one* more. I wish I could figure out how to gulp stuff down fast enough to get that one final satisfying drink. I must be doing something wrong. It's too bad Drunn Kanhigh steals my resolve, takes all my motivation, and kills my curiosity. Other than that she's pretty cool. I'm just glad Drunn Kanhigh is *my* bitch and not the other way around.

When I'm with Drunn Kanhigh everything is cool. I'm excited. But the next day I'm usually sort of irritable. I guess it's because she plants the seed of discontent. I didn't even notice this until we stopped hooking up every day. But the seed was always there – and most of the time I didn't even know it. I guess we only have so much happiness in our brains. When I keep everything under control, it trickles out slowly, a little at a time. Feeling Drunn Kanhigh causes a whole bunch to spurt out all at once, and it takes a while for that steady trickle to start up again.

I've spent a lot of time eating out Drunn Kanhigh in restaurants, and I'm always lying down on a weight bench, pumping Drunn Kanhigh as I sweat and grunt.

One day I was even fucking Drunn Kanhigh at the Buffet Bar while I was playing pool, and before I knew it I had nearly cleared the table. I was on fire that day. "I've got two balls on the table!" I bragged. "And I'm gonna win!" Then I knocked in the eight ball and ran around the bar holding it and the cue ball. "Look at my balls!" I cried. Everyone was laughing. They couldn't believe how great I was. But that didn't last long. I wasn't in very good condition the next morning, and I was beginning to feel irritated about being irritated. Drunn Kanhigh wasn't as great as everyone was telling me. And then I realized something. The seed of discontent makes it tough to enjoy the moment – unless you happen to be Drunn Kanhigh. I didn't realize this until it was gone. But I can see all the small stuff now. Before I was only happy with Drunn Kanhigh and unhappy without her. And I was really only happy for about the first hour every time we hooked up. The rest of the day just wasn't very good.

Drunn Kanhigh used to take me on some crazy roller coaster rides. I can't lie. Sometimes it was fun. I never knew what was going to happen with her around. I guess I enjoyed the unpredictability since I was stuck in a pit of boredom without any motivation or resolve. At first she was fun. But every time seemed a little less fun than the time before. Seems like boredom is the first sprout that comes out of the seed of discontent.

For some strange reason people don't want to play pool with me anymore. I guess they're all afraid to lose. Anyhow, I've raised my game up a notch lately. With lowered inhibitions I wound up doing a lot of stuff I wouldn't normally do. Maybe there's a reason we all have inhibitions? I rarely remember the highs, but everyone remembers the lows, and it doesn't take too many of those until no one wants to hang out anymore. How come people always remember the negative? If I tell someone about ten strengths I have and one weakness, they just file away the weakness and forget the rest.

Lately I've found a new drug. I think I'm going to do her for a while. She's *perfect* – the one I've been searching for my entire life. I love her. And I can't believe I never thought about trying her before. Taking her keeps me amazingly stable and well-balanced. I've got that steady trickle going now and I'm unstoppable. Well, I guess there are *some* side effects. I don't need a go-between with friends anymore. And my seed of discontent is gone. I'm not sitting around recovering all day long either. I've become a lot more productive too – it feels good to get stuff done! I no longer feel like there is some far-off, unreachable thing I'm grasping for either. That seems to have gone away with my seed of discontent. I wonder if there was any connection? I guess life works on a sliding scale with hedonism on one end and hair shirts on the other. You don't want to go too far in either direction, so I'll still have a beer. My new friend's name is Nadrunn Korhigh.

A Good Licking

I woke up late and for some reason I was all curled up on the floor. The spot seemed really comfortable, though, so I didn't think too much of it. I lifted up my head. Then I opened my eyes and began to check out my surroundings. I saw a fly – it was zipping back and forth in the air up above my noggin. The thing was annoying. Without even thinking I reached out, grabbed the bastard, and stuffed it into my mouth. I had never eaten a fly before, but today it just felt so *natural*. And I have to admit – the fly was tasty.

I was bored so I got up and ambled around the house for a while. Some bacon was lying on the floor, so I scarfed it down and let out a proud belch. Next I stared out the window for a couple of hours. For the life of me – I just couldn't think of anything better to do. I had already satisfied the beast in my stomach and that seemed to be about all there was to life.

Finally, I decided to make my way to the bathroom for some water. The toilet lid was down so I hopped up onto the counter and – all of a sudden – I caught my reflection in the mirror. It was the most shocking moment of my entire life! I couldn't believe my eyes – I was a cat. I leaned to my left in front of the mirror, and then to my right. I was hoping somehow to juke my reflection, but it was no use. The cat followed my every move. Next I turned around and checked out my backside. A couple of cat balls were jutting out. This gave me some small measure of relief. Sure, I had been randomly transformed into a cat – but at least I still had a sack. I wouldn't have to kill myself.

I was puzzled by my predicament. This was not how I had hoped to start the day, so I zoned out for a few hours. Then I hacked a furball up onto the floor. After that I clenched a paw and shook it at the sky. "Why God?!" I meowed. "Why me?! What kind of cruel joke is this?!" And then it hit me. The Creator had decided to punish me by turning me into a cat. It was divine retribution for all the times I had tortured cats in my life.

I covered my eyes with both paws and thought back to childhood. We had always had great fun tormenting the family cat. I remembered the time me and Craig had put the thing into a dresser drawer with only its head sticking out. Then – slowly – we slid the drawer in until it was trapped. The cat had no way to either pull its head in or get its body out. It was stuck. It didn't seem to know what was going on at first, but once the thing put two and two together, it went full-on postal. The cat started yanking its gray matter all around in the most insane panic I had ever seen. Its eyes were popping out of its skull and it was making a crazy face. Me and Craig were dying laughing. It was the greatest thing we had ever seen.

"Hahahahahahaha!!!" Craig laughed. "Check out its eyes!"

"Yeah!" I cried. "This cat sure is dumb! How come it doesn't know it can't escape?"

The cat was about to break its own neck, but some quick thinking by Craig saved its life. He jerked the drawer open and the cat leaped out. Right away the thing tried to play it cool. It flicked its tail high in the air and sauntered off, showing us its ass as a sign of disrespect. The drawer game was a great prank, but none of that mattered today. All at once the horror hit me and my fur all stood on end. *I* was the dumb cat now and *I* was doomed. I was going to live life as a feline! And now *I* would be subject to the whims of the human torturers! I was very afraid.

Not knowing what to do or where to go, I bolted out of the house and ran down the street as fast as my legs would take me. Tears were streaming down my cheeks and off my whiskers. I was truly lost. Finally, in an alley, I stopped to take a break. All of a sudden I just felt so dirty, and something way down deep inside told me I had to fix the problem. I hadn't cleaned myself the entire day. So I started licking my body all over, grooming my fur, and it was the greatest feeling I had ever had. I kept licking and licking – it was just so enjoyable. I couldn't stop myself. I took my paws and rubbed them behind my ears, and I had no idea why I was doing this. It all just felt so *right*. Instinctively, I lifted a hind leg, but then a feeling of apprehension swept over me. I didn't want to think about what was next. It was a terrible thing I was about to do. It was a vile and repulsive act – but all cats did it. I took my sandpaper tongue and stuck it out as far as it could go. Then I got my head down in between my legs and started licking my own ass. I just *had* to get it clean. At first I thought licking my own butt might bother me. But it didn't. My ass tasted great! There was maybe even a hint of oregano down there. And cleaning the thing was as easy as tossing a salad. Everything I did now seemed to come second nature, so I decided to chill out about the whole cat thing. It was starting to look like this new gig might work out after all.

All of a sudden I caught a whiff of something in the air. The aroma wafted past my nostrils and made my tail stand on end. It was a beautiful stench. I didn't know exactly what to call this smell but I *knew* what it was. This was lady cat! There was a lady around who needed a little servicing.

Instinctively I followed the odor. I kept walking and walking and the smell kept getting stronger and stronger. Finally, I tracked it down into an alley. I came around a corner and saw the dame. She was all flowing fur with a diamond collar and had a set of eyes on her that would've knocked most cats dead. "Meorrr..." she cooed, trying to act coy. Then she batted those baby blues at me. But there was no time for small talk – I had to break me off some of that! Without hesitation I got up on the booty and started to work it like I owned it. After a moment or so she let out a contented purr. I was the cat for this job! I just kept on waxing that ass and after a minute or so I busted a nut. My work was done so I turned around and scampered off.

I was beginning to like this cat thing. It was easy – I could do whatever I felt like whenever I wanted. Everyone liked *easy*. But I was starting to miss my grandma and the rest of my crazy family too. I thought about college. I had been in school for almost a decade. I needed to finish up because a guy couldn't be a cat forever. I had to find some way to become human again.

I started heading back to the apartment. But on my way out of the back streets, I was confronted by a gang of alley cats. "Hey punk!" one yelled. "That was my sister! You can't treat her like that!" This cat was pissed off. I took one quick glance and saw I was outnumbered, so I turned tail and ran. But these cats were fast. They caught up to me in no time flat and started ripping me apart. Fur was flying everywhere. All I could see were claws. There was a lot of blood. And then – I passed out.

I came to several hours later. It was afternoon now and I was lying in a motel bathroom in a puddle of water. Looking down I caught my reflection. I was human again. I was starting to wonder if the whole cat thing had been a dream, but then I looked a little closer. I was a mess. My face was all cut up and there were claw marks running up and down my body. Next I saw the leader of the alley cat gang. He was walking away, showing me his ass. All of a sudden he turned and looked back at me over his shoulder. "Bitch," he said, "if she's pregnant I'm gonna kill you. Either that or you're gonna marry her." I thought about it. The alley cat was right. She'd be screwed without me. Cat world didn't have a system to help the needy. Instead it had a Code of Honor to help keep everyone in check. I hadn't lived up to that code. I was embarrassed and looked down at the ground. I kicked some dirt off my shoe and then I looked back up again. "Okay," I said, "I'll marry her." After that the alley cat jumped out a window and ran off. I just sat there for a moment. I had no idea about what kind of ring to buy for a cat.

I was standing there scratching my head when I realized that something was twitching behind my back, so I reached back and grabbed the thing. It was my tail. I was still part animal. But I didn't want to be an animal anymore. An animal did whatever it felt like all the time – it had no control over its actions. You could train an animal, but then it just did whatever it was trained to do. An animal didn't understand *why* it did anything. And it never did the right thing when no one could see. Human beings had free will. We had the ability to understand the difference between right and wrong and to act it out. I wanted to be human. I looked at the nightstand in between the two motel beds. Then I pulled the drawer open and peered inside, but what I saw next sent a chill down my spine – it was a copy of the Evil Book. At first I was afraid to touch it, but deep down I wanted to know all the secret things too. I had been searching and searching for Zong Zong Boogaloo. I had been looking and longing for something that was perfect and unchanging – but there was only one perfect thing that never changed. I glanced to my left and then to my right. After that I spent a few minutes checking the room for hidden cameras. Finally I realized the coast was clear. No one could see me so I picked the thing up. I read and read and nothing ever made more sense in my entire life. And all of a sudden everything seemed perfect.

Made in the USA
Middletown, DE
29 November 2018